The Garden of Fragile Things

The Garden of Fragile Things

Richard J. O'Brien

Dark Alley Press

The Garden of Fragile Things

© 2015 by Richard J. O'Brien

ISBN: 978-0-692-39322-2

Dark Alley Press
http://www.darkalleypress.com

An imprint of Vagabondage Press LLC
PO Box 3563
Apollo Beach, Florida 33572
http://www.vagabondagepress.com

First edition printed in the United States of America and the United Kingdom, June 2015

10 9 8 7 6 5 4 3 2 1

Front cover art by Salajean. Cover designed by Maggie Ward.

The Garden of
Fragile Things

This novel is dedicated to the old gang
from the Fairview section of Camden, N.J.

Many thanks to everyone who read this novel in various stages, including my wife Jessica, Thomas E. Kennedy, and, of course, Nanette.

The Garden of
Fragile Things

Prologue

22 Aspen Trail
Hillsboro, NH
January 17, 2008

Dr. Martin Cambridge
714 State Road
Mays Landing, NJ

Dear Dr. Cambridge:

I am writing to seek permission for an interview with a patient of yours at Ancorra State Hospital. The patient's name is Joseph Michael Godwin, age 44, who has been a ward of the state since 1977.

As a writer and an independent researcher (see attached C.V.), I am aware of the sensitivity involved with subjecting a patient to an interview with a stranger. However, I am currently working on a book concerning a history of missing children who disappeared in Franklin State Forest not far from Yorkville, N.J. where your patient grew up.

My research has uncovered more than thirty reported disappearances dating all the way back to 1865. The last reported vanishing was in the summer of 1963. Granted, your patient Joseph Godwin was not alive in 1963, however, my research thus far has led me to believe that your patient may have been exposed to certain anomalies in Franklin Forest, the very same anomalies that may have lent themselves to the unexplained disappearances of more than two dozen children over the past century and a half.

My phone number is included on my C.V. if you wish to call me. I eagerly await your reply.

Sincerely,
Reginald T. Crawford

Department of Abnormal Psychiatric Care
Ancorra State Hospital
County Road 7
Ancorra, NJ
February 2, 2008

Mr. Reginald T. Crawford
22 Aspen Trail
Hillsboro, NH

Dear Mr. Crawford:

Thank you for your inquiry.

I am well aware of the local lore concerning Franklin Forest, as well as the greater Weyrd County area here in New Jersey. Over the years, there have been many inquiries about my patient, Joseph Godwin. Many writers, though not so many with the publishing credits you possess, have expressed interest about the so-called "'anomalies" in Franklin Forest and how those anomalies relate to my patient.

Urban legends have grown up around the events that led the very tragic end of three young boys back in 1977. It would not be remiss to add that even a cottage industry of sorts has sprung up with curiosity seekers poking around Franklin Forest. Over time, sadly, people have lost sight of the fact that a grisly crime was committed by a boy who, for all intents and purposes, suffered a calamity that left him with a fractured mind.

Many independent "researchers" who requested access to my patient maintain that Joseph's psychosis is not real, and that we, the citizens of Weyrd County and beyond, are the ones who are, in fact, delusional.

Psychotics are, as you may well know, easily manipulated by leading questions. Regrettably, with my patient's best interest in mind, I will have to willfully decline your request for interview.

Ordinarily, I do not accommodate any researcher seeking material on the events of Joseph's life between 1976 and 1977. However, given the nature of your research, and the history of missing children you attribute to these alleged anomalies, I have included in this package a manuscript my patient wrote during his time here.

Now an adult, Joseph was twelve years old when he committed a heinous crime. He continues to sink further into the delusion that first took root back in 1977. As previously stated, I cannot allow access to my patient on these grounds, as well as the wishes of his family. However, Joseph's legal guardian has granted consent for me to share this manuscript with you. It turns out that Joseph's legal guardian is a fan of yours.

If you seek permission to use any of the enclosed manuscript in your own work, please contact my patient's legal guardian whose information is attached.

As for the land, I am sure you are aware that the area within Franklin Forest that you intend to write about was taken over by the United States Government via imminent domain in the late 1990s. The portion of the forest that was handed over to U.S. Army is a sizable tract of land that is used nowadays to conduct readiness exercises. If you wish to visit that land, I am confident that you will seek permission through the proper avenues with the Army.

Sincerely,
Dr. Martin Cambridge

cc: Mr. Scott Freeman
Mr. Armand Hope, Esq.

Chapter 1

It was Bobby McMahon's idea to go camping. He was my best friend. It was the summer of 1976, and we were both twelve years old. Bobby was afraid of everything under the sun including, but not limited to, swimming, darkness, closed-in spaces, strangers, people of lesser intelligence, and people in uniform: be it the police, the mailman, soldiers, or the Abbotts Milk delivery guy. What possessed him to want to go camping was beyond me, but he kept at it all afternoon. He insisted we pick up a tent and supplies. I assumed he wanted to go to Franklin Forest. I was wrong. Too bad we didn't listen to Bobby that day.

"We don't have a tent," I told him.

"Don't be so smug," said Bobby.

Bobby was forever using words like "smug." On a good day, his lexicon was peppered with big words that even adults in our community didn't use. It was like he became possessed by the ghost of Montgomery Clift or some other Golden Era movie star.

"I'm not being so anything," I replied.

If there was one thing I hated, it was being made to look stupid, and Bobby was good at that.

"Listen," he said. "Let's go visit the Swanson Brothers. I shudder to admit it, but I think they can help us."

I was friends with Jack Swanson. He was a year older than Bobby and me. He had a younger brother named Tim, and everywhere Jack went, Tim followed. When Jack was six years old, his father was sent to prison for manslaughter. Children were rarely privy to the embarrassing affairs of adults, so I never learned all the details. Before that, Jack and Tim and their parents lived over in Tracktown out near the rail yard. Less than a year after Mr. Swanson went to jail, Jack's mom took off with some biker from Delaware. That's when the brothers went to live with Granny Swanson.

The house, a dilapidated, colonial-style home, stood on a dead-end road called Tanner Street. There were three other houses on the street. In one house lived Mr. Von Braun. He was old. The Swanson brothers treated him like shit, convinced that Mr. Von Braun was some Nazi war criminal who narrowly escaped the wrath of the Nuremberg Trials. Fortunately, Granny Swanson didn't share her grandsons' sentiment. To her chagrin, Jack and Tim were never lacking when it came to imaginative ways by which to torture their elderly neighbor. Their campaign was relentless. A child psychologist may have said that Jack and Tim were simply projecting their anger at their father's imprisonment toward an innocent victim incapable of defending himself. For Jack and Tim, it was more like a personal vendetta against a remnant of evil that once manifested itself in the form of black-clad SS officers, death camps, and Nazi stooges marching to the demented beat of a failed artist madman.

That Heinrich Von Braun was German, there was never any doubt. My parents told me that Mr. Von Braun had come to America in the early 1930s shortly after the Reichstag Fire. Bobby's parents told a slightly different version. Everyone in Yorkville, N.J.—that tiny working class town near the Delaware River where I grew up— had their own version of Von Braun's story.

"Mr. Von Braun was a member of the Berlin intelligentsia," Granny Swanson told me one afternoon after she finished beating Jack and Tim with a stick and sending them off to their bedroom.

Next door, Von Braun busied himself by raking leaves. Fifteen minutes beforehand, he chased off Jack and Tim as they attempted to toilet paper the huge mahogany tree in his backyard.

"That means he was very knowledgeable in his field, Joe," she went on.

"Which one?" I asked.

Granny Swanson wrung her meaty hands together. She was always doing that, as if she constantly imagined strangling her grandchildren for the sins they committed against the elderly man next door. Or maybe it came from spending most of her adult life keeping her own son out of trouble, as if Mr. Swanson's incarceration was somehow her fault. A failure that she never learned to live with.

"He once wrote books," said Granny Swanson. "Rumor has it that Mr. Von Braun knew Thomas Mann."

I knew about Thomas Mann from my dad. A long time ago, my dad read some tired, old book about a guy who goes to a spa in the mountains to recover from some illness. The yawn factor in that story was overwhelming. I knew nothing of the nuances of language. Nor did I grasp how the human psyche often split: On one side, the true artist who possessed an uncanny insight into the human condition; on the other, the potential to become a murderous monster.

Somewhere behind me a window opened. Granny Swanson was busy praising the genius of Heinrich Von Braun. I heard Jack and Tim whispering as they crept along the side of the house. The only word I understood, as they high-crawled beneath the ranch-style fence between both yards, was "firecrackers."

"Thomas Mann," I said to keep Granny Swanson's attention. "You don't say."

I'd heard the story before, but my parents told me it was rude to remind my elders of how forgetful they'd become in old age.

"Now, mind you," she went on, "Mr. Von Braun was a promising poet and novelist."

The look on her face went sour, the way it always did when she reached that part of the story. Her hand-ringing routine kicked into overdrive.

"Then that Austrian monster and the brown shirts ruined everything," she cried.

I wondered where Jack and Tim had snuck off to, but it didn't take long to solve that mystery. The *pop-pop-pop* of firecrackers erupted like machine gun fire. I expected to see Mr. Von Braun dive for cover. Instead, he just shook his head and kept on raking leaves.

Granny Swanson beat the living daylights out of Jack and Tim. For an old woman, she moved fast, and in order to even the odds, she often used whatever weapon she had on hand. Tim wailed loud enough for me to hear him all the way down the block as I retreated from the melee.

Jack, I knew, was another story. He never cried, never showed the slightest sense of fear, whether he faced a beating from his grandmother or the unending taunts from Sean McClusky, a local degenerate, the fifteen-year-old scourge of younger boys throughout Yorkville. Jack took his licks and showed no emotion. His inability to show emotion caused alarm in people. Bobby McMahon believed that Jack, if he remained in his self-imposed cocoon for too long, may one day turn into a sociopath. I had to look up that word. I didn't like it, but Bobby was usually right about that sort of stuff.

Tanner Street was like a different world. Between Von Braun and Granny Swanson, Bobby found that whole section of town the most depressing. His parents considered the Swanson brothers a bad influence, as if the brothers Swansons' knack for finding trouble was contagious. Bobby always waited on the sidewalk whenever I knocked on Granny Swanson's door, never letting me forget that Jack and Tim were my friends, and not necessarily his. Nothing reminded me more of that fact than Bobby's unwillingness to go near Granny Swanson's house.

"It's too bad we don't know anyone else with a tent," Bobby said as he tapped a crack in the sidewalk in front of Granny Swanson's dead lawn.

"How about Billy Federov?" I asked.

Bobby shoved his hands in his pockets. "Did you ever notice that Billy smells like cabbage?"

That much was true. Billy and his family moved to Yorkville two years ago. His mother was a school teacher and his father wrote sci-fi novels. I'd read a few of his father's books I found in our town library. They were racy tales set in space that celebrated man's conquest of the universe, the equality of the sexes, and battles between human spacefarers and aliens that, as far as I could tell, just wanted to be left alone. Most of the kids at school thought Billy was weird, and men like my dad spoke in hushed tones about Mr. Federov being a "conscientious objector" who spoke at anti-war rallies. It took nearly a year before Billy came out of his house. He tagged along with the Swanson brothers whenever he caught up with them near Tanner

Street, but Jack always gave him the slip. I felt sorry for Billy Federov. Still, no matter how unfairly he was treated, he always came back.

"Joe?" Granny Swanson appeared at the front door.

She looked past me through the screen door. As her gaze settled upon Bobby, she wrung her hands.

"Is Jack home?"

"He and Tim went to the square," she told me.

"Okay, thanks."

"Say hello to Mr. and Mrs. Godwin for me."

"Will do."

Bobby looked relieved as soon as we left Tanner Street. We walked six blocks to Yorkville Square. Jack and Tim were easy enough to find. They liked hanging out at The Roost, an arcade that served Ellio's Pizza, cold-cut sandwiches, and soda. Every other kid in Yorkville that summer thought they would become the next Pinball Wizard, though I suspect that none of them would part with two of the five senses that made The Who's *Tommy* a true prodigy.

Bobby shuddered as we stood in front of The Roost.

"A den of inequity if ever I saw one."

I liked The Roost for one reason: Her name was Marcella Carbone. We met in the first grade at St. Bonaventure School, but it was at the arcade two years prior, when we were both ten years old, that I developed a full-blown crush on her. It was an autumn afternoon on a Saturday. There were high cumulus clouds blowing over Yorkville, and, on the wind, the scent of approaching winter. She wore a yellow T-shirt, blue jeans, and Converse All-Star sneakers. Her black hair was cut short like Joan of Arc's, as Bobby noted that day.

That was the thing about Bobby. He worshipped the ground that Marcella walked on, but on that day, he knew I'd been struck by a bolt that made me uncomfortable. I was too young to know what romance was, but I knew in my heart that I loved her. By the time we were eleven years old, Marcella and I had decided, against Bobby's wishes, that we were going to run away together when we were old enough. Our plan, though not etched in stone, was to be rich and famous. Marcella wanted to be an actress. She didn't care what I did, so long as we were together.

My mood lightened when as Bobby and I stepped foot into The Roost. Marcella was playing pinball on a rather garish machine that depicted big-boobed women in camouflage and their muscular mercenary counterparts. Flanking Marcella on either side were Annie Gallagher and Kim Whalen. As soon as Marcella saw me, she let Kim take over her game.

"Hey, boys." Marcella wore shorts and a halter top.

Her bronze shoulders bore the marks of her bathing suit straps. That summer marked a milestone. Marcella's little bud breasts beneath her halter top made me blush whenever I looked at them for too long. Around her neck, she wore a choker made from thin black leather with a triangle-shaped opaque crystal attached.

"Good afternoon, Marcella," said Bobby.

"Cool necklace," I remarked, unable to look her in the eye.

Marcella stepped forward and took me by the arm.

"Thanks," she said.

"Where did you get it?"

"My dad and I were hiking through Franklin Forest," she informed me. "I found it there."

"Splendid," Bobby's voice cracked. "Have you seen the Swanson brothers? Boorish pair about this tall? Sometimes they drag their knuckles—"

"Joey." Marcella tugged on my arm. She leaned her head against my shoulder. Her hair smelled like sunshine and hyacinths. "Buy me a Coke."

"I don't have any money," I said, embarrassed.

In the summer, my parents gave me a couple of dollars a week. My dad always said to spend it sparingly—whatever that meant. His reasoning was this: On some public service commercial, he had heard that a whole family in a third-world country, a country without a name since my father forgot it by the time he doled out this little life lesson, could be fed on two dollars a week. If he possessed one quality, it was his ability to pontificate endlessly on the importance of being thrifty. When my friends like Bobby and the Swanson brothers went to Woolworth's or Korvette's for new school clothes every year, I looked forward to a bus ride into Philadelphia with my dad, where he'd treat me to used clothing at any one of the numerous second-hand stores he had mapped out. That was all part of the thrifty plan, I guess. My old man even took the bus to work. It was that or he walked, since we didn't own a car; even Granny Swanson owned a car, and she made no bones about being the poorest old lady in Yorkville.

"Hey," Marcella's voice snapped me back to the present. "There's Jack and Tim."

I bolted out of The Roost. The Swanson brothers ran full-tilt straight toward me as they cut across the square.

"Joe!" shouted Jack.

"What's up?" Tim wore a devilish grin when he passed me.

Before I could answer, the brothers Swanson ducked down an alley a few doors down from The Roost. At first, I didn't know what the hurry was, but then I spotted Sean McClusky and four of his cronies high-tailing it through the square as they gave chase.

McClusky was fifteen years old. By that age, he had already flunked the sixth grade twice and spent one summer at the county juvenile detention center. As local bad seeds go, McClusky was the quintessential class-A degenerate. He kept his distance from me, however. I was friends with Marcella, and her sixteen-year-old brother Gale (short for Galileo) had it in for McClusky and his crew. By the time I turned twelve, I already lost count how many times Gale Carbone had kicked the snot out of Sean McClusky. While Marcella's older brother offered me protection, Gale couldn't stand the Swanson brothers, and he offered them no clemency. He thought they were trash. More than that, Gale told me that Jack had only one thing on his mind when it came to his kid sister. I guess that's what made him think that Jack and I were so different; in truth, the only disparity between us was that, unlike Jack, I hid my real intention much better than my less-fortunate friend.

That summer, Jack and Tim had decided, despite having no one to protect them from the retribution that older boys often doled out, to see how far they could push McClusky. Jack and Tim weren't afraid of anyone, and, judging from the crazed look on McClusky's face as he sprinted toward the alley now, it was plain to see that the brothers Swanson had finally pushed the right button.

"Get them motherfuckers!" McClusky screamed at his buddies.

He stopped, barely able to breathe, and stared at me. His eyes looked wild as he clenched his fists. He took three steps toward me, and I nearly pissed in my pants. Suddenly, McClusky stopped; his shoulders slumped as his hands went all limp. That's when I smelled hyacinths and sunshine again. Marcella stood beside me, taking my hand in hers.

"Hello, Sean," I heard her say.

McClusky gave me a dirty look. Then he turned on his heels and set off down the alley at a quick pace.

Bobby emerged from The Roost holding two ice-cold bottles of Coca-Cola. I held my free hand out, but he passed one of the bottles to Marcella.

"Have the barbarians retreated?" Bobby asked. He made a big show of looking around all nervous.

"They won't bother you, Bobby," Marcella told him.

"I'm not so sure about that."

"Don't be a moron. My brother—"

"Likes Joe more than he likes me," Bobby cut her off. "I don't think he'd go gunning for the likes of Sean McClusky if—"

"We're thinking about camping out," I interrupted.

"Don't think too hard, Joey," said Marcella. "You'll bruise your brain."

She took a long sip from her soda bottle and handed it to me.

"That's why we were looking for the Swanson brothers," I informed her.

"Camping, huh?" She kept her eyes trained on the alleyway. "That sounds cool. Can I go?"

"Yeah, Joe," Bobby chimed in, "let's bring some girls."

"No," Marcella poked a finger against his chest. "Just me."

"We have to go find Jack." I handed the soda bottle back to her.

Marcella squeezed my hand and let it go. Bobby and I promised her we'd catch up with her again soon. By the time we reached the alley, I turned to see to see Marcella was following us. She was joined by Annie Gallagher and Kim Whalen. The girls kept their distance, huddling close as they walked and whispered to one another.

Chapter 2

Hobbs Creek began north of Yorkville and south of the Raritan River, running deep into the Pine Barrens. It separated Yorkville from the eastern edge of Franklin Forest. Less than a football field's length from Jack Swanson's backyard, Hobbs Creek reached its widest point, measuring a little over a quarter-mile from the Swanson dock to the Franklin Forest side. Long ago, Jack's grandfather built a sturdy dock for locals to use for fishing. Back then, Yorkville was a boomtown, built specifically for shipbuilders who were employed in the Philadelphia Naval Yard. Jack's grandfather issued an open invitation to anyone in town to come fish off the dock. He passed away long before I met Jack. Not long after, Granny Swanson closed the dock for fear of someone falling off and drowning. It was just as well. By the late 1960s, all the catfish were gone. During summer months, the muddy banks smelled to high heaven at low tide. In winter, it wasn't much better, unless a thick blanket of snow and ice covered the creek.

A well-worn trail wound its way from Granny Swanson's backyard to the dock where Bobby and I found Jack and Tim. Even at her advanced age, Granny Swanson remained vigilant about who passed through her yard. There was no chance that Sean McClusky and his goons would give chase that far, not without having to explain to everyone in Tracktown how they got their asses beat by an old woman. McClusky was a brute, the lowest form of degenerate, but he was no idiot. If he ever landed in the clutches of Granny Swanson, he would never live it down.

Just as we reached the dock, I heard Granny Swanson's voice. Turning, I saw that Marcella and her friends had followed us. The girls were halfway down the trail when Granny Swanson spotted them from the back porch.

"Pardon me, girls," Jack's grandmother called out. "That trail is no place for young ladies."

"Hi, Mrs. Swanson," Marcella said. "We're with Joey."

"Joey Godwin doesn't keep company with adolescent trollops," she countered. "Now run along before I call the vice squad."

"Did she just call us whores?" Annie Gallagher cried, as Marcella herded her friends back up the trail.

Granny Swanson stood like a sentry on her back porch, a broom in hand, as she surveyed her domain. Sure, I felt bad for Marcella, but, given her age, Granny Swanson was about as old-fashioned as they came. If she did not want girls and boys together in the sparse woods behind her house, then that's the way it would be. In Granny Swanson's mind, no good could come from adolescent boys and girls cavorting with one another. If anything, she reasoned, left to follow the natural course of things without proper adult supervision, it would all lead to unwanted pregnancy. The old woman would never risk having her own name stained when the truth came out. Old people were like that. They avoided scandal at all costs.

"Bobby and Joey sitting in a tree," Tim sang from the dock when he spotted us, "K-I-S-S—"

Jack belted his younger brother in the gut. "Stop it," he said.

Tears welled in Tim's eyes. He had a hard time catching his breath, and he looked scared.

Bobby coaxed Tim into standing up straight. After a few attempts, Tim was able to draw a deep breath.

"Don't touch me," he told Bobby.

"I'm only trying to help," Bobby said.

"I don't need it."

Jack shook his head and sat down on the dock. His bare feet dangled over the edge. Tim marched up the trail, away from us, toward home.

"I didn't mean to—" Bobby started to say.

"Don't worry about him," said Jack. A mischievous grin flashed. "Did you see McClusky?"

"What did you do?"

"Nothing."

"Jack," I said.

"Okay." He rolled his eyes as he leaned back on his elbows. "So I might have stolen something from him."

Bobby and I ribbed Jack about having a death wish. What he didn't tell us that day was the object of the theft.

The three of us sat on the edge of the dock. I told Jack about the camping idea. Bobby seemed agitated. It didn't take long for him to explain why.

"Even if we do go," said Bobby, "we need something to keep the rain off of us in case it storms."

"My dad's tent," Jack told us. "I'm sure he doesn't need it."

"Where did he get it?" Bobby asked.

"The fuck should I know," he told him.

There were many times that summer when I noticed Bobby acting a certain way toward Jack. He could complain all he wanted to about Jack, but I knew that he was sweet on him.

"How big is it?" Bobby asked.

"What? Oh," said Jack. "Sleeps four. When are we going? Tonight?"

"No good," I said. "Today's Thursday."

"What? You got a job?"

"No, what kind of job would I have?" I asked. "You know how my parents are."

"But it's summer."

"I have chores."

"Whatever," Jack waved me off. "Anyway, I heard on the radio that it's supposed to rain."

Bobby and I sat down next to Jack, watching the murky water. Twenty yards upstream were the thick moorings from another dock that washed away a long ago. Two summers ago, a long, coffin-shaped chunk of wood washed up on the bank adjacent to the Swanson dock.

"Looks like a coffin," Jack had said that day.

Upon closer inspection, we discovered that the "coffin" was just a bunch of rotted planks nailed together.

"It stinks," I told him, as the shallow water lapped against the old wood.

Bobby had been with us that day. He wouldn't come near the water. From the time he was able to walk, Bobby McMahon always had his nose in a book. His parents had never taught him to swim. One winter, when we were just seven years old, Bobby and I had followed some older kids down to the creek to do some ice jumping. The stretch of Hobbs Creek that ran through the south end of Yorkville always iced over from the Swanson's dock all the way out to Crescent Island, which lay a half-mile downstream.

When the first thaw had arrived, the frozen creek had cracked apart, turning the ice into giant sheets that, once they shrunk in size and thickness, had eventually floated downstream to where the creek fed into the Delaware River. So it had been on one wintry February afternoon when I had tempted fate by performing my first ice jump. Some of the teens from our neighborhood had jumped all the way down to Crescent Island. Bobby, frozen with fear that day, had stood on the creek bank and watched, waiting for me to slip off and sink into the cold depths below. Bobby never participated, satisfied, instead, to remain a spectator.

"Bobby," Jack had said, "help us pull the coffin out of the water."

Nothing doing: That had been the look on Bobby's face. He hadn't cared if it was six inches of water or six feet. Bobby had wanted no parts of the creek.

Tim had soon joined us. He just had stood on the banks, staring at the coffin-shaped planks.

"Dracula?" Tim had asked.

"What?" Bobby had responded.

"Nah," he had said. "Probably one of his minions." Tim had looked like he was in a trance. There were times he went all creepy like that. "Vampires," he had gone on, "tend to do that. They breed worse than rabbits."

"Vampires don't breed."

"Sire," Tim had countered. "That's the word. Vampires sire other vampires."

"Wouldn't that be cool?" Jack had asked.

That's how we had spent the rest of that hour, the four of us arguing the possibilities and probabilities of the existence of vampires, and, more to the point, whether or not we had just discovered a vampire's coffin in the creek's shallow waters along its banks.

Every neighborhood in America had its own monster buff. In Yorkville, in the mid-1970s, the monster buff was Tim Swanson. From the time he learned to read, he consumed comic books, novels, and short story collections that fell into one of three categories: science fiction, fantasy and, his personal favorite, horror.

If you needed to dispose of a vampire, a werewolf, a mummy, a zombie, or any variation of supernatural entities that meant you harm, then Tim was the kid to seek. Extinguish a dragon's fiery breath for good? Ask Tim. Bring a sleeping beauty out of her comatose state when kissing her failed? Tim knew the remedy. Likewise, he knew the weakness of elves, the power behind magic mirrors, the physics involved that kept the leprechaun's pot of gold perpetually beyond the treasure-seeker's grasp, the difference between dawn magic and twilight enchantment, and even the origin of the fairy folk in all of their mysterious guises, from sprites to brownies, from ogres to hobgoblins, from banshees to trolls—something, as I recall, that had to do with angels cast out of heaven who did not fall as far as their more zealous brothers. Tim was the only person I ever met who knew why the bricks that led to Oz were yellow rather than any other color.

Sadly, where Tim's mind worked overtime concerning all things fantastical and phantasmagorical, he lacked the ability, as so many geniuses did, to pay attention in school. As a result, he was subjected to a special needs class where all the kids fell into one of three categories: the retarded, the hyperactive, and the degenerate offspring of degenerate parents.

"It's like a circle in Dante's *Inferno*," Bobby had remarked one day.

I didn't know what the hell he was talking about. Then again, half the time none of us did.

Ultimately, it was Tim who had gone into the water that chilly afternoon to find out if there was indeed a vampire cloaked in the sleep of the undead inside the water-logged coffin. For Tim, that day proved one of the lowest when he had quickly discovered that the coffin turned out to be rotted pieces of plain old wood hastily tacked together with penny nails.

"Did you guys see Marcella's necklace?" Jack asked.

The mere mention of my beloved's name brought me back to the present.

"She said she found it," Bobby was saying.

"I heard differently," said Jack.

"Oh?" I felt light-headed. I swore I could smell Marcella's skin on the wind. Or perhaps it was just some private reverie, a mid-summer adolescent dream.

"Kim told me someone gave Marcella the necklace."

"Who?"

"She didn't say."

"That's bullshit," I said.

Jack knew how I felt about Marcella. He made it a mission that summer to supply me with enough doubt and jealousy to last a lifetime. And even though we all knew that Jack liked Kim, the reverse wasn't applicable since Kim was, at the age of twelve, no longer a virgin, courtesy of some rich kid from the suburbs she had met Memorial Day Weekend while staying at her aunt's house along the Jersey shore. Marcella confided as much to me after Kim told her about the experience in all of its gory details. The boy was supposed to be eighteen years old, but I suspected that he may have been even older, since Kim was far more developed than the rest of the girls her age.

"Don't worry, Joe," Jack told me. "If Marcella said she found it, then she found it."

"Why would Kim say someone gave it to her?"

"I don't know. Girls are retarded, I guess." He shrugged and made a face. "And, oddly enough, smarter than us at the same time."

"So," Bobby said as he stood up, "it's settled then. Tomorrow night we go camping."

"I have to tell Granny Swanson we're camping out in Joe's yard," said Jack.

"We are?"

"No peckerbreath."

"Then where?"

Jack shook his head. "For the smartest kid in the class," he said to Bobby, "you're pretty stupid most of the time."

Whenever someone tried to insult him, Bobby's jaw always set a certain way, as if the grim expression he wore were a mask meant to deflect such vituperation. And he never wavered until the other person quit.

"Franklin Forest," Jack announced.

"We can't," said Bobby.

"Why not?"

"For one, you need a permit," he answered. "And I was thinking of camping out in someone's yard."

"Nothing doing," he countered. "Besides, we sneak into the forest after dark."

"We have to cross the creek."

"Unless you have a hot air balloon."

"What about Dover Bridge?"

"No way," Tim spoke up now. "That's like five miles away."

"We could use our bikes," Bobby countered.

"Tim and I don't have bikes," Jack reminded him.

Bobby looked embarrassed. "Sorry," he said.

"So how do we get across?" I asked.

Jack mumbled something about being surrounded by imbeciles. For the next five minutes, the conversation degenerated into a laundry list of opposing views on what exactly imbecility and intelligence meant and how it was measured. Once Bobby laid waste to the brothers Swanson, he stood there beaming like a young Socrates.

"Just leave it to me," said Jack. "We go at sunset on Friday night. Meet us here with your packs. You know the drill. Bring food and soda. Tim and I will take care of the rest."

Chapter 3

In a small town, trouble always found you. It didn't matter if you went looking for it or not. No matter how hard you tried, it just came upon you like angry hornets cooped up in the nest you just picked to beat with a stick. Once you stirred it up, there was no stopping it.

After we left the dock, Bobby asked me to walk him some of the way home. It was nearly time for dinner, and I was already late. My mother liked for me to be there on summer afternoons to help her prepare meals. Still, I couldn't let Bobby down. He was an innocent lamb in a small town teeming with no-good wolves. It didn't matter that he lived ten blocks away from me. And no matter what, he always started out asking me to walk him part of the way, but somewhere near the half-way point, he always egged me on, pleading, almost, because he was so afraid of everyone and everything. The truth was that Bobby always ran the risk of running into some kid or another who he had insulted. If my best friend had one fault, it was his acerbic wit. Kids in Yorkville didn't grasp the nuances of a friendly verbal joust. Once Bobby got started—running at the mouth as my father called it—there was no letting up. It was this sort of tenacity on Bobby's part that usually led to some less-than-intelligent kid punching him right in the kisser. I was hardly a tough kid, but if Bobby was the king of playful insults, then I was the peacemaker. I got along well enough with most kids in Yorkville. Lucky for us, that was enough to keep the wolves at bay.

"Are we really going to cross the creek?" Bobby asked.

We were headed toward the square. Along the way, we passed Morgan's Corner Store. As we neared the little shop, I saw Mr. Von

Braun exit the store and march down the steps like some Schutzstaffel on parade. Jack Swanson told me once that he saw Mr. Von Braun buying adult magazines at Morgan's Corner Store.

"Since when is *Playboy* a crime?" I had asked Jack that day.

"The other mags," he had said with a wink. "Under the counter."

It was long rumored in Yorkville that Peter Morgan, the proprietor of the corner store, trafficked in illegal publications that ran to more extreme tastes: namely, underage boys, men on men, underage girls, and any one of the aforementioned with farm animals.

I never believed the rumors. My father and Mr. Morgan both served in the same unit during the Korean War. And my father was a straight-laced insurance guy who rode the bus every day into Philadelphia where he worked in a high-rise building. He and Mr. Morgan belonged to the same VFW lodge, and I knew that my father would never be chummy with a degenerate who pedaled illegal smut magazines.

"It's just that the bridge is so far." Bobby was still going on about crossing the creek.

"The tide will be low," I told him.

The truth was I didn't know shit about the tides, but I learned early on that if a guy sounded convincing enough, he could get away with just about anything.

"So, the boat might get stuck in the mud."

"At least nobody drowns if they fall overboard."

"Not funny."

"I wasn't trying to be funny. Christ, you worry too much."

As we passed Mr. Von Braun, I saw Peter Morgan exit the store.

"Mr. Von Braun?" Morgan called out.

"Coins." Bobby ducked into the phone booth located outside the store.

That was the code word—coins—for eavesdropping. I don't remember now if Bobby started that one or I did, but it didn't matter. No one ever considered some kid fishing for coins in a pay phone or crouching down in a gutter searching for spare change to be suspect. Adults were stupid that way. Most of the time, we remained invisible to them; unless, of course, we were in trouble, then it was as if a miracle turned their blind eyes into perfect instruments of perception.

Bobby and I crowded into the phone booth. I pretended to look for coins in the change slot, while Bobby kept his eyes trained on the two men. The previous summer, Bobby had ordered a pamphlet on lip reading from the back of one of my comic books. He swore by what the pamphlet had taught him, but I had my doubts about the pictures of people's mouths in different shapes. Bobby told me that the shape of the mouth determines if a vowel or consonant was being uttered. With practice, he told me, you could read lips like most people did books.

"What are they saying?" I asked. "Shit."

"What's wrong?"

"Some moron put out a cigarette in the change slot."

"German."

"The cigarette?" I rubbed my fingers on my pants. "How should I know?"

"No," said Bobby. "They're speaking German."

"Mr. Morgan doesn't know—"

"Something about searchers, I think."

"Are you sure?"

"My grandmother speaks German," he told me. I knew that. I had met the woman only a few times. She was Mr. McMahon's mother. She always smelled like potatoes fresh from the ground. "Anyway," he went on, "Mr. Morgan—"

"You boys get out of that phone booth," said Mr. Morgan as he climbed the steps toward his shop. "That isn't a playground ride."

"Hi, Mr. Morgan." I stepped out of the booth first.

"Joe," he said, smiling. "Everything okay?"

"Sure, I'm just walking Bobby home."

"There's a shortcut through the phone booth?"

"Sir?"

"Never mind. What's the matter? Your friend afraid of walking home by himself?"

"Uh, I was going to borrow a book from his dad," I said.

"And what book would that be?"

"*The Count of Monte Cristo*," Bobby spoke up.

"Dumas," the store owner said. "Come by the store some day when you finish the book, and we'll discuss the Count."

"Sure thing."

"Say hi to your dad for me."

"I will," I assured him. "Good night, Mr. Morgan."

Bobby ushered me away from the store. I sniffed my fingers. They stunk of ash.

By the time we reached the square, Bobby was shaking his head and moaning like he was sick. He was always doing that, but, as I learned, it had nothing to do with being physically ill. Bobby did the same thing when he screwed up a question on a test, as if he were berating himself for being such a dunce.

"What now?" I asked, far too familiar with the routine.

"It wasn't searcher," he said. "The word was suchender."

"What's that mean?"

"Seeker."

Far across the square, I spotted Sean McClusky surrounded by a handful of his regular goons. Bobby looked troubled.

"Don't worry, man," I told him. "It's cool."

"For you, maybe." He kept his eyes on McClusky.

"What do you think they were talking about?"

"Von Braun?"

"Not McClusky," I said. "Hell, I can read his lips."

I did my best Neanderthal impression. Bobby didn't crack a smile.

"Von Braun was telling Mr. Morgan that the seekers were here."

"Are we talking spies, maybe?"

"Don't be ridiculous."

"Commie spies?"

"And what would communist spies want in a town like Yorkville?"

"Good point," I said.

We crossed West End Street and entered an alley between Dave and Di's Luncheonette and Schmidt's Pharmacy. Bobby knew I was pressed for time. He figured the shortcut would do us good. Halfway down the alley, we found out he was wrong. McClusky and his goons followed us into the alley and cornered us right behind the pharmacy. A long line of big metal dumpsters stood between us and McClusky's gang.

"Hey, girls," said McClusky, "where are you going?"

"How original," said Bobby.

"Your buddy's got a smart mouth," the cretin told me.

"Maybe he needs his mouth stuffed," Mike Gruber announced. He was a friend of McClusky's from Tracktown. At fifteen, Gruber had been in and out of juvenile hall so many times, he'd lost count already.

McClusky grabbed Bobby's neck. I moved to stop him. A big mistake. Mike Gruber kicked me in the balls. I dropped to my knees. One of the other goons booted me in the back of my head. It took me several seconds to catch my breath. After I wiped the tears from my eyes, I looked up to see McClusky and his goons shuffling Bobby behind the long row of dumpsters. I followed, scurrying along like a four-legged spider on my hands and feet. My stomach felt like it was twisted in a huge knot. By the time I reached the row of dumpsters, I glimpsed Bobby as three goons held him in place on his knees. McClusky stood over him and lowered his pants. That's when Mike Gruber stepped into my path.

"Get lost," he said.

"What are you going to do him?" I asked. I couldn't see Bobby anymore, but I could hear him. The sound disgusted me.

"We're not going to do anything," Gruber said. "It's what that sweet mouth is going to do for all five of us."

Gruber was a big fat slob of a teenager. He held up a meaty fist to his mouth and pretended to suck a boner.

Bobby didn't fight them off that night. More than that, I wish I could say that I was able to save my friend. Or that I ran screaming back into the square searching for help. But I didn't.

McClusky exited the hiding spot behind the dumpsters, zipping up his jeans.

"Go take your queer friend home," he told me. "And if you rat on us, I'll kill you and that cunt girlfriend of yours, Marcella."

Mike Gruber punched me hard in the stomach. My knees buckled, and I collapsed. I high-crawled it to the other end of the dumpster row. That's where I found Bobby dry heaving as he bent over at the waist. He didn't say anything once he pulled himself together. Instead, he punched one of the dumpsters and ran off, leaving me alone.

Chapter 4

The next morning, I woke up late. My stomach still hurt, but I didn't tell my parents. Before breakfast, I called Bobby. His mother answered the phone.

"Bobby can't talk right now, Joe," Mrs. McMahon told me. "He's not feeling well."

"Tell him I called?"

"Sure thing."

"Did he—"

"Look, Joe," she said. "Bobby told me all about what happened."

Shit, I thought. "He did?"

"Now, Joe, I don't approve of boys fighting," said Mrs. McMahon, "but I can't keep Bobby home every day."

"I understand."

"Bobby is not like other boys. And other boys don't understand him."

"Uh, yeah, well—"

"You know that Bobby's different, too."

That much was true.

"He's my best friend," I told her.

"I know, dear," Mrs. McMahon cooed. She was always doing that. My father called her The Pigeon. "Just remember what I told you."

No way, I thought. *How could Bobby have told her about McClusky?* It was one thing to bear the stigma of what had happened, along with the constant chastisement that would follow, but telling your parents that you were victimized by a degenerate troglodyte like Tim McClusky was something else altogether.

"Anyway," Bobby's mother concluded, "try waiting until you are older before you go picking fights with teenagers. Honestly, Joe. Does your mother know that you and Bobby walked to the Bellshade Shopping Center?"

"No, ma'am."

"Well, I won't tell her this time," she said. "The next time you and the Swanson boys go hitchhiking over to Bellshade, just leave my Bobby out of it."

My head was spinning when I hung up. I felt torn. In a way, I knew that the only reason Bobby had lied about what happened the previous day was because he couldn't take being ridiculed by his father. I had no doubt that Bobby, despite being victimized by McClusky, would have endured his father blaming him yet again for getting into trouble. Sometimes, when I visited Bobby's house and his father was home, it was plain to see how his father seethed with the knowledge that his son was growing up queer. Bobby's father would never address the issue of his son being assaulted by an older boy, but instead he would go on ad nauseum about the dangers of walking down dark alleys. On the flip side, I was disgusted by the fact that Bobby somehow implicated me in a fabricated wrongdoing that never took place.

"Joe," my mother called from the basement. I opened the door in the kitchen that led downstairs. My mother stood there with a large laundry basket on her hip, stacked high with wet clothes. As the years would go on, that's how I would remember her: a perpetual task master who did not know what it meant to relax. "I'm taking the bus into Philadelphia later today," she announced. "Time to pay a visit to Uncle Scott. You want to go?"

Uncle Scott was my mother's older brother. He was a retired firefighter with a penchant for Sinatra music, whiskey, and Chinatown massage parlors. Uncle Scott may have been a walking cliché, but he was always there to help us when we needed it, and he was never afraid to let my father know as much.

"Do I have a choice?" I asked.

"I can call Mrs. McMahon. You could stay at Bobby's."

"Bobby's not feeling well."

"Oh, well, in that case—"

"Are we staying overnight at Uncle Scott's?"

"You like hanging out there."

"The spare room smells like ashtrays."

"I didn't plan on going back and forth," my mother said. "Besides, Uncle Scott will treat us to dinner."

"I was going to camp out at Jack's."

My mother commenced her march up the steps. I moved aside as she passed and headed for the back door.

"Can you remember to come home later today to take down the laundry?" she asked.

"You never leave me here alone," I said. "Besides, what do I do for dinner?"

"So you want to go?"

"No."

"You're just like your father."

"Will dad be home tonight?"

Dinner with dad. The choices were limited. My mother rolled her eyes when she saw the look on my face.

"Tell your dad I said to order a pizza from Angelo's," she said.

"I'm going over to Jack's now," I told her. "I have to help him clean the tent."

"Come out back with me."

My mother busied herself by hanging wet sheets on the clothesline that stretched between the house and the garage. Funny thing, the garage. My father didn't own a car. He and my mother inherited the house from my grandmother, my dad's mom. My grandmother died when I was just two years old. I didn't remember my grandmother at all, but I often wondered if I would one day inherit the house from my parents. If I did, I knew I'd spend the rest of my natural-born life disposing of all the crap my father collected and stored in the garage.

My father was a hoarder. All of his curios and crap ended up in the garage. There was never rhyme or reason to the things he collected. He kept old newspapers in bundles tied up with twine, car tires, parts to washing machine engines, spare mufflers, lamp shades with no lamps, boxes with old, mildewy books—some of them in English, others in Latin, Greek, Spanish, and German—weird statuettes that ranged from angels to gargoyles, and other oddities that served no purpose other than to take up space and drive my mother nuts.

"You should make an inventory," Bobby had told me one day when I showed him the garage.

There were file cabinets positioned way in the back of the garage. Locked or not, they stood completely inaccessible.

"Inventory?" I asked.

"Yes, it would be cool."

"To rummage through three tons of crap? No thanks." Bottles, some of them very old. Metal cases with padlocks. I wouldn't know where to begin.

"Joe," my mother's voice rang out like a song behind a canopy of bed sheets.

"Yeah, mom?"

"Promise me you won't go near the creek at night?"

"Why would I—"

A sheet snapped back in the gentle breeze. My mother stood there glaring at me, one hand holding back the sheet and her other hand planted firmly on her hip. Did she know already?

Once, when I was nine years old, my father told me I could go to church on my own. For me, it was a like a rite of passage. My mother wasn't so hip to the idea. The following Saturday after my father gave me his blessing to fly solo at mass, I invited Jack Swanson to go with me. He was raised by his grandmother as a Lutheran—a faith of which I knew nothing about. Jack always thought that all the saints and angels of the Roman Catholic Church were cool.

"All we do," he had confessed to me once, "is sit there and sing and listen to some blowhard drone on about Adam, Eve, and the serpent."

Given Jack's position, I thought it was time for a change, but I never dared to tell my parents that he would go with me.

Amongst all the crap in the garage, my father kept two three-foot-tall statues. One was a rosy-cheeked St. Dominic, the patron saint of astronomers in the Dominican Republic and also the athlete of God, known so because of his tireless effort to serve his Maker. The other statue was of the angel Michael, the warrior of God who fought in the War for Heaven, adorned with helmet, breastplate, shield with the words "Quis ut Deus," and armed with sword in hand. Christ knows where my father found these two unlikely companions, but it was the archangel Michael who made Jack a convert. Or so I thought until Jack accompanied me to a vigil mass.

St. Bonaventure Church was the oldest church in Yorkville. Across the street from it stood my school named after the same saint. When you stepped inside the church, you could smell the scent of old wood mixed with the ever-present aroma of incense. In a grotto to the left, as you entered the church, stood a life-sized stature of Saint Bonaventure, a plaster reminder that all who stood in his presence could, if they chose to, fly the straight and narrow, develop stainless character, and avoid, just as Bonaventure did, the curse of Adam's Sin. In the grotto on the right, a life-sized likeness of the Blessed Virgin whose facial expression, when you stood close to her, hinted at a spiritual ecstasy often associated with Saint Theresa D'Avila. Bonaventure's mug, and on the other hand, belied the envy he harbored toward the Queen of Angels. In truth, for a twelve-year-old boy, the vestibule where the two statues stood was creepy.

Vigil masses on Saturday afternoons always went by faster than the regular Sunday mass. And the best part was that confession was heard thirty minutes prior to the vigil mass, so in theory, parishioners could absolve themselves of whatever sins they carried, hear the Gospel, and partake in Holy Communion in about as much time as it took to run a load of laundry through the washer and dryer.

That Saturday afternoon, I took communion like a good Catholic boy. Afterward, I returned to the pew where Jack sat, waiting for me as he stared in awe at the celestial murals painted on the high cathedral ceiling. No sooner had I sat down, preparing to pray for my parents and all those who had gone before me, I noticed Jack had become more anxious.

"Man,"—I never forgot the unholy words he muttered in the church that day—"I can't wait to get the fuck out of here."

Later, when I went home, I met my mother in the yard where she was hanging the laundry out to dry. She stood there with her hand on her hip the way she always did, a disappointed look etched on her face.

"Joe," she said, "you can go to church on your own any time you want."

"Thanks, Mom."

"Let me finish."

"Sorry."

"But you will not be going to church with Jack Swanson ever again."

That summer day, when my mother mentioned Hobbs Creek, my mind replayed the memory of that ill-fated visit to St. Bonaventure Church with Jack. That wasn't the only time, however, when bad news traveled fast. Throughout my childhood, I had the unfortunate luck of being somewhere in public when one of my friends muttered a curse word or rendered some obscene gesture. By the time my mother reprimanded me for the church incident, I was convinced that someone bolted from the church after mass to the nearest pay phone and dialed my house. There was no other explanation, unless my mother had St. Bonaventure Church bugged with sophisticated electronic surveillance equipment.

"Joe, are you listening to me?"

"Stay away from the creek. I got it."

"I'm serious."

"Mom, I heard you."

"What is it with the Swanson brothers and that creek, anyway?"

"I won't go near the creek. Okay?"

"Your father and I don't need that sort of trouble," she told me. "Do you remember Sean Pullman?"

Who could forget with a mother like mine? Years before, when I was maybe three years old, a teen named Sean Pullman had decided to dive off the Dover Bridge on a bright summer day. To hear my mother tell the story, Sean took the dive on a dare. My father's version was a bit different. He told me that Sean was out to impress a girl. Never mind that my father could never remember the siren's name that called young Sean toward ruin, that Sean risked life and limb, and ultimately his life, for the fleeting approval of some small-town harpy was the convoluted lesson my father offered. No matter the story's version, or who told it, Hobbs Creek claimed the life of the teen, and that loss, in turn, served as a warning for any child who wanted to go near the merciless creek.

Ever since that time, my parents kept a constant vigil. Still, no parent can protect their son or daughter all the time. This much I learned by the time I was twelve. I managed to sneak off to the creek, but as often as I did, my parents somehow always found out. There were times when my mother whipped my ass, and there were times when my father did. Such was the power Hobbs Creek had over our lives.

Chapter 5

The day's last light had given over to twilight's magical hue when I met Jack by the creek. He busied himself by laying two knapsacks into a canoe. Next, he hoisted a folded, olive drab tent into the canoe along with a half-dozen or more poles. While Jack labored to ready the vessel, Tim attempted to light a Coleman lantern without much success.

"Where's Bobby?" Jack wiped his hands on his jeans.

"He's not coming," I told him.

"Did he say why?"

"Tell you later," I nodded at Tim.

"Did you bring food?"

I handed him a small gym bag filled with sodas, Tastykakes, chocolate bars, potato chips, fresh rolls, luncheon meat I stole from my refrigerator, and a small jar of mayonnaise.

Earlier that evening, after my mother left to visit Uncle Scott, my father and I walked to the square. I was nervous as hell since I figured my father was going to somehow relay to me that he found out about Bobby's predicament. Instead, we went to Dave and Di's Luncheonette. My father loved that place. He ate there two or three times a week. What he didn't know, and only a little boy would, was that I went in there once when I was five, and I could see beneath the countertop where patrons sat on stools and ate their sandwiches. There were countless chunks of dried chewing gum and snot on the underside of the counter beneath which the stools rested.

For my father, there was no better on-the-go meal than the pastrami and rye at Dave and Di's. All I could think about was the dried snot and gum. My father was capable of putting away three pastrami and rye sandwiches in one sitting. That night, however, he took it easy and consumed just two of them. I knew the old man enough to understand that something made him agitated that night. For me, I barely made it through a single slice of pizza. I was pretty sure there were no chunks of dried snot or gum inside the pizza oven, so I figured I was safe. As to what bothered my father, I didn't have a clue.

If there was one redeeming value about going into Dave and Di's, it was the magazine section. Unlike Mr. Morgan at his corner store who hid adult magazines behind the counter, Dave or maybe Di, or perhaps both of them, saw fit to line the top shelves of the magazine section with all kinds of adult entertainment magazines. Some of the regular titles included *Playboy, Penthouse, Swank, Genesis*, and *Mayfair*; and every now and again, there were more exotic mags placed on the top shelf for patrons, both young and old, to see.

A rumor went around Yorkville that Di Schlesinger, Dave's wife, was some sort of former stag film star, but I never saw how she could have made any money doing it since her blond hair looked like dried straw and she had a wandering eye.

The perv section aside, however, Dave and Di's offered the most diverse comic book collection of any store in Yorkville. Bobby and I spent countless hours getting our fix there, always careful to avoid eye contact with the errant, seedy stranger who perused the adult mags. The previous summer, Dave and Di's shut down for a week. Many adults, my mother included, speculated that one of these perverts got a hold of a little girl or boy and ushered them into the dark restroom in the back corner of the establishment. That rumor, like the one about Di doing the nasty on film, turned out to be not true. My father, a long-time champion of Dave and Di's, set the record straight. He informed my mother and me that Dave and Di's was closed down due to renovations. The odd part was that when they opened for business, the place looked exactly the same.

Sitting in the luncheonette that night, I listened to my father drone on about the merits of trying out for Little League baseball that summer. The problem was that tryouts began back in May, and the season was nearly over that August, with the start of a new school year only weeks away. It was this sort of miscommunication, or dare I say, sheer ignorance on my father's part, that summed up our relationship. My father never really took to having a son; instead, he tried to relive his own guarded boyhood through me. My mother once told me that my grandparents never let my father do anything except study hard and pray. Even a boy like me knew enough to understand that such a life might leave a man empty inside or at least yearning for all that he had missed.

So I let my old man go on ad nauseum about building friendships and bonds through sports while building a stronger body. Meanwhile, I could see the adult magazine shelf just over his head as he sat facing me. I studied the faces of all the pretty women on the covers of those magazines. Immediately, I thought of Bobby McMahon who, while ordinarily seeking to avoid any form of confrontation, risked it all to glimpse between the covers of those magazines. He got away with it from time to time, but the whole scene made me a bit uncomfortable as he would leer at the naked men in those magazines. Before long, once Dave or Di shooed us out of the luncheonette, Bobby always got around to talking about the human body, more specifically, the male body and how each guy's pecker looked different than the next.

The other thing about Bobby, his other weakness besides naked men in magazines, was his secret taste for comic books. In school, everyone knew he was a smart kid who read more classic novels than anyone else in town. Bobby's addiction to comic books came in part from his parents' refusal to allow them into their home. I felt sorry for him. But what bothered me more than his fancy for pictures of grown naked men in various sex acts with women, more than his jonesing for comic books, was how at that moment—as my father sat there with a sliver of pastrami hanging from the corner of his mouth, going on incessantly about the magic of baseball—Bobby sat in his room, afraid to come out. For the time being, he refused to let me or anyone else into his closed world.

"Tim," Jack's voice pulled me back to the present, "go get the life jackets in the basement."

"You go," his brother said as he finally got the lantern lit.

"The lantern and the life jackets were your responsibility."

"Don't let the lantern go out."

"Tim, come on. Save the lantern until we need it."

"We need it now. It's dark out."

"Thanks for the update, shit cake. It will be darker when we cross the creek. Now, go get the life jackets."

"But the lantern—"

Jack kicked the lantern over. The flame inside jumped and went out.

"Forget the lantern." Jack stepped close to his brother. "You want everyone to see us crossing the creek?"

"No." Tim took a step back.

"Then quit fucking around, and—"

"Grandmom will catch me."

"Not if you sneak in through the basement window."

"Yes, she will."

"She's probably watching McCloud by now with the volume turned way up."

Tim turned his back on us and took off at a slow trot. He vanished into the humid, hazy darkness. No sooner than he did, Jack picked up the lantern and put it in the canoe.

"The other night," I said, "McClusky and his goons cornered me and Bobby in the alley behind Schmidt's Pharmacy."

Jack sat on the ground as he listened to me spin the whole yarn about how McClusky forced Bobby to do things behind a dumpster while Mike Gruber used me as a punching bag.

"Fucking Gruber," he said when I finished. "I hate that fat cocksucker."

"I should have done something," I said.

"Like what?"

"I don't know. Maybe run for help."

"So you think McClusky forced Bobby to...you know?"

"I didn't see it, if that's what you mean."

"Ah. McClusky and Gruber are queer."

"How do you know that?"

"Did you ever see them hanging out with any girls?"

"We don't hang out with any girls, Jack."

"What about Marcella?"

A twig snapped. Tim's muffled curses drifted toward us through the dark. Out over the creek, fireflies lit their tails like errant stars blinking in some chaotic constellation. Jack stood up, and held a finger to his lips.

"Dickheads." Tim emerged holding a huge bag of Wise brand potato chips.

"Life jackets?" Jack asked.

"What did you do with my lantern?"

"In the canoe. Life jackets?"

"I couldn't hear the television," Tim stammered. "It felt like Grandmom was watching me."

"Where did you get the chips?"

"I slid through the basement window like you told me. Then I remembered I was hungry."

"So you grabbed the chips from the kitchen and forgot the life jackets? What's wrong with you?"

"I'm sorry, Jack. I forgot."

"Did you close the back door?"

Tim shoved the bag of chips into my hands. He took off running again back toward the house.

"It's getting late," said Jack.

"We don't need life jackets," I told him. "Bobby's not here."

A few minutes later, Jack, Tim, and I boarded the canoe and pushed off into the dark. The Swanson brothers fought each other over the stupidest things when they were on dry land, but when they were on the creek in a boat or a canoe, their differences dissolved like a snowflake in a hot frying pan. There was no oar for me, so the brothers rowed slowly across the cool, stagnant water. There were mosquitoes clumped in little clouds every few feet. Jack and Tim seemed impervious to the onslaught. I flailed my hands like a drowning man, attempting to part the sea of bloodsucking insects.

"You'll tip us," Tim said quietly.

I stopped. At night, the creek looked different. When Jack and I were a few years younger, we used to go down to the dock behind his house with the hope of catching a glimpse of Sean Pullman's ghost. We never saw the drowned boy's spirit, or any other spook for that matter, but that night, crossing Hobbs Creek in a stolen canoe, we were only ten or twenty yards from the far shore when I saw something move in the high reeds.

The mosquito clouds lifted as Jack steered us clear of the reeds, and we ran aground on the far shore. Tim sat ahead of me, his oar resting on his lap. As his brother steered, I busied myself by holding the sides of the canoe until we came to rest in the wet sand.

"Look." Tim pointed at the reeds.

To our left, the reeds parted, and a small inflatable raft emerged. I heard a girl complain about the mosquitoes. She wasn't visible, but the teen boy maneuvering the raft sat up straight. He cranked a small outboard motor. The remainder of the couple's conversation was drowned out by the engine's noise. If they saw us, they didn't pay us any mind.

"Love is in the air," Tim sang.

"Shut up," Jack cut him off. "All ashore and all that bullshit."

Tim stepped out of the canoe from the front, bounding in one leap onto the dry land. I followed, but my feet landed in mud.

"I'll bet they were doing it over there," Tim whispered.

"Doing what?" I asked.

"Don't be a moron, Joe."

"Hey, Columbo," Jack called out. "I need you to help me pull the canoe."

The three of us slid the canoe out of the water. After we stood on dry land again, I unloaded our supplies while Jack and Tim gathered fallen tree limbs. The woods lay ten yards from the creek bank. Once I moved our packs into the tree line along with Tim's lantern, I went to get the tent.

"Be quiet," said Jack.

I stood still.

"Sometimes the Tracktown kids come over here to party," said Tim.

"And worse," Jack whispered.

He took the tent, poles, and pegs from me.

"Where?" I started to say.

"You and Tim carry the canoe into the woods," Jack instructed. "We'll need to hide it so no one steals it."

"But it's—"

"Just help Tim!"

Across the creek, shadows moved along the water. Tim showed me how to lift the canoe by the front tip. Then, he gripped the back end and counted to three. As we hoisted the canoe up, I nodded toward the water.

"It's a trick of the clouds," said Tim. "The water reflects them and the moon and the stars. It gives you a false sense of where the water ends and the land begins, so you think you see things moving—"

"Okay, Marlin Perkins," his brother cut him off, "if you're finished with your *Wild Kingdom* pitch, I'd like to get going."

We stood there as Jack marched forward and vanished in the shadows beyond the trees.

"Jack has no respect for nature."

"You're going to respect my foot up your ass in about two seconds," Jack's voice rang out, "if you don't get going."

"I thought I saw something moving," I said.

"The reeds and the reflection," Tim said as we shuffled the canoe into the tree line. "It plays tricks on your eyes."

We found Jack waiting for us. He already had his pack on his back with the rolled up tent, the poles, and the pegs affixed to it. He looked like he was ready to go on a safari.

"Everything's cool," he said.

"I don't feel like dealing with any of those Tracktown kids tonight," I told him.

"Joe, if they were around, we wouldn't have seen that couple in the raft."

"That's true," Tim added. "Some girl from over on Downey Street was raped here last summer."

"What girl?" I wondered.

"It doesn't matter."

"Tim's right," said Jack. "But it wasn't Tracktown kids that did it."

"Who did it?" I asked.

"Derelicts that come over from the rail yard in Hagerstown," Tim said. "Real lowlifes."

"Throw some branches over the canoe," Jack told me after Tim and I set the canoe down against a big oak tree. "We'll come back for it before first light."

After I finished camouflaging the canoe, I picked up my knapsack and my gym bag. A strong wind blew through the woods.

"Smells like rain," Jack announced as he led us into the forest.

Chapter 6

As we moved further into the woods, we discovered evidence of past expeditions made by others. Their refuse littered the ground all around us. Beer bottles, soda cans, and food wrappers were strewn near pine needle-covered fire pits. One two occasions, we passed half-buried beer kegs. Near the buried kegs, there were old, rusted ten-gallon canisters of gasoline. That summer, a commercial on television depicted the ills of pollution. An Italian-American actor masqueraded as a Native-American tribal chief with tears in his eyes. If he had visited the banks of Hobbs Creek, the chief, imposter or not, would have had a stroke. Besides the aforementioned litter, I spotted a rusted, old washing machine and a refrigerator missing a door.

"Maybe we can loan your old man the canoe," said Jack.

"I think the garage is full," I told him.

"The ground's wet," Tim said.

That much was true. My Converse All-Stars were soaked. We trodded nearly a hundred yards before there were any signs of dry land.

"The ground here is lower than the creek," Jack explained. "When we get to higher ground, it will be okay."

He led the way up a gradual incline. The trees appeared larger and more foreboding there. Looking up, I noticed the stars had all gone away.

"Get out the compass, Tim," Jack said.

Tim pulled the device out of his pocket. He held the compass at his waist as I looked over his shoulder. The arrow pointed to his right.

"That's north." Tim jerked his right thumb out. "Me and Jack found a trail that leads west about a mile into the woods."

I already harbored second thoughts about the camping expedition. I wasn't the outdoorsman that the brothers Swanson were. And unlike other kids in Yorkville, I never went camping with my parents on vacation. My mom and my dad were pure city types. Nature, for them, was a place where landfills bloomed; untamed acres simply invited developers to build housing communities, shopping centers, and industrial parks. Nowhere else was it more true than in New Jersey. Franklin Forest was a small portion of the Pine Barrens that covered much of the state and, much to my parents' disappointment, was protected from development.

In school, we learned all about Franklin Forest and how it came to be named. In the early 1800s, a contemporary of Charles Darwin came to America to study a peculiar rumor about a site that had been excavated by some locals. Within a year, Rhys Franklin, the friend of Charles Darwin, had, with the help of an archeology team, unearthed an entire Lenni-Lenape village, complete with fire pits, pottery, arrowheads, and deerskins upon which murals were rendered. The soft, boggy earth preserved most of the items from ruin. but the deerskins had been rolled and placed in tubes constructed from bark centuries ago. And now, those skins were in bad shape.

Rhys Franklin rendered reproductions of the deerskin murals in his book *A Vanishing: The Fate of a Lenapi Village*. One drawing made by Franklin in his book depicted a variety of stick people fleeing a pyramid shape. Inside the pyramid stood what appeared to be an angel with Raphaelite wings. Franklin explained in his book that while the Lenapi could not have possibly known anything about pyramidal structures in places like Egypt, Peru, Greece, Mesopotamia, and India, the recurring image on all the deerskins may in fact have represented a doorway or a portal into the dreamtime. Until the publication of his book, Rhys Franklin had been a respected scholar who taught at Oxford as well as at the universities of Paris and Munich. By the time he arrived in America, Franklin was wealthy beyond measure. His book, *A Vanishing*, proved nearly fatal for both his reputation and his livelihood. In *A Vanishing*, Franklin surmised that perhaps the particular Lenapi settlement he had unearthed bore witness to one of the strangest disappearances in human history. The muddy bog where the settlement lay also housed weapons, food reserves, and the mummified remains of infants and toddlers, all of which were preserved for centuries. Franklin's theory regarding portals to other dimensions made him an outcast.

In the years that followed the publication of *A Vanishing*, an entire cottage industry erupted as a result of Franklin's work. There were numerous tours to the excavated site. And countless self-styled "spiritualists" visited the New Jersey Pinelands in search of the famous portals. By the time of the First World War and the subsequent stock market crash some years later that heralded the Great Depression, the excavated site was all but forgotten, trodden over by curiosity seekers and various self-appointed mystics throughout the ensuing decades. Before long, the site was consumed once more by the Pine Barrens.

After World War II, a vast tract of the Pine Barrens covering nearly 110,000 acres of the Pinelands was designated as the Rhys Franklin State Forest. It turned out that despite concocting a theory concerning parallel dimensions and secret doors, Franklin had left a boatload of money to the state of New Jersey to be used for the preservation of the Pine Barrens. Somewhere within the new state forest, covered over by pine trees, vines, and moss, lay the Lenapi settlement that had plagued the explorer and scholar throughout his adult life.

In the early 1960s, or so the story goes, a graduate history student named Carl Huffington came from the University of Michigan at Ann Harbor to visit Franklin State Forest. Huffington wanted to find the original settlement first revealed nearly a century beforehand. He intended to write his thesis on how all myths were based on historic fact, but they were distorted by collective embellishment until the original truth was lost.

Three weeks into his jaunt, Carl Huffington vanished. An extensive search of the state forest and points beyond turned up nothing save for a copy book with notes and sketches rendered by Huffington himself. The last entry Huffington made was on June 7, 1963: *Ohta*, the name the Lene-Lenape gave to a trickster spirit who often led men toward ruin. Poor Huffington. He roamed the forest the Lenape once did, but the alien gods there turned a blind eye to him.

"That's weird," Tim said.

The sound of his voice made me jump. Every stick we trampled as we moved further into the woods sounded like bones breaking. I kept thinking about Franklin and Huffington. *Were their ghosts out here?* I wondered.

A warm, humid wind blew through the woodland. Far to south, lightning illuminated the sky, turning the dark gray clouds into ghastly shades of green, purple, and blue. Each time the lightning flashed, the trees moved in the wind like skeletal monsters slowly making their approach.

"Shit," Jack exclaimed.

"Are we lost?" I asked.

Tim slapped the compass. "Fuck," he muttered.

Jack cupped his hands to his ears. "I don't hear anything," he said.

"Like what?" I asked.

"The compass has gone all haywire," Tim announced.

"Meaning," said Jack, ignoring his brother for the moment. "I don't hear anything. No crickets, no owls, no frogs. Nothing."

"We're lost," I said. "Just go on and say it."

"We're not lost," the brothers Swanson said in unison. Tim handed Jack the compass.

Lightning revealed the sour look on Jack's face as he shook the compass several times. Thunder rumbled in the distance at first, but ended with a sharp report right over our heads.

Chapter 7

We were beyond lost. First, Jack failed to find the trail he mentioned after we had hidden the canoe. Then I found out that Tim wasn't kidding about the compass. I had hoped he was just playing a prank, a sort of initiation into the tedium of outdoorsmanship. The compass needle spun continuously in a counterclockwise motion. I didn't know much about the great outdoors and camping, but I knew enough about compasses to understand that something was definitely wrong.

"They say this happens in the Bermuda Triangle." Tim flipped the compass closed.

That summer, *Jaws* and the Bermuda Triangle were all the rage. Tim reminded me time and again of a case in Matawan, N.J. where a boy died from a shark attack in a tidal river. Sharks in fresh water creeks and rivers never deterred the Swanson brothers from venturing out on Hobbs Creek. Of course, I knew that Tim loved to play with people's heads as much as his older brother did, and what better way than to tease someone like me who never really developed their sea legs—or creek legs in my case—but, when it came to the unknown, Tim never teased about that. So, when he likened the compass going all haywire to a phenomenon that happened in the Bermuda Triangle, I listened well.

"Joey, don't pay my brother any mind," said Jack. "He's just fucking with you."

"I don't know, Jack," I started to say.

"But there are documented cases from the Bermuda Triangle," Tim cut me off. "Of course, Jack, if you ever visited a library, you would know this yourself."

"You want to know what else I know?" Jack turned on him.

I stepped between the brothers. Lightning flashed, illuminating the woodland around us. When it did, that's when I saw him. He was thin, with skin the color of white birch bark, and a head full of wild, matted hair dotted with leaves and tiny tree branches. From fifteen yards away, he looked like a wild little boy. I scanned the dark, but I lost sight of him. Lightning flashed once more. The wild boy was gone.

"We should set camp," Jack was saying.

"Someone was there," I said.

"Where?"

"Behind you," I told him. "About fifteen or twenty yards over that way."

"I don't see anything," Tim announced. "Set camp here?"

"No," his brother said. "We'll end up waking up in an inch of water. No, let's head for the next rise."

"Jack," I said, "there really was someone there."

"Yeah, right."

"He wasn't wearing any clothes."

"You're not going all homo on me, are you?"

"What? No. Listen to me—"

Tim patted me on the back as thunder rumbled closer to us. "The woods are weird that way, Joe," he said. "Especially with the lightning and all. It was probably just a fallen tree."

We moved further into the forest. After another two hundred yards, we came upon a clearing on a rise that satisfied Jack. As the first drops of rain began to fall, I felt confident once more in his ability to survive. He knew, as well his brother did, that I harbored serious doubts about the excursion that night. The only thing that would have made it worse was for Bobby to have come along. At the first hint of rain, Bobby would have pleaded with the brothers Swanson to take him back across the creek, and that's to say nothing of the lightning and thunder. Anyway, Jack decided that since the compass wasn't working, he'd mark our direction the old-fashioned way by reading the moss on the north side of the trees.

While Jack pontificated on the merits of old-world land navigation, Tim gathered long sticks with spindly twigs on their ends and used them to sweep clean the clearing. Afterward, the three of us set up the tent. Jack used an old army excavation tool to dig a trench six inches deep all the way around the tent. The instrument was a small folding shovel with a wood handle and collapsible blade identical to the type that soldiers carried on their rucksacks. Next, he carved a short trench, eight or ten feet long, down the rise to lead the water away from the tent.

"Break out the food," Tim said.

"Smell that?" Jack asked.

I shook my head.

"Ozone," he told me.

"Get the fuck out of here," I told him.

A sharp report exploded overhead like artillery fire as lightning turned the dark woodland into a bright white wasteland.

I didn't have time to argue any more. Tim was the first one into the tent. Jack left me standing out there when the first part of the storm hit. Wind whipped around the tent from all directions. I could smell smoke on the wind, too, but I didn't stay outside long enough to see where it was coming from, choosing, instead, to dive head-first into the tent.

"The sleeping bags!" Jack exited the tent.

"Throw them to me," I called to him.

Less than a minute later, we were comfortably sheltered from the passing storm outside. I passed sodas around. Jack insisted we wait to eat once the storm passed. He and Tim agreed that food inside the tent was bad news. I figured we ate in our homes so it was okay to feast inside the tent.

"Wrong," Jack told me. "We'll have every critter within miles sniffing and snuffling their way—"

"Snuffling?" I felt a little like Bobby now.

"The point is—"

"Hey, Joe," Tim cut him off. "Did you ever read Swamp Thing?"

"Why?" I asked. "Did the Swamp Thing invade a tent full of food?"

"He came out of the swamp," he ignored my snide comment. "But don't worry. There are no swamps around here."

"That's a relief."

Tim shrugged. Jack stared off into the darkness.

"Of course," said Tim, "there is the Jersey Devil. Now, that's a documented fact."

"Here we go," his brother muttered.

"You see, Joe, this forest is part of the Pine Barrens. And the Barrens, everybody knows, belongs to the Jersey Devil."

"My dad says there's no such thing," I told him.

"Adults are like that," he said. "They always put down what they can't easily categorize in their ordered universe. You know the deal. Death and taxes. In between, there's no room for magic or mystery."

"The Jersey Devil's a myth."

"No, the Devil's a fact. Before the first World War, people as far away as Philadelphia claimed to have found strange tracks in their yards. And this with the Delaware River separating the two states."

"I still say it's a myth."

"What my brother's saying," Jack spoke up, "is some people think otherwise."

"Yeah, and some people believe in the Easter bunny," I argued. "That doesn't make it so. You guys are just trying to scare me."

"Listen," he said. "Be quiet."

Tim took hold of my arm.

"You hear that?" Jack asked.

"What?" I said and held my breath. It was a good thing I did. Jack let loose a fart so loud it was enough to wake the dead.

"Okay," said Jack when the air cleared, "let's get our packs into the tent. I don't think the rain will let up any time soon."

Thunder rumbled overhead as we worked. When the rain came, it fell hard. The brothers Swanson and I slipped into the tent along with our packs. It was difficult to situate the sleeping bags just so owing to the room our packs took up inside the tent, but we managed to do so by working in concert, slithering over one another as we muttered curses.

Soon, each of us settled onto our stomachs, our packs placed toward the back of the tent, and watched the rain through the open flap. The rain drummed against the tent exterior and onto the forest floor, the syncopated beat at once hypnotic and soothing.

"Do you think Kim Whalen is cool?" Jack's voice sounded far away when he spoke.

My eyelids felt heavy. "I think she's cool, sure," I told him.

Kim lived with her mother and her older sister, Theresa, who spent most of the year away at college. She was pretty in a plain Jane kind of way; her mother and her sister were the same. When we were in the second grade, Kim's father went out one night after dinner for a pack of cigarettes and never came back. At night, all over Yorkville, couples took inventory of themselves and their respective relationships, including my parents; such was the stigma of abandonment. Suddenly, all the married men in our town were thrust under the microscope. The ripple effect Mr. Whalen's vanishing act had on the whole community continued in the years that followed. Many an evening, I heard my parents speaking in hushed tones about what would make a man leave behind his family. Divorce was one thing, they reasoned, but abandoning a family was something altogether different. There was more to it than running to the arms of another woman, my father surmised. My mother agreed, whispering in a conspiratorial tone about the emptiness modern man experiences despite appearing outwardly satisfied. My parents' musings aside, I felt bad for Kim. How she managed to deal with her father walking out on her was beyond my comprehension.

No one of us lived a typical life. For me, by the time I reached my teen years, most boys attempted to come to grips with the hormones raging through their bodies, mostly after girls, or, in other cases, after other boys, with the hope of either losing their virginity or at least satisfying some deep, unfilled adolescent sexual desire. For me, it was different. For me, it was more than that; for me, there were powers beyond my comprehension existing within the real world but largely ignored by people who would rather bask in the security of linear thinking than wade into the chaotic abyss that existed just beyond the veil of immediate reality.

Still, I was twelve years old, and I thought I knew a little something about human nature. Namely, that everyone possessed holes in the fabric of their being, a void, separate from the stain of original sin, that existed within the human soul, that the emptiness we experienced was fundamentally misunderstood—and that human beings everywhere, no matter their race or creed, no matter the age in which they lived, sought to fill that void with any number of temporary remedies. There were people who turned to drink or drugs; still others sought solace in cults and cliques. Kim's father was no different; though his actions appeared outwardly self-serving, egocentric, even irrational, he suffered from the chronic condition all men suffered: the perforated soul.

In a small town like Yorkville, however, the sudden absence of a family man not taken by war or a murderous crime punched a hole in the collective fabric of the community's soul. It reminded everyone how fragile a thing the human soul was, and how the emptiness the soul experienced made man forever incomplete.

"Are you going to run away with Marcella?" Jack asked.

My eyes opened wide. "No way," I answered.

Boys were such cruel creatures. At our age, we were obligated to deny the love we felt for a certain girl even when pressed for truth from a close friend.

"Sure."

"I'm serious, Jack."

"So am I, Joe. Me and Kim, we're going to stay right here in Yorkville."

"Not me," Tim piped up now. "I'm going to join the army when I get older."

Coming in the heels of the Vietnam War, Tim's plan for the future carried some weight. Yorkville was like so many towns; young men saw few options to get out, so they ended up serving in uniform.

"No you're not, jackass," his brother said. "A lot of guys get killed in war. You want to end up like them?"

"Maybe I'll live," said Tim.

"You can get maimed," Jack said. "Look at Futnut. You want to end up like him?"

"Don't make fun of Futnut, Jack. It's not right."

Futnut was the nickname we gave to a neighbor of Bobby McMahon's. His real name was Stan McClure. He was barely twenty-five years old, serving in Vietnam as a rifleman in the 28th Infantry, when a mine strapped to a banana tree riddled his left side with shrapnel. Stan "Futnut" McClure lost his left arm and a good portion of the left side of his head which military doctors put back together as best they could with steel plates and screws through the jaw bone. Though his skull had been made new, McClure lost a good chunk of his brain matter when the mine blast hit him. Some kids from Tracktown were making fun of him two summers ago at a Little League baseball game, calling him all kinds of names. McClure's face turned red as he frothed at the mouth; his left eye secreted a mix of tears and mucus the way it always did when he got excited, and when he muttered a curse, it came out sounding like "futnut." In a perfect world without war, Stan McClure would have told those kids "fuck you," but fate had left him half-crippled with a speech impediment. The nickname stuck.

Mrs. McMahon told my dad that, late at night, she often heard Stan McClure screaming in the dark. I felt sorry for McClure. Mrs. McMahon said that she didn't know which was worse: the physical pain boys endured in war or the way playing a part in such mayhem tore asunder their very souls. As if the price paid for survival, Bobby's mother maintained, was to have one foot in this world and the other one planted firmly in Hell.

"That is the very definition of anguish," Mrs. McMahon told my dad, "not knowing whether you belong among the living or among the dead."

My mother always said that Mrs. McMahon possessed the soul of a poet. My dad, on the other hand, maintained that Bobby's mom was probably a harlot in a past life. I didn't know who was right, but I knew that Bobby's mom had a knack for saying things like no one else could.

Presently, the rain fell in torrents, blocking our view of the woods. I don't remember what time it was when the rain finally stopped. All I knew was that Jack and Tim slept right through the worse part of the storm and, in so doing, missed the spectacle I witnessed right outside our tent. Things may have been different if the Swanson brothers were awake, but since they were asleep, the boy standing in the rain-soaked woods, not ten yards from the tent, beckoned me alone. He was about my height, sickly thin with skin as pale as the moon, and naked as the day he was born. The hair on top of his head was long and knotted in dreadlocks. When the boy beckoned me, he left me no choice. I followed him into the darkness.

Chapter 8

The trees glistened as a pale moon broke through the parting dark clouds; the familiar splendor of the nighttime woodland turned at once alien and spectral as I followed the boy deeper into the forest.

It dawned on me too late to turn around and stay within sight of the tent. My attention, instead, was drawn to the strange boy ahead me. He seemed at home in the woods, as if he had lived there without ever knowing town life with its grid of streets and anonymous façade of row homes. Was there, I wondered, some errant family, perhaps even a whole clan, who lived in the forest, a secret enclave as yet undetected by the surrounding communities? My mind raced as I followed him up a gradual incline until we reached a low ridge. He raced down the slope on the other side, dodging saplings and underbrush with ease. Halfway down the hill, continuing my pursuit, I fell, face-first, into a thicket. When I pulled myself up again, I looked around. The boy was gone.

Ten or fifteen yards away, a stream ran beneath a footbridge. At the bridge's entrance, there was a natural arch formed by two trees. As I drew near, I saw that the trees arcing toward each other were stripped of their bark.

Now, having lost sight of the boy, panic seized me. As fast as I could, I slogged my way back through the woods. The full moon cast its gray-white glow, and, before long, I saw the tent through the trees. Jack and Tim emerged and stood facing each other, their arms gesticulating wildly as they argued with each other. As I made my approach, it was Jack who saw me first.

"Where did you go?" he demanded.

Tim busied himself by turning on the flashlight and turning it off again.

"I..."

"Maybe he had to take a shit." Tim held the flashlight beneath his chin, turning the light on and off again.

"You're going to wear out the batteries, dipshit," his brother told him. Then, "Joe, don't go disappearing like that."

"There's an old bridge over the hill," I said, pointing, "that way."

"Tim," said Jack.

"Let me guess," he said. "Stay here and guard the stuff?"

Jack took the compass from inside the tent and put it into his pocket. Next, he wrestled the flashlight from Tim and handed it to me.

"Listen, Tim," he said, at last.

"What?" his brother snapped.

"Over the next rise is a stream," said Jack. "If we're not back in an hour then go to the stream and follow it south until you come out to the creek."

"Don't—"

"When you get to the creek, turn right," he cut him off. "Follow the creek until you get to Dover Bridge. You know you're way home from there."

"Oh," said Tim, "don't get all morbid on me. You guys will be back in no time."

"Just in case, little brother," Jack told him.

"Then what?"

"Tell Granny to call the police."

"Come on, Jack."

"I'm sure we'll be fine," I said.

"Anyway," Tim said, "Granny will just get pissed off and wail on me like it was my fault."

"Just do what I say," said Jack.

"Okay, don't be pushy. How about two hours?"

Jack looked at me. I nodded, not knowing what lay beyond the bridge or even if it was sturdy enough to get across. Whatever the case, I thought it best not to talk about the feral boy in Tim's company.

"All right," Jack said. "Two hours."

"I'm not hauling all this shit out of here by myself," Tim told us.

"Leave everything."

"Then why don't I just go with you guys?"

"Come on, Joe," Jack took me by the arm. "Let's go."

Minutes later, as Tim's protests faded into the distance, Jack and I found the footbridge. I still didn't say anything about the boy I had followed. Tim may have believed me, but I knew that Jack, even at the age of thirteen, was too much of a pragmatist to ever consider such a notion. He would have ribbed me from the moment I told him until the time we reached high school. Worse, he would have made sure to tell everyone in town. It was too much of a risk. All of Yorkville would consider me a raving lunatic. It was better to keep it a secret, for now.

What I first took to be two trees growing toward one another at the bridge entrance was, in fact, an arch constructed from oak trees stripped of their bark and branches. The tops were fastened with thick vines, calling to mind a handmade bow for some long-ago Titan.

Up close, with the flashlight shining on the arch, I realized that someone, perhaps a group of artisans, had taken painstaking care to carve intricate scenes up the length of either side of the arch. Detailed images of flora, fauna, and fairies lined every inch of the wood's surface.

"That's just weird," Jack said as he studied the carvings.

Wild vines grew up and across the bridge, forming a lattice that slowed our pace. More than once, I tripped and fell, but I wasn't alone. Jack didn't do much better.

The planks on the bridge creaked with every step we took, as if at any moment they might give way beneath our combined weight. Peering over the side, Jack trained his flashlight on the stream below. There were large rocks, some of them as large as trashcans, and fallen trees whose sharp, broken, dead branches pointed straight into the air.

"That's like twenty or thirty feet down," I said. "I didn't think we were up that high."

"Yeah, a fall like that will kill you," said Jack.

"Maybe we should—"

Jack took off at a full sprint, jumping over the low vines that stretched the width of the bridge and dodging the high ones.

"—turn back," I managed to say.

A few seconds later, I lost sight of Jack. At least he was kind enough to leave me with the flashlight.

"Joe," Jack's voice drifted from the other side. "Come on over. You'll be safe."

Halfway across the bridge, at a pace considerably slower than my friend's, I envisioned some trap door or rotted plank giving way and triggering my ultimate demise. On either side of the narrow bridge, there were railings made from long timber stripped of its bark. Each railing was adorned with graven images identical to those carved into the arch.

The first thing I noticed on the other side was how different the forest looked. The trees were taller, older, and the vines and underbrush looked as if they had been growing for a thousand years. Even the shadows between the great trees looked darker, despite the pale full moon overhead.

"There's a path." Jack appeared beside me.

"Christ." I gritted my teeth. "Make some noise next time."

"Sorry about that," he said.

I handed over the flashlight. He shined the light to the left and to the right.

"I was saying just before you left me behind that maybe we should go back."

"Why? Scared?"

"This might be someone's property."

"What? Are you kidding me?"

"Someone made that bridge."

"Right. Maybe a hundred years ago."

"Jack."

"Don't jack me, Joe." He held the flashlight in front of his crotch and pretended to masturbate.

When Jack turned off the flashlight, the woods appeared even darker. Somewhere a woodpecker hammered a tree in rapid succession.

"Look over my shoulder," he said. "Tell me what you see."

I didn't see anything save for the darkness hunkered between the trees.

"What am I looking for?"

"Give it a second."

"But I—"

"Let your eyes adjust."

As I stared into the darkness over Jack's shoulder, oblong luminescent stones, set in two parallel waving lines, slowly revealed themselves. The stones snaked their way deeper into the forest.

"What kinds of stones glow in the dark?" I asked.

"The fuck should I know," Jack replied. "Come on, let's go."

Along the path, there was no need for a flashlight. The glowing stones lit our way as we traversed the serpentine course. Moving further into the forest, I noticed that the shadows were darker, perhaps a trick of the dim light emitted by the stones. The trees looked less like trees and more like the skeletal remains of deformed ancient giants now frozen in time. The path was devoid of the dense underbrush that grew across most of the forest floor. Someone had gone to great lengths to keep the path clear. I wondered if it had something to do with the stones. It was more convenient to believe that Jack and I simply stumbled across a path that belonged to some campground. Still, the air along the path felt considerably cooler than it did in the forest before we crossed the bridge. I wanted to believe that there was nothing supernatural about the path or its stones, but on either side of the path, the shadows shifted and swirled like smoke. Here and there, barely visible, were humanoid forms that danced in the darkness only to vanish behind the great trees. As we moved along the path. I heard the woodpecker's drum roll once more. Next, a high-pitched scream forced me to stop.

"What was that?" I was so scared I could hardly breathe. "Was it Tim?"

"Screaming like a girl?" Jack dismissed the idea with a wave of his hand. "No, Joe. That's the *megascops asio*."

I did my best to look cool, despite the disturbing noise I just heard.

"The Eastern Screech Owl."

"Sounded like a person."

"Sometimes they do, Joe. Sometimes they do. I read in the library that there are over twenty species. Even in Puerto Rico."

I decided that high-tailing it out of there would have been anti-climactic. Jack and I continued our trek along the stone-lit path. After another quarter mile, I mentioned my theory about the path being part of some campground. Jack grunted his approval, but I knew he wasn't buying it. Wherever the path led, it wasn't to a campground. The answer came soon enough.

Chapter 9

The path ended abruptly before a vast lawn whose green expanse appeared well-manicured for being situated in the middle of such a dark, formidable forest. Right where the glowing stones stopped, there were four obelisks spread out at even intervals across the front of the lawn, each one fashioned from the same glowing stone as the ones that marked the trail. The obelisks stood nearly nine feet high. Upon closer inspection, they revealed odd, circular carvings on all four sides.

Jack turned on the flashlight and shined it across the wide grassy stretch. At the very edge of the light's halo, there was a stone-bordered pond. As we moved forward, Jack turned the light up over the man-made body of water and stopped in his tracks. I bumped right into him, mouth agape, as I stared like some village idiot watching a fireworks display for the first time.

"It's a house," he whispered.

A house was an understatement. Overgrown with creeping vines, a dilapidated Gothic revival Victorian mansion stood three stories high. Two towers that called to mind old English castles flanked either side of the mansion and reached another two stories over the main house. A long porch at the front faced us; vines, withered and old, looked as much a part of the porch as it did its wood and wrought iron frame.

"Let's take a closer look," he said.

I was afraid of that. The mansion looked as if it had been abandoned long ago. Even so, I'd read too many scary comics. Just because a place looked empty didn't make it so; whatever ghosts remained were no doubt lying in wait.

Halfway across the wide lawn, we reached the man-made pond, a perfect circle bordered by natural rock. Unlike the stones that marked the trail leading up the mansion, the rocks that spanned the circumference of the pond were dark—granite, maybe—and though they stood only a couple of feet high, they were shaped like shark's teeth. I imagined that once upon a time, the owner of the estate had them placed, perhaps to keep people out of the pond or maybe to keep whatever may be lurking in the pond from leaving it. I glimpsed the moon's reflection in the still water as I gave the pond a wide berth. In that moment, something rippled just beneath the surface, creating concentric waves that broke up the moon's reflectioninto a thousand shards of pale light.

"You saw that, too?" Jack asked.

"What was it?"

"Water moccasin, maybe. Come on. Let's go."

"Jack."

"Look," he pointed the flashlight at the house. "I think the front door is open."

"Maybe someone still lives here," I said. "Maybe a shut-in or some witch."

"Joe, don't be a douche bag. Look at this place. No self-respecting witch would live here."

I followed Jack up to the porch steps. When he shined the flashlight again, beyond the web of vines that covered the porch like a loose net, a black hole gaped where the front door should have been.

I thought about Tim back at the camp site. If he'd been with us upon first discovering the house, he would have surmised a whole host of supernatural culprits occupying the mansion. In truth, I wondered all the time about such things: about how ghosts and spirits fall into play with the world that we see and the world beyond as chronicled by the saints and sages of the Catholic Church. The greatest hurdle for me was the notion of guardian angels. As if God would ever farm out a person's well-being instead of Himself looking out for us. There were places where not only angels feared to tread but that seemed utterly devoid of God's presence. Someone once said that Hell was the absence of reason. They weren't even close. Hell was the complete absence of God's presence, a place teeming with every torment imaginable. A void that swallowed up every plea for mercy, every yearning for hope, and every desire for solace. When Jack and I first discovered the house, I thought about how superstition and what-ifs shaped Tim's psyche, and how, when you got down to it, he was no more equipped to deal with what followed than we were.

Jack traversed the vine-strewn steps. The moon vanished behind a cloud, And a great shadow blanketed the grounds for a moment before the cloud released its grip on the moon. With the grounds graced once more with pallid moonlight, I took a few steps back and took in the house in all its Gothic glory. Most of the windows were shuttered closed. The exterior was constructed from dull gray stones and black mortar. In the moonlight, I could barely make out the parapet gables.

Jack jammed his flashlight into his belt, raked the vines aside at the porch's edge, and entered the house.

"Hey," he shouted, "there are bottles in here."

A few seconds later, Jack emerged holding a small Mason jar.

"Don't," I said, but it was too late.

He wound up like an old-fashioned pitcher and threw the glass jar over my head. The Mason jar broke against the jagged rocks that bordered the pond behind me. The sound was insulated by the surrounding forest. When I turned back to face the porch, Jack stood ready to throw a second bottle. I could see that the bottle was a relic of some kind, topped with a rubber stopper and sealed with thick wax. Before Jack could throw the bottle, the front door slammed shut behind him. A sonorous echo rattled the entire porch.

Jack nearly bowled me over when he leapt from the porch. He dropped the bottle in the grass. By the time I caught up with him, he had already skirted the pond and was headed for the trail.

"Why did you do that?" I asked.

"Fuck it," was all he said.

We didn't stop running until we reached the end of the moonstone path. Jack wheezed as he doubled over, feeling his pants pockets.

"Oh fuck me, man," he grunted.

"What?" I kept my eyes on the path, hoping we weren't followed.

"I lost the compass."

"We're not going back."

"I have to get it."

"It's a stupid compass," I said. "Who cares?"

Jack pushed me to the ground. He straddled me and cocked a fist back.

"That was my father's compass," he said. "He gave it to me to keep until he comes back."

Jack always spoke of his father as if his old man was away on a business trip or he had gone off to war. That Jack maintained his father's innocence, there was never any doubt, but a son will defend his father, even a murderous one, until the very end. I didn't pretend to know what it was like to be in his shoes. Often I imagined Jack and Tim, night after night, looking out their bedroom window—the crickets' lament their musical accompaniment—as they envisioned their father sitting in a cramped jail cell, counting the endless days until he was a free man again.

"You won't find it in the dark," I told him.

Jack helped me up. He brushed dried leaves and dirt from my shirt.

"I think I dropped it on the porch," he said.

"You can't go back."

"But I have to."

"I'll wait here."

"Chickenshit?"

"You're damned right I'm scared."

"Keep your voice down."

"Who's going to hear us?"

"Come up the trail a bit."

I followed him as he slowly made his way back up the trail. When we reached the strange markers with the circular carvings at the edge of the wide lawn, I stopped.

"Wish me luck." He darted across the lawn.

Another cloud embraced the moon and smothered her pale light. I couldn't see Jack anymore. The seconds felt like minutes and each minute a day. At last, I spotted a shadowy figure running across the dark lawn.

"So, did you get it?" I asked.

"Motherfuckers!" Jack shouted. Then, "Come on. Let's go."

I didn't look back until, some minutes later, we made it the safety of the footbridge. There was no feral boy waiting for us there, no spectral ghosts or demons closing the gap down the trail.

When we made it back to the camp site, Jack and I found his brother fast asleep. Jack gave him a swift boot in the leg.

"Hey, fuckwad," he said, "wake up."

"Are you going to tell him?" I asked.

"Tell me what?" Tim forced the words from his mouth the way somnambulists often did upon first waking up, unaware that they are conversing not with the chimeras of their dreams but with flesh and blood people.

So Jack and I told him the whole story. In the end, Jack left out the part about the compass. Of course, Tim wanted to go out and explore on his own, but we were able to dissuade him by lying and telling him that we almost ran into some older boys from Tracktown who were camping out near the house. Jack and I both knew that the lie would work, of course. As a rule, Tim avoided kids from Tracktown like the plague.

"Did you see any ghosts?" Tim mumbled. He stirred, stretched out his arms, and opened his eyes. "I had a dream that you guys were in a haunted castle."

"No shit?"

"There were little people in jars."

"Like *Bride of Frankenstein?*" I asked.

"Yeah," said Jack. "Homo-unculesis."

"Homunculi," his brother corrected him. "Grown from seeds by Dr. Pretorius."

"Go back to sleep, Tim," said Jack.

I crawled into the tent, followed by Jack. The place stunk to high heaven on account of Tim dropping fart bombs all night while we were gone.

"Hey," Tim said, "I had another dream that Dad was following you through the woods."

"Go to sleep," said Jack.

I closed the tent flap and curled up facing away from the Swanson brothers. When sleep came, I dreamt of the mansion. Somewhere deep in the house, the feral boy beckoned me. There were dried leaves blowing everywhere inside the house as I searched for him. Everywhere I turned, I saw spindly stick men in the shadows gesturing for me to join them. Their heads were slanted, their mouths grotesque cavities of fetid waste. I kept after the feral boy, but I never caught him.

Chapter 10

The day after we discovered the old mansion, Jack and I went over to Bobby McMahon's house. I was exhausted, having slept little the previous night, but I wanted to let Bobby in on the secret. Compared to Jack's pragmatism and Tim's lofty ideals concerning the supernatural, Bobby stood alone as the voice of reason. If anything else, he was smarter than the rest of us. Since he was removed from the experience thus far, Bobby's input was just what we needed to put things into perspective.

"I can't believe school starts next week," Jack said as I rang the doorbell. "That fuh...hey, Mrs. McMahon," he caught himself when Bobby's mother opened the door, "looking good."

Mrs. McMahon stood there in a pink summer dress with her hands on her hips. She wasn't the best looking woman in Yorkville, but her big hips and full bosom were proportionate enough to make men turn their heads, often to the chagrin of her husband. I heard my dad tell Mr. Morgan one night that Bobby's mother was the kind of woman who could lead a man toward ruin.

"The siren of Yorkville," he called her. "That's what she is."

I didn't know enough back then to know anything about Greek legends and Ulysses and all that. Even as young as I was, however, I somehow knew that what my dad said about her wasn't exactly a compliment. There were some mornings, especially in the beginning of the school year, when Mrs. McMahon walked Bobby to school. She wore dresses that you could practically see through when the morning light hit her just right.

"Every morning through September," Bobby confided when the previous school year began, "I pray for rain."

Mrs. McMahon was a head shorter than my mother, and her long, curly red hair shone like fire in the morning sun. Old men in the square were forever tipping imaginary hats at her and bidding her a good morning. Of course, you'd have to be a moron not to know what those old lechers were really thinking.

Jack remained fixed where he stood, no doubt imagining what Mrs. McMahon's naked breasts looked like. I know I did, especially that year. It was the beginning of a new era for us, and, like most of the men in Yorkville, Jack and I both harbored sordid, secret thoughts about Mrs. McMahon.

"Hello, boys," said Mrs. McMahon. She sounded like Alida Valli in *The Third Man*.

"Can Bobby come out?" I asked.

"Bobby!" her shout rang out sharp and melodic; her voice, no matter the tone, possessed that musical quality so prevalent in Irish-American women.

"Where's Mr. McMahon?" Jack asked.

"You better come inside," she told us. "I wouldn't want the neighbors to get the wrong idea."

It was an odd thing, inviting Jack Swanson into the McMahon home. Neither of Bobby's parents cared much for him, nor for his brother, Tim. Long before any of us were born, Mr. McMahon and Jack's father had been friends. My father said that Jack was named after Bobby's father, John McMahon. Sometime shortly after Jack was born, the two men experienced a falling out; no one talked about it much, especially other men. Whatever the case, Mr. Swanson went one way, toward chaos and despair, and Bobby's father flew the straight and narrow.

The past was history, and the bad blood between both men didn't affect Jack that much. He was a good friend to Bobby. And Jack understood just how close Bobby and I were without feeling the need to interfere. Still, that fact didn't bother Jack or his brother. But Tim and Bobby were now closer than ever. As for Mrs. McMahon, her condescension toward Jack never made a dent in his armor. The same went for Tim. The brothers were cast from the same devil-may-care mold. Rather than play into Mrs. McMahon's attempts to undermine the relationship the brothers shared with her son, Jack attempted to kill Bobby's mother with kindness. And if that didn't work, he turned on the charm. In some ways, it was obscene the way Jack flirted with Mrs. McMahon. For better or worse, that was the way of things. And over that year, in some twist of anxious fate, Bobby's mother came to accept it.

Presently, we followed her into the foyer. The living room just beyond was off-limits. It was kept impeccably clean, and the only time the McMahons ever used the room was when they "received" visitors.

"Might as well put up a velvet rope," Jack remarked once when Mrs. McMahon shooed him off the garish floral-patterned couch and straight out of the living room.

"Bobby," she called out as she ushered us into the kitchen. "Joe's here."

That was the other thing about Bobby's parents. Neither of them ever mentioned Jack by name. A great figure and a sheer dress did little to hide the fact that Mrs. McMahon could be a bitch most of the time.

A thunderous rumble of footsteps sounded on the stairs. Seconds later, Bobby entered the kitchen with a book in his hand.

"What are you reading?" Jack asked.

"*Tess of the d'Urbervilles*," Bobby answered.

"A girl's book?"

Mrs. McMahon crossed her arms over her big, beautiful chest as she looked toward the ceiling. Her fragile lips trembled as she mumbled something not meant for our ears.

"It's a novel," Bobby explained. "Thomas Hardy? Ever hear of him?"

"The Hardy Boys' dad?"

"No."

"Monsters?"

"Not one."

"People from outer space?"

"Honestly," Mrs. McMahon weighed in now. "Anyone who's anyone knows that people do not live in outer space."

"Technically," Jack replied, "we live in space on a planet called Earth. Seven continents, polar regions on either end of said planet, oceans—"

"I know more about Earth than you do, thank you very much."

"—and all that. But you catch my drift," he concluded. Then, to Bobby, "Does anybody get killed?"

"As a matter of fact," a glint shined in Bobby's eyes now, "yes, they do."

"Feeling better?" I asked.

All emotion left Bobby's face. "Yes, thanks."

"Let's go out."

"Where?"

"The square?" Jack asked.

"No. I'd rather not."

"Why don't you boys go up to Bobby's room," Mrs. McMahon suggested.

Bobby was the only kid in Yorkville whose bedroom was a converted attic. He had one single bed tucked neatly in the far corner opposite the stairs. The bookshelves that lined the walls were crammed with Bobby's personal collection of books and magazines that rivaled the Yorkville Public Library; not that the local library was a huge bastion of the printed word, but Bobby's was as good a start as any for a twelve-year-old kid. Opposite the top of the stairs, a chair and desk were positioned against one wall beneath a window that overlooked the street. Atop the desk sat an old Royal typewriter.

Bobby wanted to write novels. There were numerous times when I visited him in his room, hoping to catch him typing away furiously like Kerouac or Thomas Wolfe, but that never came to be. The only time I came close to catching him, he quickly slipped the paper out of the roller and jammed it into a footlocker by his bed. Bobby never let anyone read his work. In later years, I heard rumors that his mother pried opened the footlocker where Bobby kept his secret writings. One story told of how Mrs. McMahon was heard to scream "Filth, filth!" over and over again. I didn't doubt it. My mother told me that Mrs. McMahon was institutionalized shortly after my fifteenth birthday. Where Bobby's literary efforts were concerned, no one ever liberated those secret writings from the McMahon household. How often did genius ended up discarded in local landfills or garbage heaps that bordered big cities? Among the abandoned literary efforts of unknown writers, Bobby's pages were also added. I knew this much, since Mr. McMahon was too much of a law-abiding prude to ever burn those papers, despite his wife's maniacal petitions to do so.

"Don't touch anything," Bobby told the Swanson brothers. "I just finished cleaning up here."

"Relax, neatnik," said Jack. He made a deliberate show of shoving his hands into the front pockets of his jeans. Then, with that same old mischievous twinkle in his eye, he plopped down on Bobby's bed.

"*The Subterraneans*," Tim read a title aloud, with his head cocked sideways, as he stood in front of one of the taller bookshelves.

"Jack Kerouac," Bobby told him.

"Hey," Tim said to his brother, "that's your name."

"My uncle gave that to me before he died," he reminded us. "My Uncle Roland."

The infamous Roland McMahon. Roland was the older brother of Bobby's father. A veteran of the Korean War, Roland McMahon never took to the rank and file life of post-war America. Instead, he spent most of his time drinking in Philadelphia bars and fist fighting men half his age. True to his Irishness, Roland McMahon took to whiskey like oil to water. Mr. McMahon did what he could for his older brother, gave him money when he was able, helped him find whatever menial jobs he was capable of working. But in the end, it wasn't enough. One cold winter evening back in 1970, Roland McMahon found himself outnumbered five to one in an alley in South Philly. It was all over the papers. The police found him cut to pieces with his head caved in like some dumb cow at a slaughterhouse. Nobody went to his funeral, not even Mr. McMahon. Roland McMahon left the world with as little as he had when he came into it, except for a box filled with his favorite books, which Mr. McMahon turned over to his dead brother's only nephew, Bobby.

"Wasn't he famous for something?" Tim asked.

"Excuse me?" Bobby said.

"Jack Kerouac."

"Oh, yes. He wrote another novel called *On the Road*. It started the Beat Generation."

"Right on, daddy-o," said Jack.

"The beatniks, yes."

"What's *The Subterraneans* about?" Tim asked. "Underground people?"

"Perhaps you should read it sometime," said Bobby. "Of course, some of his books were good and some not so much. Why, I believe it was Truman Capote who said Kerouac was more a typist than a writer."

Back then, I didn't know who Truman Capote was, but Kerouac's name was more familiar. The brothers Swanson, however, appeared more mystified than I did.

"Yeah," Jack yawned. "Whatever."

"How was the camping trip?" Bobby switched gears now.

"It was okay."

"It rained," I added.

"Yes, I was thinking about you boys out there roughing it in the dark."

He lay down on his bed and gave Jack an alluring look. Marcella made that same face at me a few times. We all knew how Bobby was, but it didn't matter. The uncertainty of life carried in it the seed of mystery, and from that mystery sprang forth both splendid and horrid wonders. At twelve years old, there was hardly any mystery left to Bobby's leanings toward boys. It drove his parents crazy, but they were powerless to do anything. And in a weird way, Jack Swanson took it all in stride.

"Hey," Jack had said one day a few months before the camping trip, "a smart, well-read guy has a crush on you? I guess that's something, if you're queer like him."

Presently, Tim took an old *Life* magazine off one shelf and sat down at the desk.

"Spread out," Jack pushed Bobby's face away from his before he stood up. "Can I use your bathroom?"

"*May* I use your bathroom?" Bobby corrected him.

"What am I? In school?"

"Go." He waved his hand dismissively.

After Jack left the bedroom, Bobby indicated I should sit down on the bed next to him.

"You told your mom we got into a fight at the Bellshade Shopping Center?" I sat down next to him.

"Hey, doll!" Jack's voice carried up the stairs from the second floor.

A muffled curse from Mrs. McMahon followed before a door slammed shut.

"So, I guess shaking it for me is out of the question?" Jack's voice rang out.

Tim, his back to Bobby and me, shook his head as he gently leafed through the old magazine.

"You didn't tell anyone?" Bobby asked as he lay back.

I followed suit. Together, we stared up at the ceiling.

"No," I assured him, "why would I?"

"Not even Marcella?"

"No one knows."

"Except McClusky."

"And his goons."

"Strictly speaking," Bobby whispered, "nothing happened."

"I thought—"

"He waved it in front of my face," he said, "but it wasn't like he shoved it into my mouth."

"Did what?" Tim asked, not really paying attention.

"Nothing," he said, "go back to your magazine."

"I shouldn't have left you."

"Don't worry, Joe," Bobby said, patting my left leg. "You can make it up to me."

A toilet flushed. A door opened. That's when I heard Mrs. McMahon's voice.

"I don't know how you do things at Granny Swanson's house," she exclaimed, "but around here, we put the toilet lid down when we're finished. And we wash our hands."

"When I turn eighteen. I'm going to be your mom's other man," I told Bobby.

"Not a chance," he said. "Besides, I couldn't call you Uncle Joe."

"I didn't say I'd marry your mom."

"So your intentions are less than noble?"

"I found a house in Franklin Forest."

Bobby sat up. "Are you moving?"

"Very funny."

"Some shotgun shack?"

"A mansion. Jack and I went there."

"And you got lost?"

"That's weird."

"What?"

"Did he tell you already?"

"No," said Bobby, "I had a dream that you guys were lost in the woods."

"Anyway," I said, "Jack lost his compass. We had to go back and get it."

When I sat up, Bobby brushed his hand against my leg again. I pretended not to notice. *Sooner or later,* I thought, *we'd have to help him find someone who could help him explore whatever it was he was going through.* I shuddered then, thinking about my friend in the back of some old guy's car or some place worse.

"Are you okay?" he asked.

"Jack went on and on about the compass," I said. "We had to go back and get it."

"My dad gave him that compass," Tim said.

"Now it's gone for good," I whispered to Bobby.

"I don't understand," Bobby said.

"Jack insisted we go back and get it," I told him. "I didn't want to go back, but Jack did. I think something scared him off."

"Do you think someone took it?" Bobby asked.

Jack's footsteps sounded on the stairs. I held my finger to my lips. Bobby nodded.

"Well, gaybirds," Jack bellowed as he clasped his hands together. "What's it going to be? Are we going out or are we going to get that circle jerk going?"

"I heard that," Mrs. McMahon screamed from downstairs, "you wretched little creature."

"Sorry," he shouted, "no girls allowed."

A telephone rang on the second floor. After the third ring, I heard Mrs. McMahon giggle over something the caller said.

"Oh, yes. I will right now," Bobby's mother announced. Seconds later, she stood at the top of the stairs. "Well, I'm sorry to say, but Granny Swanson called. The Swanson brothers are to return home at this instant. That's what Granny Swanson said to me. 'This instant!' Don't keep your grandmother waiting."

"Did she say why?"

"I'm not your secretary. Now run along, young Jack. And take Tim with you. I wouldn't make Granny Swanson angry. Not if I were you—"

"Okay, okay," he said. "We're going. We'll see you guys later?"

"Sure," Bobby told him.

"I'll show you boys the way out," Mrs. McMahon announced. Her sarcasm was not missed.

"Hey, you know what we haven't done in a long time?" Bobby said after Jack and Tim had followed Mrs. MacMahon downstairs. "We haven't had a naked party."

A few summers back, Bobby, the Swanson brothers, and I had decided it would be okay to show each other our dicks—a little compare and contrast session—all very perfectly innocent since we were, what, nine years old? None of us thought anything of it, at the time. At twelve years old, I wasn't sure it would be a good idea.

"Let's go out," I climbed off the bed.

"Not the Roost," said Bobby.

"Morgan's Corner Store?"

"Excellent. I'll ask my mom for money."

Downstairs, we found Mrs. McMahon on the front porch talking to Mr. Silas, a neighbor. Evan Silas was tall, dark, and unquestionably enigmatic to all the local ladies since he wasn't married, nor was he queer as far as anyone was able to tell. Bobby's dad didn't care for him too much, but his mother went all ga-ga over the guy whenever she saw him. Sometimes even when Mr. McMahon was standing right next to her. My mother said it was shameful the way Mrs. McMahon carried on like that, but, even so, she wasn't above all the gushing that went on in Silas's presence.

Once we left Bobby's house, he marched a few paces ahead of me to the corner. Since his mother had been too busy flirting with Evan Silas, he didn't get to ask for money; instead, he went into her purse and took a ten-dollar bill.

"She won't miss it," he remarked before we left his house.

At the corner, he grabbed me by the shirt and pulled me as he ran down the alley that bisected his block.

"Where are we going?" I asked.

"Shut up," he said. "Be quiet."

Halfway down the alley, there was a garage overgrown with vines and trees. The garage belonged to a shut-in named George Fowles, but that wasn't what interested Bobby that day. He pulled back the rotting door on the side of the garage, beckoning me to join him. Once inside, he led me to a dirty window that overlooked the alley and gave him plain view of his backyard.

We stood atop an old steamer trunk. From our perch, I saw Mr. Silas helping Bobby's mother over the railing that separated the McMahon's back porch with his. After Silas opened his back door, Mrs. McMahon kissed him on the mouth, briefly, before Silas spirited her into his house.

Bobby turned from the window and sat down on the steamer trunk.

"My mother's a whore," he said, his voice bereft of emotion.

I sat down next to him and wrapped my arm around his shoulders. We stayed like that for several minutes, not saying a word. Bobby eventually patted me on the thigh the way some old aunt might in an effort to cheer you up.

"Come on," he said, "let's get out of here before old George finds us."

Chapter 11

"Are you boys going to loiter there all afternoon?" Mr. Morgan asked.

Bobby and I sat on the steps outside Morgan's Corner Store. Not many kids in our neighborhood liked the corner store, mostly because it was away from all the action in the town square. For Bobby and me, at least on some days, it suited us just fine. That afternoon, we splurged on candy: Swedish Fish, a bag of Bottlecaps each—my favorite were the root beer ones—Hawaiian Punch for Bobby, a bottle of ice-cold Coca-Cola for me, and a comic book each all courtesy the ten bucks Bobby had hoisted from his mother's purse.

I was a total nut for Marvel Comics. My favorite that summer was The Incredible Hulk. I couldn't get enough of the big, green, mean guy. Bobby opted for Swamp Thing. He called it a guilty indulgence, owing to how he spent most of the time with his face buried in a book more fit to collect dust in a public library than it did being read by a twelve-year-old boy. His mother called comic books *déclassé*, and his father viewed them as just plain vulgar, a vehicle, Mr. McMahon maintained, meant to keep young people from learning. Given his parents strong dislike for comic books, ownership of such materials for Bobby was not an option. His parents forbade him to bring comic books into the house. That was the word Bobby used once— forbade—as if people actually talked like that in Yorkville. What a gas. That meant I was usually left to maintain Bobby's inventory of comic books, the aforementioned Swamp Thing being among his favorites next to Doctor Strange.

Bobby would have had a better chance of smuggling porn mags into his home than he did a comic book. Mrs. McMahon possessed the superhuman ability to sniff them out—comic books, not porno mags as near as anyone knew—so Bobby learned early on that it wasn't worth the risk. Maybe his mother smelled the fresh newsprint. Maybe she questioned his taste in comic books; aside from Swamp Thing and Dr. Strange, Bobby went in for the likes of Conan the Barbarian, Kull the Destroyer, Prince Namor of Atlantis, and Tarzan. Whatever the case, I ended up holding his stash at my house.

"Mr. Morgan," Bobby was saying, "if you don't want kids loitering in front of your store then perhaps you should post a sign."

"Why should I post a sign?" he asked. "It's my joint, see? I can do—"

"Clearly," Bobby agreed. "No one is disputing ownership here, sir."

"Good, because—"

"It comes down to a question of litigation."

"Don't you mean liability?"

"That too, I'm afraid. With regard to discrimination, of course."

"Who's discriminating?" Mr. Morgan asked. "I just don't want any young punks scaring away business. No offense, Joe."

"Oh, none taken," I said.

"Joe, why don't you explain to Mr. Morgan," Bobby began.

"Don't drag me into this."

"What's at stake here is our rights as free citizens—"

"No," said Mr. Morgan, "what's at stake here is me booting your snotty, little, know-it-all ass off my stoop with a size thirteen shoe I just polished this morning."

"Victory attained by violence is tantamount to defeat," said Bobby, "for it is momentary. Mahatma Gandhi said that."

"Victory by ass-kicking is the sweetest berry," the store owner replied. "Peter Morgan."

"Come on," I grabbed Bobby's arm. "Let's go."

Bobby handed me his comic book. He sighed as he stood up, willing to concede defeat.

I looked down the street and saw Mr. Von Braun making his way toward us.

"Hello." He waved as he called out.

"*Gutentag*," Morgan responded.

Bobby saw the look on my face and rendered the same expression his mother did whenever she faced some imbecilic inquiry. I knew Bobby and his mother both spoke German, but, as usual, my friend wasn't in the mood for a tutorial. So, I let the matter go.

"Do you have a minute?" Von Braun asked. He stood in front of us now. "If not, I can come back."

"Uh, well," I began before Mr. Morgan cuffed me lightly on the back of my head.

"Well, boys," the store owner said, "thanks for visiting. Joe, tell your dad I'll give him a call soon."

Morgan and Von Braun entered the store. Bobby and I watched as Morgan flipped his "Come on in, We're Open" sign to the "Sorry, We're Closed" side.

"It's killing you, isn't it?" Bobby asked once Morgan pulled down the shade on the glass door.

"What is?" I asked.

"You think the old guy is buying some illicit material?"

"No way."

"Let's go around to Marcella's."

That sounded like a good idea, but as much as neither of us wanted to admit it, there was still the business of Mr. Morgan closing his store in the middle of a summer afternoon. Very few men, I surmised, could persuade Mr. Morgan to close shop altogether like that. Given that Mr. Von Braun was one of those few men added even more to the mystique surrounding the old German.

"We could wait," I said.

"Mr. Morgan has a screen door in the back of the store that leads out the alley."

"You want to sneak around there and listen?"

"No, not me," said Bobby. "You. That way if you get caught, you can smooth it out with him."

"How would I smooth that out?"

"Morgan and your dad are friends, right?"

"What if they're speaking German?"

Bobby's eyes narrowed. "Good point, Joe," he said. "We will need a cover story."

"I have to use Mr. Morgan's bathroom."

"Now?"

"No, that's the cover story."

Bobby moved down the alley first. He made a big show of pretending to be one of the Mod Squad members, holding his hands up near his face like a handgun. The way he pranced made me think of Julie instead of Pete or Link. I liked Link, even though my mother said the portrayal of such a character was contrived and that the network just force-fed viewers racial stereotypes in order to placate the liberal masses. Whenever my mother got started on one of her rants like that, my father always made a big show of moaning like Archie Bunker and leaving the room with a newspaper under his arm to seek solace in the bathroom. Sometimes I'd tell Bobby about such episodes, and his advice was always the same.

"When you turn eighteen," he said, "you should run away. That's probably your best bet for survival. Your parents are going to slowly drive you insane."

Morgan's Corner Store was located on the corner of Creek and Turner Roads. The alley was a narrow one, lined with tall fences on either side. I knew from experience that there were no dogs behind those fences. It was a good thing, too. Bobby was scared to death of dogs. In life, there were constants like the sun rising in the east, snow falling in the winter, the brothers Swanson using every possible means at their disposal to make Mr. Von Braun's life a living hell in their pursuit to expose him as a Nazi, and all dogs giving chase to Bobby McMahon.

Despite his fear of dogs, Bobby and I were initiated into the town-wide game of jailbreak. Kids between the ages of twelve and fifteen met on one of the commons near Yorkville Public School. Teams were divided into two, and each team had anywhere between eight and fifteen. Before girls were permitted to play, the boys resorted to the old shirts and skins routine to tell who was on what side. The complexities of the game grew exponentially when we boys decided that girls were allowed to join the game. Surely, none of the girls wanted to run around without their shirts on, so, one of the girls, I forget who now, suggested hats and scalps in lieu of shirts and skins. Half the kids that played that first night after the hats and scalps sides were chosen ended up losing their baseball hats, and Ralph Gruger, a fourteen-year-old boy from our neighborhood, decided he would psyche out his opponents by wearing a ski mask despite the hot, humid weather that evening. He was arrested after being accused of peering through Claire Billingham's bedroom window near Morgan's Corner Store. Poor Ralph claimed he was simply hiding in the Billingham's backyard, but the police didn't see it that way when Claire's dad explained to the cops that he caught Ralph Gruger on his porch roof right outside his nineteen-year-old daughter's bedroom window. No one wanted a repeat of that night. So, leave it to Bobby to come up with a remedy.

"Let's just use flags," he announced from his perch atop a tree stump like some old-timey politician.

Crickets chirped in the field where I stood along with twenty other kids. At any moment, I expected the impromptu rally to disintegrate into chaos over not finding a permanent solution regarding who was on what side during the jailbreak game.

"Uh," Bobby spoke up once more, "like in flag football."

There were murmurs of approval. The excitement soon faded though as Jerry Cummings stepped forward to be recognized. Jerry was a kid from the Tracktown side of Yorkville. He and Bobby shared an insatiable appetite for literature and proper grammar, as well as a secretive penchant for comic books. Bobby and Jerry were cast from the same mold. Everyone knew it. And somehow, in the world of jailbreak, no one cared if you were smart or dumb, queer or not.

The first few nights, we played jailbreak centered around the commons just north of my street. It wasn't long before our numbers grew, and with that came the inevitable expansion of boundaries. The alley behind Morgan's Corner Store offered plenty of hiding places. At night, jailbreak players ran the risk of running into any number of transients who found their way into town via the highway. Most of these nameless strangers wanted to be left alone, but Yorkville, like so many communities, was not immune to predators that preyed on unsuspecting children. Mr. Morgan did his best to keep his end of the alley devoid of any such characters, but there was always the chance that some pervert junkie alcoholic might defy residents and lay in wait. The prize, I guess they figured, far outweighed the risk.

Stories circulated every summer throughout Yorkville about some poor kid who got his ass gang-tagged by a sex-hungry group of degenerate winos. And every summer, it was always the same thing: No one ever knew the kid's name. Variations on the story included runaways from Tracktown on their way to Philadelphia, visiting cousins of a Yorkville family, or some kid who belonged to a group of born-again Christians bussed in from out of state to attend the two-week bible camp at the New Yorkville Methodist Pentecostal Holy School, or as we liked to call it, the NYMPH of God, which consisted of a bunch of disadvantaged kids sitting around listening to Pastor Clement Hopkins, who was like 104 years old, pontificate on why young boys and girls should not fornicate before marriage and how the Whore of Rome (the Vatican) will one day lead to the ruination of the world. The out-of-town kids slept on cots in the basement of the church. At night, Pastor Hopkins and his cronies played wholesome movies outdoors in the yard against the side of the whitewashed church. Twenty or thirty minutes into the movie, there was always a gang of these Pentecostal kids who would jump the fence and seek entertainment elsewhere. One summer, it was even rumored that Pastor Hopkins himself was the degenerate rapist who lingered in the alley behind Morgan's Corner Store. Never mind that the good pastor was nothing more than skin and bones, that one swift kick to the old man's shins would cause him to crumble into dust like a statue made from ash.

"I know the perfect spot," said Bobby.

He picked the caged-in area behind Morgan's Corner Store where Mr. Morgan kept his trashcans. At night, the caged bin offered plenty of concealment. During the day, it was another matter. The sun high overhead obliterated any shadows that may have kept us hidden.

"What happens if they're sitting on the back porch?" I asked.

"It's screened, isn't it?"

"So?"

"Keep asking questions," Bobby warned, "and he'll hear us before we even get close."

The gate to Morgan's backyard was open. Bobby moved in first. I thought he'd find his way into the trashcan corral. Instead, he pulled a fast one and darted for the back porch. Before I knew it, he scrambled beneath the porch and vanished. I was left with no choice but to follow. Beneath the porch, I smelled cat piss. The stench was so bad, my eyes watered. Bobby used his shirt to mask half his face, but it didn't do any good. I knew Morgan didn't own any cats, but that didn't stop neighborhood felines from turning the area beneath his back porch into a collective litter box.

Footsteps sounded overhead as I pictured a platoon of stray cats pissing on the very ground where I lay. Bobby held a finger to his lips, as if I was about to break out in song.

"Have a seat, Heinrich."

"Thank you."

Chairs shuffled. Dust bits rained down on our heads. Bobby drew a quick breath. I clamped my hand down over his mouth and nose. If I'd been any slower, it would have been all over for us. Bobby's eyes went wide for a moment before he exhaled slowly into my hand. When I was sure his sneezing fit was over, I let him go.

"Peter," Von Braun was saying. "I've seen the seekers."

"Where?" Morgan asked.

"Last night. Across the creek."

"How many?"

"Two."

"The threshold?"

"Nein."

"You want me to check it out?"

"No need," he said. "The threshold remains stable."

A chair slid.

"You're leaving?" Morgan asked.

"I have my garden to tend to."

"The garden that faces the creek?"

"How many gardens do I have?"

"Barring Hobbs Creek drying out," said Morgan. "I don't think we have anything to worry about."

"Those boys went camping in the woods over there not long ago," Von Braun announced.

"Oh?"

"They found the bridge."

"The bridge leads to nowhere," Morgan assured him.

"I'm not so sure anymore."

"Have you been over the bridge?"

"No," Von Braun answered. Then, "There's a girl."

"In addition to the seekers?"

"No," Von Braun said. "She wears a pendant. The moonstone."

Silence followed. Bobby shifted his arms and legs. When he did, his left foot kicked an empty can. Beneath the porch, the echo from the tin sounded like a church bell. *There was no doubt about it,* I thought. *We were dead.*

"Cat," Morgan said, at last. Then, "Do I know this girl?"

"I'll take care of it," Von Braun informed him. His tone reminded me of one of those villains from a 1940s movie.

"Let's not get ahead of ourselves."

"Fine. Do you have a better idea?"

"We should call a council."

Bobby looked at me. I made a face. He kept staring, his expression grim.

"Now, hold on," Morgan's voice boomed. "You are the one who initiated all of us all those years ago. The very rules of the group you founded—"

"I didn't establish the order," Von Braun said. "The order has been around for—"

"Several centuries. Yes, I know," the store owner quipped. "Maybe longer. At any rate, no action can be taken without consent of the council."

"Gather them," the old German told him. "It's high time we've checked the wards anyway."

The two men went on to discuss the current political situation. Neither man spoke highly of President Nixon, but even so, they were slightly kinder than my father had been whenever the subject came up. Several minutes passed in this fashion, and I hoped that Mr. Morgan and Von Braun would get back to the secretive subject of the council, but, the conversation concluded rather lamely when Morgan announced that he should re-open his store.

Bobby and I waited until after we heard the back door shut and the lock catch before we moved. I started to crawl out from beneath the porch, but Bobby stopped me. One of the boards overhead creaked. Through the boards, I saw the shadow of two large shoes before they descended the wood steps only a mere three feet away. Mr. Von Braun made his way to the back fence and paused. His long fingers drummed a moment atop the gate before he opened it and exited the backyard.

Chapter 12

"I smell cat piss," my father said.

He arrived home from work just minutes after I came out of my room wearing a fresh set of clothes. As the front door opened, I heard my mother dash down the cellar steps, two at a time from the sound of it, to shove my soiled clothes into the washer.

"Smell what?" I asked.

"Where's your mother?"

"Doing laundry?"

I went into the living room and turned on the television. It was too late in the afternoon to catch any cartoons, so I decided to watch the news. My mother and father stood in the kitchen conversing in hushed tones. Slowly, I lowered the volume so I could hear what they were talking about. Sitting in my father's armchair, I turned on the tall lamp and opened one of my comic books I kept stashed behind the short bookshelf my mother and father shared for the few books they owned. Those titles included *East of Eden* by Steinbeck, *A Death in the Family* by James Agee, and the Bible. Not just any Bible, but a real fancy one in a wood box that smelled like camphor when you opened it; as fancy Bibles go, it was a nice one with color illustrations of New Testament highlights that included twenty-four plates from the Annunciation to the Crucifixion, maps of Israel and the Mediterranean during "biblical times"—whatever that meant—and even a section where a family could fill in generations of names: a genealogical who's who. That was the bible I wasn't allowed to read; my folks were weird that way. Also, along with the Steinbeck, the fancy Bible, and the Agee, there were other books like J.D. Salinger's *9 Stories* and *A Catcher in the Rye*. I cared less about Holden Caulfield and his ridiculous hunting cap. No self-respecting kid would wear a hat like that in an urban environment, not unless the aforementioned kid was looking to get his ass kicked. The short story collection by Salinger I liked, my favorite being *Bananafish,* even if I didn't understand it. The first time I read it, I had nightmares about the guy who sat down on the bed and shot himself in the head. Tough break if you haven't read the story, but then that's your fault, because that tale is like a hundred years old by now. Anyway, as I perused my comic book, I listened as best I could to my parents, hoping to pick up something. Whenever they began a conversation in hushed tones like that, it usually ended in a full-blown argument. I thought about breaking open the fancy Bible, but they would have caught me red-handed the way they always did.

"Joe, stop that," my mother was fond of saying whenever she caught me thumbing through that Bible, like she had just caught me masturbating.

My father was no better. "Joe, don't," he often said as soon as he heard the latch give on the wooden box containing the Bible.

Both my parents acted as if I'd go blind or grow hair on my palms if I thumbed through the Bible for too long.

That evening, while the newscaster droned on about some bank robbery in Philadelphia, I leaned close to the doorway that led out of the living room. A foyer separated the living room from the dining room. Our house was an acoustical nightmare. Sound from the dining room drifted straight up the stairs in the foyer. Whoever designed the house was either a paranoid secret-agent type who didn't want conversations to be overheard from room to room or an imbecile.

"Tonight?" my mother shrieked.

"Keep your voice down," my father told her. His next words were so muffled, I couldn't make them out.

Silence followed for several seconds. I thought about going out into the foyer until I heard my mother speak up.

"Well," she said, at last, "you have to tell him."

Suddenly, the television went blank, and the light from the lamp went dark.

"Dad!" I shouted.

He didn't answer. Power outages in a poor neighborhood like mine were nothing new. My father exercised an almost Pavlovian response whenever it happened. He immediately dropped what he was doing and proceeded to the basement. Depending on how heavy his footfall was when he came back up the steps once he tampered with the fuse box, my mother and I were able to tell whether our house had lost power or the whole neighborhood. Power outages coincided often with summer thunderstorms. And since there was no storm outside, I found it peculiar that a fuse blew. Tim Swanson once told me that electrical outages, on a local level, that is to say on a level confined to one's home, was often caused by a rare form of telekinesis often brought about by stressful situations.

Presently, my father descended the steps to the basement. I left the living room and found my mother seated at the kitchen table toying with her checkbook. My father rarely allowed me to go into the basement except to go to the far corner where the washer and dryer were located. The rest of the basement, much like the garage filled with curios and oddities, was off limits, according to my father, on account of the excess crap my father horded down there that didn't fit in the garage.

The real reason I wasn't allowed down there all that often had less to do with the extra junk my father collected and more to do with the steel door on the wall behind the furnace. The door was shaped like the typical damage control barrier found inside a submarine, a small rectangular thing with rounded corners, complete with a dog-type hatch. A huge stainless steel padlock with a U-shaped bar thicker than a man's thumb dissuaded me from exploring what lay beyond the hatch. The first day I saw the hatch, I could tell by the cob webs and grime covering every inch of it, including the Goliath padlock, that no one had used the barrier for a long time. When I asked my father about it, he dismissively informed me that the padlock was there when we moved into the house. That was it. No explanation, no speculation as to why it was there in the first place. My father conveniently avoided the fact that he had inherited the house from his parents. Naturally, I searched high and low through the house for a key that fit the giant padlock, but I was never successful. That hatch behind the furnace remained the greatest single mystery in my life.

Everyone I knew wanted to see what was behind the steel hatch. It was hard to sneak people into the basement. My parents maintained that I had no business being there in the first place. On separate occasions, I managed to get Bobby McMahon to come into the basement to see the portal and the Swanson brothers as well. Bobby kept mum about where the door came from or what its use might have been at one time. Tim Swanson offered more colorful hypotheses: a) the steel hatch led to some kind of underground tunnel, b) the barrier led straight to Hell, or c) it was a portal to another universe. Like many of his explanations, Tim offered no hard evidence to support his claims. Bobby and I ruled out the gateway to Hell right away.

"Maybe it's a back entrance," Jack offered. "Like you go through it, and you end up on a dead-end street in Hell."

"Or like the wardrobe," Tim said.

"Or it could be a bomb shelter," Bobby said. "Plenty of people built them in the 1950s."

"In this neighborhood?" Jack asked.

"Are you saying that only rich folks could afford bomb shelters?"

"Well, yeah."

"That would mean it came later," Tim said.

"How so?"

"Most of these row homes in Yorkville were built after the First World War," he explained. "The atom bomb wasn't invented until World War II."

As far as we knew, my house was the only one with a hatch in it. Somehow, out of sheer speculation, the brothers Swanson and Bobby surmised that if any other house in Yorkville had a steel hatch like the one in my basement, it had to be inside Von Braun's home.

"One of us should check that out," Jack said.

"Like who?" said Bobby.

That settled it. Jack may have been many things, but crazy wasn't one of them. Igniting firecrackers and other illegal explosives on

Von Braun's property was one thing. Breaking into the old German's home, however, was something entirely different.

Presently, my father marched up the basement steps. He walked through the kitchen, took hold of the back of my neck and led me into the living room. The lamp beside the bookcase and the television were back on again.

"Your mother says you've been wrestling cats who like to piss on young boys," my father said.

"I don't—"

"Joe, don't lie to me."

I didn't know what to say. My mother had already started the wash when my father came home. How did he know about the cat piss? Fortunately, I didn't have to enmesh myself further in a web of lies. My mother came to my rescue.

"Don't you worry about Joe," she told my father. "You just get ready for your meeting."

"What about dinner?" I asked.

"Get a load of this guy," my father said. "Work up an appetite wrestling cats did you?"

"That's enough!"

My father turned up the television volume on the early evening news. My mother executed an abrupt about-face and threw her hands in the air as she exited. I started for the stairs to go up to my room.

"Hold on, Joe," my father said. "I want to talk to you."

Here it comes, I thought. There was no place in Yorkville that smelled to high heaven of cat piss the way it did beneath Mr. Morgan's back porch. Not that I figured my father for the kind of guy to go crawling around beneath people's porches, but I didn't doubt for a minute that Morgan must have told my father about the plague of cats beneath his back porch.

"I don't know how to say this," my father announced. "Maybe you should sit down."

Shit, I thought. Was my father about to tell me he and my mother were getting a divorce? If they did, would my father move out? Or would I go with my mother and live with Uncle Scott in Philadelphia?

"It's about your friend Marcella Carbone." He put his arm around me when I sat down next to him.

Before I could move, he wrapped both his arms around me and held me close. When he told me that Marcella was dead, I wailed like a baby. My cries may not have reached heaven that day, but I was sure they could hear me all the way over in Tracktown.

It was already dark out by the time I quit crying. I ended up huddled next to my father on the couch. As soon as he let me go, however, I bolted for the front door. My mother tried to stop me; but she was too late. I didn't have to look far to find the one responsible for sending my love away from me.

Something inside me that night snapped. I ran until I reached the town square. Once there, I ducked into Stevenson's Supermarket. As always, there was Mr. Stevenson, seated on a bar stool near the entrance. When he greeted me, I made no reply. Inside the supermarket, in the last aisle before the produce section, I searched the kitchen utensils until I found the largest butcher knife Stevenson's sold, snatched it from the hook, and hid it beneath my shirt. As I exited the store, I mumbled something to Mr. Stevenson about forgetting my money at home. The store owner, a rather fat specimen who seemed permanently attached to his bar stool, guffawed and waved good-bye. It was no wonder that Bobby McMahon considered the man mildly retarded.

The night air felt cool as I strode across the square. My destination: The Roost. The windows there were all aglow with pinball machine lights. As I approached, I spotted Sean McClusky as he exited the place. He made his way down the alley. So I followed him.

McClusky slipped behind the dumpsters where weeks ago he forced my friend Bobby to suck his prick. I crouched between two dumpsters on the end, not six feet from the cretin as he pissed. The whole time he whizzed against the wall, I thought about how my father told me they had found Marcella face-down beneath three feet of water at Hobbs Creek. My dad was reluctant to tell me how she died, since he had heard that Marcella was already dead before the killer dumped her body. Strangled? Stabbed? I didn't know. Once

McClusky finished pissing, he zipped up jeans and started humming *Iron Man* by Black Sabbath.

He passed in front of me with that stupid grin on his face. I imagined the same grin Bobby saw that terrible night. A light caught his silhouette. That's when I noticed the bracelet on his left wrist. The bracelet had once been the choker I saw Marcella wearing only a few weeks ago.

I was all set to stab the degenerate from behind until he turned into a raw, bloodied fat mess of useless meat when the alley went all aglow with flashing red lights. I heard men shouting from behind bright orbs emitted by flashlights. McClusky raised his hands in the air. When he did, the light caught the moonstone on Marcella's necklace now wrapped double around McClusky's fat wrist. Just beyond the flashing red lights atop two squad cars parked at right angles to thwart an attempt of escape, I saw—for only a split second—Marcella's ghost. I lost it after that and leapt out from behind the dumpsters.

Looking back, it was stupid of me. Everything slowed down. McClusky turned, offering that same toothy grin he did when he assaulted Bobby. Screaming, I thrust the knife.

A big fat uniformed cop stood between McClusky and me, brandishing a nightstick. Suddenly, a pain shot through my wrist. The blow from the nightstick knocked the knife free from my hand. My whole arm stung like a bitch.

"Is it broken?" the big cop asked.

I held my right hand beneath my left armpit. My tears flowed as the other policemen cuffed McClusky and whisked him away into one of the squad cars.

The big cop wore a name tag that read "Malone." He reached out his hand and put away his nightstick. At first, I thought he might apologize, but instead he spun me around, ordered me to place both hands on the dumpster directly in front of me. Malone frisked me without muttering a word.

"Hey, Mike," another cop called out. "Are you bringing that one?"

"No," Malone answered as he took me by the arm. "I'll just run him home. No harm, no foul."

Lucky bastard, I thought as I watched McClusky be driven away. It still hadn't occurred to me how much trouble I was in for trying to stab that fat slob. Worse, I started shaking and hyperventilating, something that had never happened to me before that night.

"Easy, son," Malone said, his voice calm. "Take deep breaths."

We stood alone in the alley for a few minutes. I wiped the tears from my eyes as Malone offered quiet words of solace until I was able to calm myself. Afterward, I felt foolish. Trouble with the police was the last thing I wanted. I just wanted to go home.

"What's your name, son?" he asked.

I told him.

"Tell me where you live," said Malone, "and I'll take you there."

"Am I in trouble?" I asked.

Malone chuckled. "You got a beef with that kid McClusky?" he asked.

"He killed Marcella," I told him.

Malone stooped down to pick up the butcher knife. He opened the dumpster lid, placed the flat edge of the blade on the lip of the dumpster, and closed the lid. Then, holding the lid down, he pulled up on the knife handle and snapped the blade in two. Satisfied with his work, he opened the lid a second time and tossed the knife handle into the dumpster.

"Jesus," he said after the lid was closed. "That stinks."

"It's worse behind them," I said.

"I bet it is, son," he told me. Then, "Do you know why we are here?"

"McClusky?"

"Well, yes," Malone said. "But do you know why we picked him up?"

"He killed Marcella Carbone."

"That's something the courts will decide," he informed me. "But what I meant was to stop angry young men like you from exacting revenge. You follow me?"

"Yes, sir."

"You knew the deceased?"

"I...I loved her."

"Then honor her memory," said Malone, "by not doing anything else stupid. Now, come on. Let's get you home."

I rode upfront in the squad car. Malone drove with one hand on the steering wheel as he smoked a cigarette. He gave me the typical cop talk about keeping my nose clean, indicating that maybe one day I could grow up to be a police officer just like him.

The last thing I wanted that night was for any other kids in the neighborhood to see me, especially those who were close to Marcella. Fortunately, there was no one on the street when Malone stopped his car in front of my house. And for the second time that day, I went home smelling like I had taken a bath in urine.

My mother was in complete hysterics when she opened the front door. My father, despite attempting to sound cool about the whole affair, looked as if he was in no better shape.

"What did he do?" my father asked.

"Nothing," Malone held me by the nape of neck. "He was alone down by the church."

My mother cocked her head. From the look in her eyes, I knew that her bullshit meter was working overtime that night.

"Come inside, Joe," she said, curtly.

Malone let go of me. "Well, good night," he said. "You folks have a good evening."

"Thank you so much," my mother told him.

"No trouble at all," he replied. "Tension runs high whenever a young one passes on. He'll be okay."

My father nodded and pulled me close. "Your summer is over," he told me.

"Go easy on him, Mr. Godwin," Malone said.

My parents and I remained in the front doorway until Malone got back into his squad car and drove away. Afterward, my mother stripped me out of my soiled clothes right there on the front porch. Up and down the street now, our neighbors stepped out of their houses and onto their porches to watch the spectacle, their faces hidden by shadows.

My father took me inside and marched me straight up to the bathroom. I had a quick bath as he stood guard at the bathroom door. When I was done, my father led me to my room and tucked me into bed. He stood in the doorway for a several minutes. The voices of other adults along the street drifted through my window screen. The sound reminded me of soft static, interrupted now and again by the mention of Marcella's name.

I drifted off to sleep like that with my father standing post in my bedroom doorway, listening to those voices. Later, I dreamt of Marcella and her soft tan skin, her brown eyes, and her dark hair that smelled like lilacs.

Chapter 13

School began, and it was already the first week of October before I mustered the courage to visit Marcella's gravesite. She was buried at St. Bonaventure's Cemetery along Route 2 near Dover Bridge. The cemetery once belonged to another Catholic church called the Church of the Annunciation. In the summer of 1955, a mysterious fire destroyed the church one night. Rumors abounded in those days as to who may have been responsible, but the culprit, according to my mother, was never caught. All of the headstones in that cemetery remained charred and blackened since the fire; even the new headstones put into place post-1955 took on the same sooty quality over time. People in and around Yorkville who remembered the fire spoke in hushed tones about how the town had fallen out of favor with God since someone had burned one of His houses to the ground. Whatever the case, St. Bonaventure's Church assumed ownership of the cemetery in 1966, but the feeling that God had turned a blind eye to our little town still plagued some of the old-timers.

St. Bonaventure's Cemetery always made me feel uneasy. It had nothing to do with simple superstitions that made Tim Swanson hold his breath for fear of inhaling some errant spirit whenever he passed a cemetery. I was different. Nothing said finality like a tombstone. And at St. Bonaventure's Cemetery, with its blackened headstones and lack of vegetation ever since the fire, the message on my beloved's gravestone meant more than any of the others inscribed over the other dead, since she was only twelve years old.

At Marcella's final resting place I wept. I lay on the ground where she was buried, and my tears wetted the dry ground there. I hugged the small granite angel atop her tombstone as if the little cherub there were a child Marcella and I brought into the world.

Of Marcella's death, I knew only what my parents told me. The night before Bobby and I hid out beneath Morgan's back porch, Marcella left her house on Harmon Street after dinner to walk to Annie Gallagher's on Downey Street. Somewhere along the way, my departed soul mate ran into Sean McClusky who led her to a stretch of woods near Hobbs Creek where the monster McClusky crushed Marcella's skull with a rock, dragged her lifeless body through the woods, and left her face-down beneath the murky creek waters. As summer ended, rumors spread like unchecked vines about the minute details leading up to my friend's death. Some said McClusky raped Marcella, but given his proclivity for boys like Bobby, I doubted that he did. Others spoke of McClusky being framed, of being in the wrong place at the wrong time, of having a nefarious reputation and being within the vicinity of the crime when Marcella's body was discovered. Those same people maintained that the neighborhood had been infiltrated by a stranger, a murderous drifter with an eye for young girls. By the time school began in September, I didn't know what to believe.

The day after I visited the cemetery, I skipped school. My father had a minor meltdown, but he learned long before I was born that it was best for him to cave beneath the pressure of my mother's demands. My mother saw my red swollen eyes that morning when I woke up and took mercy on me. She called the principal's office at St. Bonnie's.

"You can stay home," she said, "but I want you to stay in bed and pray."

"Okay," I said.

"Pray for Marcella, baby."

That bothered me. All the priests at St. Bonaventure's Church told us that, above all others, children were favored by God, and that they were guaranteed a place in Heaven. Why would I have to pray for my angel, Marcella? In my mind, she should have gone to the front of the line. So, instead, I stayed in my room that day reading comic books—Iron Man, Dr. Strange, The Incredible Hulk, and others—until my mother decided I could go outside.

Not long after my father returned home from work, my mother stood on the porch and called my name. In Yorkville, parents all over the neighborhood often stood outside and called their children home during mealtimes or when darkness fell and the hour grew late. Some nights it was hard to tell which parents were calling to what children. I remember being on the common near our block, waiting for the bats to fly overhead the way they did sometimes at that hour, especially during warmer weather when they swooped down out of the twilight to feast on clouds of mosquitoes that lingered over grassy fields, when I smelled the first hint of autumn in the air. A northerly wind blew at the same moment my mother called out my name. It was then I smelled the coming change of season. On the common that night, remembering Marcella's face the previous autumn when we hung out in the square after dinner one night, one of those rare evenings during the week when my parents thought it was okay for me to be out of the house, I knew that some part of my life was behind me, that magical portion of time when, like all children, I gave little thought to finality, to death in all of its certainty. With Marcella's passing came the end of my childhood. I understood that all of us were destined to die one day. Still, for the first time since Marcella was killed, I did not shed a tear. Instead, I went back to my yard and greeted my mother on the porch.

That evening, dinner consisted of my mother's specialty: meatloaf and mashed potatoes. My father lauded the merits of vegetables all the time, but he thought corn was simply another starch, cooked carrots devoid of any nutritional value, and spinach, like lettuce, a leafy food fit for rabbits and other small mammals. What my father did love was broccoli, and he only ate that vegetable raw. Whenever my father consumed broccoli, my mother complained that the bathroom smelled horrible after he finished relieving himself. Such was the banality of marriage between my parents. Many a night, I witnessed the most inane conversations take place between them, as if they were performing some absurd theater meant to numb anyone who experienced it. I didn't know about other couples in their houses at night, or what they did behind closed doors, but if theirs was anything like our household, it meant that the indifferent God we prayed to was dead, as the philosophers maintained, and that love between man and woman was something the poets wrote about, but ordinary people rarely experienced.

"Feeling better?" were the only words my father spoke that night.

I grunted, stabbed my fork into a slab of meatloaf and pretended that everything was okay. More than anything, I wanted to be outside again, and alone.

My mother opened her mouth to speak but, instead of saying anything, she commenced a coughing fit that lasted several seconds. Where greater men would have moved to action, my father simply sat back in his chair, looking dissatisfied over my mother interrupting the silence that surrounded us.

Chapter 14

St. Bonaventure Catholic School turned into my personal purgatory that year. Located across from the church of the same name on America Road, St. Bonaventure's was a two-story, squat, red-brick fortress of Catholic learning where the nuns of ruled over the first through eighth grades like hooded, deformed demons in some working-class Hell.

I walked to school every day, rain or shine, along with Bobby. The Swanson brothers attended Yorkville Public School. So once the school year began, I saw less of the brothers, mostly on the weekends.

In my classroom, the nuns removed Marcella's desk a few days after her death. Where there had been twenty-four desks, there were now twenty-three. The good nuns of St. Bonaventure had left an empty space where Marcella's desk once stood: a constant reminder of how fleeting life was, even though Sister Mary Ianella, our teacher, acted as if Marcella never existed.

The desks were rearranged to Sister Mary's liking, in perfect rows and equally spaced apart, and students were seated alphabetically by last name. That was Sister Mary's life, one of order in which there was no room for even the slightest variance. If a desk slid out of place even by so much as a quarter of an inch or if a student talked out of turn, Sister Mary's structured world unraveled, and so did she, judging by the tantrums she often threw in front of us.

Sister Mary Ianella was my mother's age, olive-complected with a slender Mediterranean nose and sublime lips. Beneath her uniform—a dark gray polyester affair—she was endowed with big breasts and, as my father once put it to Mr. Morgan, an ass built for sin. Of all the nuns at St. Bonnie's, Sister Mary was every father's favorite. Still, that Sister Mary was pious, no one had the slightest doubt. At mass every Sunday morning, men looked longingly at her and wondered, perhaps, how such a pretty, vivacious Italian-American siren ended up being a bride of Jesus, never to know a man's touch.

"Children," Sister Mary said, "let's take out our reading texts."

If there was an upside to removing my beloved's desk from the classroom, it was two-fold: Bobby and I now sat next to each other, and Billy Federov, the boy who smelled like cabbage, had to sit in the back of the class. Truth be told, Billy was smart enough. He didn't need to sit up front with those of us who struggled through our lessons. Still, his midget of a mother must have convinced him that children who sat in the front of the class always excelled. Never mind if a child happened to be complete dunce with an IQ in the lower double digits or not; according to Billy's mom, genius could be bestowed upon a student by simply sitting in the front row of the class.

It was true that Billy Federov smelled like cabbage, but he rivaled Bobby where brains were concerned. In all of St. Bonaventure's school, it was pretty much understood that Billy was the smartest thing on two legs. In addition, he possessed a sense of humor common among eggheads the world over, the kind of wit often mistaken for sarcasm by people of lesser intelligence; and with it came danger, since Billy's absurd sense of humor often made him the target of playground brutes who preferred to trade blows rather than verbal jibes. Billy Federov lived with only one purpose in mind at St. Bonaventure's and that was to make Sister Mary Ianella as uncomfortable as possible.

Billy waved his arm as if it were on fire. "Sister Mary," he said in his sing-song voice, "I left my reading book at home."

"Then you may partner with Susie Haupt," the teacher told him.

Bobby and I spun in our seats to catch a glimpse of Susie. She was a head taller than the rest of us. Susie's blond hair fell straight below her shoulders, and she had green eyes that made you feel like you had butterflies in your stomach whenever she looked at you. Susie also had boobs already, which made her all the more a creature of mystery to boys like us. Most days, she wore a dreamy look, and if I stared at her long enough, I often wondered if she was from some distant realm beyond our known universe or perhaps an angel tasked with enduring the awkward hardships of Catholic school.

Billy Federov sat back in his chair and folded his skinny arms across his chest. The elbows of his blazer were worn, and he looked as if he hadn't bathed in a week.

"Sister Mary," he said, "if one already knows how to read, then what is the point of participating in this frivolous exercise?"

Bobby winced. He was as much a smart-ass as the next egghead, but, unlike Billy, he knew his limits. Challenging the authority of a nun in a Catholic school classroom was tantamount to suicide.

"The answer to that, Mr. Federov," Sister Mary replied, "can be found at the principal's office. Now, run along."

Billy unfolded his arms, stood up, and fixed his eyes on our teacher.

"Your God is dead," he announced. "You and the other dykes in this school are all married to a corpse."

After Billy stormed out, the class erupted in equal parts laughter, dismay, and doubt. It took Sister Mary several minutes to calm the class down. As she went about the task of restoring order, a few of the Goody Two-shoes slid out of their desks, armed with their rosaries, and knelt down on the floor to pray. This small group consisted of homely girls who, for one reason or another, at the age of twelve, all believed they were being called to a higher purpose, whether it was to pray for wretched non-believers like Billy Federov or to join the ranks of women like Sister Mary Ianella, and they used every opportunity to wield their piety over the rest of us like the archangel Michael's fiery sword. Secretly, I envied those three girls. By the time a kid in Yorkville reached age twelve, it became no secret that every last one of us needed a ticket out. For the three pious furies, their meal ticket was Jesus, himself. For the rest of us, it felt like Heaven had turned her back on us.

Not long after order was restored in the classroom, the last bell rang. And somewhere in heaven, despite Billy Federov's protestations, another angel earned his wings.

Outside, the schoolyard was abuzz with news of Billy's one-sided philosophical annunciation. First graders ran crying to their waiting mothers, plagued with the notion that there was no God after all. Older kids stood around in close huddles weighing the pros and cons of what would ultimately come to be known as Federov's Paradox.

"You think he's finished here?" Bobby asked.

"Not much point in going to a Catholic school," I reasoned, "if you don't believe in God."

Bobby pursed his lips and whistled. "No," he said, "your logic is wrong." He took hold of me by the shoulders and spun me around. As we stood facing the mass of students, he told me, "Do you think every last of one of them is a true believer? I say no. But at least here, a kid can learn something instead of going through the motions at the Idiot Academy."

Bobby echoed his parents' sentiment in that good education could be had at a parochial school like St. Bonaventure's. The only difference I saw was that kids like the Swanson brothers didn't have to wear uniforms and ties, and in public schools, students weren't forced to pray like a thousand times a day. What? Another test? Say a prayer. Christmas break coming up? Say a prayer. War in Southeast Asia? Say prayer. Neighborhood becoming more culturally diverse? You best say your prayers loud enough for all the saints to hear, because you're going to need it. The prayers that went up from St. Bonnie's alone were enough to cause a racket in Heaven. It was hard to imagine all the other Catholic schools in the free world offering up the same amount. Maybe Billy Federov was right. Maybe God was dead; only we killed Him with our constant bantering, drove him, perhaps at long last, to commit some sort of secret cosmic suicide.

"Are you listening to me?" Bobby asked.

"No. What?"

"My believing in God or not is hardly relevant."

"How so?"

"Faith is a personal matter."

"Yeah, but without God—"

"You are missing the point."

"Which is what?"

"That Billy Federov is only here because his parents think he will benefit from learning from the good sisters."

"That's bullshit," I said, "and you know it."

Bobby whistled once more as he started down the block. It didn't take a genius to notice that the spring in his step returned the day Sean McClusky was arrested. Worse, he started getting chummy with an eighth grader named Alistair Simon. The first time I heard that name, I thought, *what kind of parent would name their son Alistair?* You'd have to think your son was going to grow up to become a secret agent or a torch singer or maybe both; but whatever case the future held for him, the present pretty much turned Alistair into a permanent target for ridicule, physical abuse, and lunch money extortion.

It was Friday afternoon, and, as was the custom, I wanted to stop at Schmidt's Pharmacy to peruse the comic book rack. Nine times out of nine, whenever I asked Bobby to go along with me, he did. That afternoon, however, he was hesitant.

"What gives?" I asked. "Is it the alley?"

"Oh, that's not it," he told me.

"Hey, Bobby McMahon," a sing-song cry rang out.

I looked across the street. There was Alistair Simon waving to Bobby with a handkerchief in his hand like some antebellum debutante. Alistair palled around with two mousy, effeminate buddies, both eighth graders, who went by the names of Geoffrey Morgan and Jonathan Overy. In a town where everyone abbreviated their names, Joe for Joseph, Bobby for Robert, and so forth, these three Catholic dandies insisted that they be addressed by their full names. There were rumors that Alistair and his two friends were already engaging in homosexual activity. Now, judging by the way that Alistair was nearly breaking his arm as he waved his fag flag, they were out to recruit Bobby.

"So, you don't want to go to Schmidt's?" I asked as he waved back to Alistair.

"Honestly, Joe," Bobby said, "comic books?"

"Excuse me, Count Fancy Pants?"

"You should come with me," he said. "Come on over to Alistair's."

"No," I replied.

"These guys are cool, Joe."

"What do you guys do at Alistair's house?"

Bobby beamed like some homely girl who had just been asked to the prom by some handsome jock. It was pathetic. Another eighth grader, a girl named Lisa Berstler, told me in the beginning of the school year that Alistair and his lackeys were caught giving one another hand jobs at summer camp. I didn't know what was more shocking when I first heard the news: the fact that Alistair and his friends engaged in adolescent homosexual play or that a normal, pretty girl like Lisa Berstler, all red curls and milky skin, knew all about hand jobs.

"Mostly," Bobby was saying, "we talk about novels and poetry."

"And when you're not mostly doing that?"

"Don't be crass, Joe," he said. "I know what some of these less enlightened children think of Alistair. They chastise him for being different."

I stood there as Bobby crossed the street and joined Alistair and company. Alistair rubbed Bobby's head and pinched his ear. Geoffrey Morgan and Jonathan Overy took turns hugging my friend as if they didn't just see him in the halls of St. Bonnie's only minutes ago. When the greeting ritual ended, the four of them went strolling down the street like the dandies they were, laughing like girls and cupping their hands over their mouths as they shared secrets.

Bobby once told me that Alistair lived with his mother, a divorcee, in Mitchell Arms Apartments. I knew the place well. My parents had friends who lived there. All of them, like Alistair's mom, were divorcees, too. The recently divorced adults at Mitchell Arms Apartments avoided one another as if there was some stigma attached to associating with someone whose marriage had failed. The Yorkville Police visited the complex regularly at night in order to keep the peace. I knew that Alistair lived in a third-floor apartment in the back of the building that overlooked Hobbs Creek. There was a fire escape on the back wall of the building. Once Bobby filled me in on his regular meetings after school with Alistair and his two new friends, I wondered if it was feasible for someone to climb the fire escape without being discovered and glimpse into Alistair's bedroom.

The reconnaissance mission I envisioned would have to wait for another day. No sooner did I watch Bobby wander off with Alistair and the others, I saw the ghost of Marcella Carbone dart across America Road as she headed straight for the town square. I barely believed in God, and Billy Federov's little escapade weighed heavily on me that afternoon, but I believed less in ghosts. And yet, there she was, the flower of my otherwise drab wasteland. I ran for all I was worth to catch up with her.

"Jesus, Joe," the girl said when I grabbed her shoulder. Up close, she looked less like Marcella now, but for the life of me, I couldn't place her.

"Hey, Catholic boy," Jack Swanson called out.

I turned away from the girl. Jack and Tim made their way toward me from the opposite side of America Road.

"What's up, boys?" I could still sense the girl behind me.

"Hey, Joe," Tim said, "what's wrong with you?"

"I was just talking to…" I started to say, but when I turned to look back the girl was gone.

Chapter 15

The town square in autumn was always littered with fallen leaves. The windows in all the stores were adorned with Halloween decorations.

Jack and Tim accompanied me to Schmidt's Pharmacy. We checked out the comic book rack, but there weren't any issues I was interested in buying. Where the selection for comics at Schmidt's was concerned, I wasn't alone in my pursuit. Old Mr. Schmidt sold out of comic books faster than he did prescription pain killers. Afterward, Jack announced that he wanted to treat all three of us to soda and pizza at the Roost. I hadn't set foot in the pinball hall since Marcella had been killed. I never expected, as I stood there in Schmidt's Pharmacy between the comic book racks and the checkout counter, that suddenly the weight of the world might crash down upon me, or that I would have to make a decision that would force me to take the first step toward getting on with my life. Of course, at twelve years old, no kid thinks that way, but, since Jack mentioned it so casually, I thought it might be a test from God. Until that day, I had the same routine after school. I walked home from St. Bonaventure's, avoiding the path Marcella used to take, stopped by the square along with a gaggle of other kids from school, and ended up either in Schmidt's Pharmacy or Dave and Di's Luncheonette to peruse comic books. If I had an extra quarter, I purchased the latest issue of Dr. Strange, The Incredible Hulk, or Iron Man.

Once the school year began, I didn't even look in the direction of The Roost for fear of seeing Marcella's reflection in the big windows that faced the square. One week after school started, I thought I saw her likeness reflected in the arcade's plate glass window. Marcella stood between an oak tree and a park bench directly across the street behind me. She didn't look dead, not the way some of the departed looked in comic books, all decayed and ghastly. Every last fabric of my being hoped that when I turned to look at the source of the reflection, I would find Marcella standing there, but it was not meant to be. Between the oak tree and the park bench, there was just empty space. Somewhere between the reality of what was and the reflection that encompassed my longing lay the truth of things: that childhood's end means understanding that there's no more magic left in the world; that each of us, as sure as we are born, will die, and, often as not, we will never be wise to the Reaper before he strikes, no matter the form he takes. So, as we stood there inside the pharmacy, and Jack asked me to go to the Roost, I figured it wasn't a bad idea to revisit the one place still replete with Marcella's energy or essence, as a test, perhaps to see if I was capable of sharing the same world with her ghost.

"Where did you get the money?" I asked Jack. "Did you win the lottery?"

"Don't be a boob," said Jack. "It's illegal for kids to play the lottery."

"We went collecting," Tim announced. "You know the old paper route, right?"

I did, only the paper route didn't belong to the brothers Swanson. The previous summer the *Evening Bulletin* newspaper began to insert billing envelopes in the Wednesday edition. It was only a dollar for a weekly delivery. Customers receiving the paper at their homes would provide payment in the envelope, more often than not in cash. The brothers Swanson quickly became hip to the process when Yorkville residents began leaving the bright orange envelopes rolled up in their chain-link fences or sticking out of their mailboxes on their porches. Late at night on Wednesday or before the sun rose on Thursday, Jack and Tim snuck out of Granny Swanson's house and went around the neighborhood hoisting the payment envelopes for their own misbegotten gains. It had been enterprising young lads like the brothers Swanson that ultimately forced the newspaper industry to forgo the old-fashioned payment in an envelope system to the more secure pre-paid billing. That change, however, lay years down the road, and in 1976, the Swanson bandits were riding high.

I begged off on the pizza. My father had a thing about thieves, especially young ones, and he made it clear to me that I should never benefit from someone else's misfortune, no matter how small the price. My parents had all kinds of crazy rules like that. Where my father broke it down to criminals and victims, my mother plotted out various activities beneath the respective umbrellas of mortal and venial sins.

"Stealing is a morally bad act," my mother echoed my father's sentiment, but she was always quick to add, "and a morally bad act is a sin, Joe. Remember that. And it doesn't stop there. Stealing leads to laziness, which is sloth. And sloth is a sin. A very deadly sin. In fact, sloth is one of the original seven deadly sins. You see where I'm going with this?"

I never did, but I pretended to understand in order to keep my mother off her fiery pulpit where every act was either morally good or morally bad. So as not to dishonor my parents, I paid for my own Coca-cola at The Roost and sat in envy as Jack and Tim scarfed down slice after slice of pizza. Between the two of them, their reprehensible act of thievery netted them close to twenty dollars each. Not bad for two kids whose father was in jail and whose grandmother may or may not have had a thing for the weird German guy living next door. We sat by the window, the same window I had seen Marcella's reflection in the previous month.

A large gang of teenagers, fresh off the bus from the county vocational school and reeking of marijuana, motor oil, and hair spray, hovered around a pool table while two teenage girls shot eight ball. For teens who attended the vocational school, there were four majors: auto mechanic, carpentry, electrician, or hairdresser. All the boys in Yorkville who attended the vo-tech, as we called it, were learning to become skilled tradesmen, and the girls studied to become beauticians or, as my father liked to call them, "miracle workers." The rumor at St. Bonaventure's that year was that Alistair Simon wanted to be the first boy at the vo-tech to become a beautician. I expected at any moment for one of the brighter vo-tech students to realize that Jack and Tim had money to burn—something no sane kid in Yorkville would ever admit to, not that any of us had it unless that money was appropriated through a morally bad act. Luckily, the teenagers were all too engrossed in watching the game of pool between the two girls who could barely bend at the waist in their tight jeans.

Tim pulled out a Swamp Thing comic book and spread it out on the table. One of the vo-tech girls, a fifteen-year-old named Molly Evers, sauntered over to our table, smiled at Tim, and peeked at the comic book for a moment before returning to the pool table.

"Girlfriend?" I asked.

Tim blushed. "Just good taste," he said. Then, to his brother, he added, "Tell him."

"We're thinking about going back into the woods," said Jack.

"Franklin Forest?" I asked.

"Yeah, that's right."

"It's a little cold out for camping."

"You are *such* a girl," Jack snapped. He waved at Molly. "Sorry, baby."

Tim coughed and turned a page in his comic book.

Jack looked around the game room. Confident that no one was listening, he leaned in close.

"It's the house," he whispered.

"And the bridge," I added.

"Of course."

"I can't stay out overnight."

"We go on a Saturday morning," Jack told me. "Same route as before. In and out same day."

"And I get to go along this time," Tim added. "I'm not sitting this one out."

"We might not find our way back there, Jack," I said.

"Don't worry," he said. "We just have to find the bridge. We find the bridge, we find the house."

Chapter 16

On a Saturday morning, I left my house a little before 10 a.m. My mother and my father were both on their way to Stevenson's Supermarket. I lied to them and told them that I was going over to Bobby McMahon's house. They didn't ask any questions. And even if they did find out that I hadn't told them the truth, I figured by the time they knew, I'd already be deep inside Franklin Forest. I waited until they were out of sight, then I went directly to Granny Swanson's. When I got there, I saw Granny Swanson standing in her yard talking to Heinrich Von Braun.

"Joseph," Granny Swanson cried. "I'm so glad you are here. Mr. Von Braun and I were just talking about you."

Great, I thought. Then, "You were?"

Mr. Von Braun busied himself with raking leaves. Granny Swanson just stood there with a stupid grin etched on her face.

"Anyway," I said and cleared my throat. "Is Jack home?"

That's when I smelled smoke in the air. I checked out Von Braun's yard, waiting to see if there was a pile of burning leaves. Despite a strict town ordinance that forbade anyone from burning leaves, Heinrich Von Braun still found that method the most effective way to get rid of natural waste.

"There's a fire in the forest across the creek," said Mr. Von Braun. He was a weird, old man who sensed what most people were thinking before they opened their mouths. "It's been burning all morning."

"I was telling Mr. Von Braun how nice it is," Granny Swanson said, "to have such a positive influence on my grandsons."

If I didn't know any better, I would have sworn I just stepped into some bizarre alternate universe; that, or Granny Swanson had already been drinking.

"I'm not sure—" I started to say.

"Jack and Tim are busy cleaning out Mr. Von Braun's shed," she told me. "Around back. That's where you will find them."

Now my suspicions were confirmed. Jack and Tim rarely helped their grandmother keep her house in order. How they got roped into doing chores for Mr. Von Braun was beyond me. Knowing the Swanson brothers, there had to be an ulterior motive. If Mr. Von Braun hadn't mentioned the forest fire, I might have suspected that the brothers Swanson had set fire to the old man's shed. Things were getting weird, and the thought of the forest fire made me nervous.

"The widow Swanson told me you might want to help the boys," Mr. Von Braun said.

It wasn't a question, so I started across the lawn. "I'd be happy to help," I told him.

Behind Mr. Von Braun's house lay a perfectly manicured lawn cut in criss-cross patches that looked like the fairway of some fancy golf course. Beyond the lawn, a small cluster of oak trees surrounded a large wood shed painted dull green and brown. The shed was as nearly as big as a one-car garage. Over the front door, which stood wide open, was a round placard with faded faint splotches. As I drew near, I could see what looked like the outline of an angelic figure. On either side of the shed, toward the rear, there were marble pylons coming out of the ground.

One quick peek into the shed proved that Jack and Tim were not inside. The interior appeared clean and the contents were all placed neatly throughout. Among the items were various rakes, shovels, and brooms; parked in the middle of the shed were an old-fashioned rotary blade mower and a small wheel barrow.

As I exited the shed, I heard a hiss. It was too loud to be a snake.

"Back here," Jack's voice called out from behind the shed.

"What are you doing?" I went around and greeted him.

"Keep your voice down," he said.

Tim stood next to his brother, looking nervous. "Check it out," he whispered.

Jack gestured to a clump of small trees. Propped between the trees was an old wood rowboat.

"You go stall the old man and Granny Swanson," he said. "Tim and I will sneak the boat down to the creek."

"What happened to the canoe?" I asked.

"We returned it."

"Yeah," said Tim. "What do you think we are? Thieves?"

I went back to the front of the house where Mr. Von Braun stood sniffing the air. Granny Swanson, I learned from the old man, had gone into her house to have a cup of tea.

"The wind shifted," Mr. Von Braun said.

I didn't want to talk about the fire, so I changed the subject by asking the old man about Germany before World War II. Mr. Von Braun was reluctant to discuss his past, as if by divulging some personal history, he lessened the memory for himself. We stood there, silent for a minute or more.

"I think the worst is over," he said at last, referring to the forest fire.

Mr. Von Braun and I made small talk after that about three topics of which I knew nothing: geometry—particularly something called the Pythagorean Theorem—the coming gasoline shortage, and the Philadelphia Phillies. Fortunately, Tim appeared behind Mr. Von Braun. It was no secret that the old German favored the younger Swanson brother over Jack, no doubt seeing the elder brother as the instigator, the source of trouble, the inflictor of mischief.

"Uh, Jack and I are finished," Tim said. "We put everything order just like you said."

Von Braun shrugged. "How much do you want?"

"Jack says—"

"One day," the old German told him as he handed him a five-dollar bill, "you will learn to think for yourself." Next, he took out three dollars and also handed them to Tim. "Give that to your brother, and don't tell him I gave you more."

"Yes sir, Mr. Von Braun."

"And don't patronize me," he barked at him. "It doesn't suit you."

"Come on," Tim led me into Granny Swanson's backyard.

Turning, I saw Mr. Von Braun walk up the steps to his porch. He paused a moment, sniffing the air once more, then pushed opened the screen door on his porch and went inside.

"Where's Jack?" I asked.

"Your ship awaits," Tim answered.

We walked down to the dock. Jack stood in the boat on the water and beckoned us.

"Get a pail," he told Tim.

"Why?" his brother asked.

"Because I want to make ice cream."

"Really?"

"No, douche bag. Because the boat has a leak. Now hurry."

"Can we plug it?"

"Later. Go get a pail."

Instead of going back to Granny Swanson's house, Tim ran to the end of the dock and jumped into the boat with his brother. A short plume of water shot up from the hole on the floor of the row boat.

"Joe, come on," Jack said. "We can make it."

I jumped into the boat. Jack got down on his hands and knees and pressed his hand over the quarter-size hole.

"Row, Tim!" he shouted. "Do it now!"

"I thought you wanted to get a pail?" Tim asked.

I squeezed into the seat next to Tim. Together, we rowed as fast and as hard as we could. We were better than halfway across the creek when Jack switched hands over the hole. There was at least three inches of water inside the row boat. By the time we reached three-quarters of the way across the creek, we had picked up another two inches of water.

"You have a hole in your hand, Jack?" Tim snickered as he posed the question.

"You're going to have a hole in your head," Jack snapped, "if you don't row faster."

"I can row faster if you want," said Tim, "but if Joe rows any slower, we'll just spin in a circle."

Jack let go of the hole. Mutiny followed. The two brothers rained blows down up one another. Tim jabbed Jack in the solar plexus with his oar, and when Jack fell over, he accidentally kicked me square in the jaw. Before we knew it, all three of us ended up fighting in the sinking boat. It was only the feel of cold water on our knees, our elbows, and our backs that saved us from further madness.

Chapter 17

The fire Jack built felt good after slogging through the wet mud. We had made it across the creek only to find that the tide had turned the far bank into a veritable marsh. My shoes were sucked right into the mud and off my feet twice as we struggled to haul the row boat onto dry land. In the end, the three of us had to lift the small boat up over our heads, which was a bitch because dirty creek water trapped in the boat rained down on us when we did. Ten yards past the marshy bank, we propped the boat on its side against a tree and camouflaged it with some fallen branches and dead leaves as best we could. In the state forest, it was illegal to light a campfire outside the designated camping areas, but we were tired, wet, and hungry, and with the forest fire miles away from, us we took a vote and decided that our little campfire could do no harm. We were more right than we knew that afternoon. Thirty minutes after Jack got the fire going, it began to rain. That was good news for the firemen out there trying douse to the forest fire, but bad news for three kids dressed in soaking wet clothes in autumn.

"Let's just go find the house," said Jack, disgusted that all his hard work went to waste.

Shrouded in a mix of smoke, cold mist, and drizzle, the woods appeared desolate, like some purgatorial wasteland. We walked through the wet woodland, our footfall padded by the dampened pine needles and fallen leaves: three shades lost in a Dantean landscape. For a change, Jack and Tim remained silent, making the trek longer than I remembered. The grayness all around me and the still air offered little in the way of direction; my sole hope for finding the house again rested on Jack's ability to navigate us through the murk of the forest.

The ground sloped downward, toward a narrow ravine. Underfoot, a weave of exposed roots and twisted vines slowed our every step. Some of the trees were bare, bent and crooked like skeletons of deformed giants; other trees still wore their coats of red, gold, ochre, and orange leaves.

"This is useless," said Jack.

"How much longer will it be?" Tim asked.

"You're wrong," I said.

"Come again?" Jack stopped, turned, and shook a low branch full of wet leaves.

"Asshole," Tim said, as rainwater from the leaves splattered all over him.

"We're in the ravine," I told Jack.

"You said it was close." His brother wiped his face clean with his shirt.

"Shut up, Tim," Jack said. Then, "I'm listening."

"The bridge crosses this ravine," I said.

"You don't know what the fuck you are talking about, Joe." He gritted his teeth now. "There are ravines all over the woods. And all of them have little streams and tributaries that lead out to Hobbs Creek."

"Let's just follow this ravine," I argued. "If I'm wrong, we turn around and come back."

It didn't take long after that to find the bridge with its hand-carved arch and railings. We were halfway across the foot bridge when Tim grabbed me by the arm.

"Joe," he said, "that looks just like you."

Tim pointed at a face carved into the railing to our left. I leaned forward to get a better look.

"Shit," Jack said as he stood behind me. "That really does look like you."

The brothers may have had their fun chiding me; my attention, however, was focused not on the carved likeness of me, but on a familiar figure I glimpsed through the bridge railing. The feral boy squatted, in all of his pale, naked glory, upon a rocky outcrop a few yards down the ravine. He looked as wild in the daylight as he did the first time I saw him during the lightning storm.

From the railing, I waved to the boy. He remained fixed, staring at me with dark eyes as big as sunglass lenses. At first, I thought maybe they were a pair of shades, but then the boy blinked. Aside from his large eyes, I noticed another attribute to his face: the absence of his nose. In place of the proboscis were two narrow slits beneath his big eyes.

"Joe?" Tim said quietly as he stood behind me.

"Look there," I nodded at the boy.

"At what?"

"You don't see..."

Tim put a hand on my shoulder. "Come on," he said. "It's nothing."

The boy stood up on the rocks. He cocked his head, scrutinizing Tim and me, perhaps, before he leapt from the rocks toward the tree line atop the ravine. Only the rustle of low branches gave away the point where the boy vanished into the forest.

"Can we go now?" Jack asked, impatiently.

New Jersey was famous for its notorious devil rumored to have been born under a curse in a ramshackle house. As Jack, Tim, and I crossed the bridge, I wondered if anyone had ever heard of the feral boy of Franklin Forest. Worse, I became afflicted with grand delusions of leading my own expedition into the heart of the forest. Once there, many important scientists and storytellers would gaze in awe at the feral boy and a magical woodland court, a fairy court in the new world. The truth of the matter was that if I couldn't convince Tim that someone had been there on the rocks along the ravine then it would be my word against those that came later. Who would believe me? And why should they? My heart raced when I contemplated the possibility that the three of us may be only the latest in a long string of backyard explorers drawn first to the bridge and later to the forest house. I kept thinking about the story of Carl Huffington who vanished without a trace, save for the notebook that he left behind.

Suddenly, Jack stopped in his tracks. He turned slowly to face Tim and me, a look of confusion on his face. Tim opened his mouth to speak to his brother, but Jack held a finger to his lips.

"Quiet," he said, and then he loosed a wet-sounding fart that seemed to echo through the woods.

"Nasty," Tim cried.

We stood on the far side of the bridge. The path there lay marked by the moonstones just as it was the night Jack and I found it. In daylight, however, there were marked differences. The stones on either side of trail lay dark; gone was the spectral glow the stones gave off in the pitch of night. Even the trail itself appeared to be longer, winding in a serpentine fashion around ancient trees, craggy rock outcrops, and dense underbrush. Scanning the immediate landscape, I saw no signs of the feral boy, but that meant little to me. The further into the forest we moved, the more I suspected he was still watching us.

Before long, the rain abated. In its place came an ever-thickening fog, rich with the smell of smoke, as we moved higher into the forest. Visibility was very poor, and it worsened the further along the path we moved. After following the path for several hundred yards, we reached a point where the trees stood further apart and then opened up to a wide expanse shrouded in fog.

When we reached that point where the woods gave way to the mansion grounds, it was Tim who loosed a muffled cry. A hulking gargantuan shadow loomed through the fog like a ghost mountain blocking out the day's light.

Chapter 18

The stench from the round, man-made pond located in the front of the colossal house gave me the dry heaves. Its dark, viscous waters were bordered by sharp, triangular rocks.

Jack and Tim held their shirts to their noses as they circled the pond. Together, they climbed the steps that led to the main porch.

The mansion in all its Gothic revival glory stood four stories at its highest part: two towers made of gray stone that looked like support columns for the low rain clouds overhead. The mansion was shaped like a "V"; the towers were located at either end of the house toward the back. The walls stretched three stories high, gray stone riddled with creeping vines and tall stained-glass windows. The house's splendor overwhelmed me. I remained planted where I stood not far from the pond. A few of the windows on the first floor were closed with decaying Venetian shutters. The rest of the first-floor windows were made from stained glass of varying yellow-brown shades. Jack busied himself by peeking through the amber windows, while Tim rubbed his hands over the intricately carved wood front door.

"Come on, Joe," he said, turning to face me. "What are you waiting for?"

"What if someone's home?" I asked.

Water lapped behind me. I didn't bother to turn and see what caused the noise.

"There's furniture inside," Jack said as I joined him and his brother on the porch.

"Someone must live here," I said.

"How can you be so sure?" Tim asked.

"Look at the lawn."

"Maybe it's dead."

"If the grass was dead, it wouldn't be green," Jack reminded him.

"Only one way to tell," Tim announced as he turned the big knob on the front door. He offered me a look of triumph as he pushed the door open. Next, he shouted as loud as he could. "Hello? Is anyone here?"

I didn't have time to react. The brothers Swanson stepped over the threshold. I took a step back, studying the intricate woodwork on the doorframe that was carved just like the foot bridge. Faces, animals, contorted trees, and fantastical beasts were all intertwined with vines spotted not with fruit but with tiny human skulls.

Suddenly, the front door slammed shut. I nearly pissed in my pants. I wanted nothing more, at that moment, than to turn tail and run all the way back to the creek.

"Did I scare you?" Tim asked as he opened the door wide.

"Jackass," I said.

"You got to see the inside."

Just passed the entryway, there were three steps that led up to a foyer as large as my entire house. To my left, there were two sets of double doors. One set was ajar. Through that open portal, I glimpsed a grand dining room. The floor of the foyer was littered with dry leaves. There was an odor that permeated the air: a dank, ancient scent that worked its way into my wet clothes.

Jack moved a dozen steps and leaned against the other double doors to the left. The doors didn't budge. He pushed hard a second time.

"Damn it," he said. "Joe, give me a hand."

It took a second, but I realized that these doors, unlike the elaborate stained glass doors that led to the dining room, slid open. I pushed Jack aside, made a show of my hands like a stage magician, or Ed Rooney from *The Honeymooners*, and slid the door on the left open.

"Holy shit," Jack exclaimed, "look at all those books."

Libraries were not Jack's forte. He was afflicted with that rare condition that made children like him uncomfortable when faced with the possibility of learning something out of a book, as if a variety of symptoms from shortness of breath to skin rashes and everything between were brought on by the very act of reading.

"Where are you going?" I asked.

"Second floor," Jack answered. "Want to come along?"

"We shouldn't get separated," Tim said.

"I'm going up the stairs," he said. "Don't be such a girl."

Jack ascended the grand stairs and left Tim and me alone to check out the room full of books.

The library consisted of four walls with built-in shelves that stretched from floor to ceiling. There were two leather armchairs in opposite corners of the room. Each chair smelled rotten, like something had crawled into the stuffing and died there long ago. I suspected that if I lifted one of the cushions, I might find a dead squirrel or a dead cat, all half-decayed with their eyes missing. Besides the walls lined with books and the armchairs, there were two desks; old mahogany monstrosities, they were, that called to mind the desks nineteenth century writers like Balzac or Dickens may have plied their craft. The blotters atop each desk were made of leather, and like the armchairs, they were ruined with age. Dried jars of India ink, rusted fountain pens and letters openers, and dust-encrusted tins of varying sizes all graced the top of each desk. To the right of the sliding door, there was a small fireplace littered with dry leaves, broken bricks, and other debris.

In front of one bookshelf stood a dark wood console table with a glass curio cabinet trimmed in brass on top of it. The cabinet looked out of place amid the dark leather and mahogany. Deeper into the room, Tim pulled a curtain back that covered the shelves. There were liquid-filled jars, identical to the curio on the desk, which lined each shelf. In each jar, there was a perfectly preserved specimen of bird. In one jar, a blue jay. In another, a scarlet red cardinal. The biggest jar in the curio contained a menacing crow that seemed to turn its head and study Tim and me as we stared at it. Several other jars held hummingbirds, robins, blackcapped chickadees, sparrows, woodpeckers, mourning doves, and even a few meadowlarks. Tim named every specimen, careful not to touch any of the jars.

I didn't know why someone would collect such specimens and store them in jars filled with formaldehyde or some other preservative. In Catholic school, I learned that the dove was the symbol of the Holy Spirit. In the Yorkville Library, I discovered in a book that humans often saw the bird, any bird, as the soul, or at least the means by which the soul was conveyed from the land of the living to the next place. In ancient Persia, for example, the vulture was not only a bird of prey but the carrier of the dead. Likewise, in other cultures, the crow served as the vehicle that transported the souls of the dead to the beyond. Armed with this knowledge on that rainy autumn afternoon, glimpsing those specimens that had been preserved in a library that looked as if it hadn't been used in nearly a century, a shiver ran down my spine. The thing I remember most about that afternoon was how those jarred birds were all missing their eyes.

"Let's get out of here," I told Tim.

From somewhere in the house came Jack's high-pitched howl followed by the sound of breaking glass. I followed Tim out of the library. We didn't have to go far to find Jack. He lay at the foot of the grand stairwell.

"What's wrong?" Tim got down on the floor next to his brother.

"It's him," Jack muttered. "It's him."

I didn't see any broken glass anywhere, and from as near as I could tell, Jack didn't look injured—scared, yes, but not hurt. It was not out of the realm of possibilities, given Jack's penchant for vandalism or otherwise defacing another person's property, that he found trouble on the second floor.

It took Tim several minutes to coax his brother back onto his feet. For me, it felt like hours had passed by the time Jack got up from the floor. Jack repeated his mantra—"It's him"—over and over again until we exited the house.

Once we reached the path that led to the bridge, I looked back toward the house. On the main porch stood a young girl in a long, tattered dress. Her curly, dark hair fell loose below her shoulders. She lingered there, the front door open at her back, and offered a coy wave of her hand before stepping back into the house.

In the short span of years I knew Jack Swanson, I never once saw him break down the way he did. Even when Granny Swanson used to beat him like a dog with a belt, a broom, her fists, a coffee mug, or whatever instrument of pain she could get her hands on, even then I never saw Jack shed any tears, not the way he did that afternoon. He scared Tim and me, but there was no pressing him for information before we left the woods. Our troubles, we discovered not long after passing over the footbridge, were far from over. When we reached the stretch of forest where we had left the row boat, we discovered that the boat was missing. All that we found were the small branches we used to camouflage it.

"It can't be gone." Jack snapped out of his daze. It comforted me to hear his familiar, biting banter again. "Who the fuck steals a boat with a hole in it?"

"Someone who knows how to plug the boat?" Tim offered.

"Don't be stupid."

"Hey, Jack," I said, "go easy now."

"Someone watched us cross the creek in that boat," he announced. "Someone on this side."

"Let's just hoof it over to Dover Bridge," Tim suggested.

Jack started back into the woods. Tim and I followed him. The trek through the forest to the road that led to Dover Bridge was less than three miles. On an open road, it may have taken us a little more than an hour. Through the forest was a different story. There were too many fallen trees to count and no discernible path to follow. Fortunately, the rain held off. Before long, the gray clouds gave way to blue skies and diffused autumn sunlight. There were a few low-lying areas in the forest we had to circumnavigate in order to avoid slogging our way through impromptu marshlands created by the recent rains. Two hours passed in this fashion before I heard the sound of traffic passing along Route 2.

"We'll be home in no time," said Jack.

Somewhere in the distance, a fire truck horn blared.

"Jack," Tim said, "let's take a break."

A fallen tree by the roadside served as a bench. We sat, resting our weary bones as we listened to more fire truck horns. Seconds later, three hook and ladder trucks raced by, going north along Route 2. I smelled smoke in the air. The rains did nothing to quell the fire that raged somewhere within Franklin Forest. Every few seconds, Jack kept peering over his shoulder as if he suspected someone, perhaps even the culprit who stole Von Braun's boat, had followed us out to the road.

"What happened?" I asked.

"The forest fire?" Jack asked.

"No, in the house."

"I'm in for a stroke of bad luck," he told me. "There was a mirror in the upstairs hallway."

"You broke it?"

"What gave it away?" Tim asked. "The shattering glass sound back there or the fact that he referred to the mirror in the past tense?"

"Who are you? Bobby McMahon all of a sudden? Mr. Grammar Police?"

Tim lowered his head. In a weird way, he was better equipped to suffer his brother's beatings when he and Jack got into a scuffle, but belittlement was another thing. Jack's constant taunting was damaging to Tim. And that was something a person carried with him for years.

"Jack," I said, "you mentioned 'him.' Who was that?"

Jack let out a long, labored sigh. He rubbed his eyes with hands.

"The mirror was a big one," he began. "Oval-shaped and tall as me. It hung on a wall on the second floor. At the top of the stairs, the hall stretched in either direction. As soon as I got up there, I felt a little dizzy. The hallway wasn't exactly straight. More like a long curve.

"Anyway, there were doors in the hallway. I didn't open any of them. At one end of the hall that curved off to the left, I found another set of stairs. They were narrow, but I didn't bother going up there. You know how sometimes you see a dark street and you know you shouldn't walk down it? Well, that's the feeling I got looking up those stairs."

He turned to look back into the woods again. When he was satisfied that no one had followed us, he continued.

"I started back down the hall toward the main stairs. Beneath one of the doors in the hall, I thought I saw a light. As I passed that door, I swore a shadow shifted beneath it," Jack said.

"So, where did the mirror come from?" Tim asked.

"It was in the hall," he said. "The mirror was covered by a blanket. Maybe more like a curtain. I didn't want to, but something made me pull the cloth back. There was this flash in my head like I knew what was under there before I did. It was like I was…what do you call that, Tim?"

"Psychic?"

"Right."

"What color was the curtain?"

"The fuck difference does that make?"

"I'm trying to help you create atmosphere."

"It was brown, all right?" Jack exclaimed. "A nice shit brown. It was heavy and musty. That's the word Granny would have used. Is that okay with you?"

"So you lifted the brown curtain," I said.

"There was a poker on the floor next to it," said Jack. "From a fireplace. The curtain slipped off as soon as I touched it. The mirror was old. My reflection looked cloudy. And that's when I saw him behind me."

"Who?"

"A dead boy." He stood up and wiped wet bark and soil from the seat of his pants. "The boy they say my father drowned."

Tim kept silent as we followed Jack out of the woods. It didn't take long after that to reach Dover Bridge.

By the time we entered Yorkville on America Road, the three of us walked in single file with almost twenty yards between us. The brothers Swanson turned south toward Harper Road once we reached the town square. They went on their way without so much as a goodbye. I kept going, even though using Harper Road would have shortened my trip home.

The sun vanished behind silver-lined gray clouds. The smell of smoke permeated the air, even in the center of Yorkville near the square. By the time I reached Beeker Street, I had the overwhelming feeling that I was in trouble. Sure enough, my mother met me in front of our house. Instead of giving me hell about the way I looked, or for being gone for so long, my mother took hold of me and hugged me close. Maybe it was something in my expression, or maybe she had some secret sight, like a shaman or a yogi, and she knew something of the strangeness the brothers Swanson and I had encountered that day. She led me into the house where I shed my dirty clothes, bathed, dressed in my warmest pajamas, and spent the remainder of the afternoon reading my favorite comic books.

Chapter 19

In my school at Halloween, there was less concentration on ghosts and goblins and more emphasis placed on the day that followed—All Saints' Day, another day in a grand scheme of days to overshadow the otherwise pagan days of celebration that came long before Christ was born. By the time I was eleven years old, I learned that Christian celebrations were no less an elaborate, albeit feeble patchwork meant to obscure powerful days whose time coincided with grand and often extreme changes in nature.

Though the school year brought many solemn changes—the absence of Marcella, Bobby joining up with what the eighth graders were calling the Gay Dapper Club (or GDC for short), and the mystery surrounding old Mr. Von Braun's stolen row boat now missing from our hiding place in the woods—I longed for the arrival of Mischief Night on October 30. The true test of any friendship, I learned, is accepting change while hoping that some of the old remains the same. Aside from a perverted indulgence in comic books, Bobby McMahon's other penchant was satisfied only once a year; on the night before Halloween, he ran amok through the streets of Yorkville like a commando deep behind enemy lines wreaking havoc on other people's property. Even Jack Swanson, himself no stranger to vandalism, offered praise for Bobby's enthusiasm.

"That boy isn't right in the head," Jack had said the previous year on Mischief Night when Bobby absconded old Eleanor Duffy's cat, a dark gray tabby, and shaved stripes into the feline's furry coat with a pair of battery-powered barber shears.

Still, it remained to be seen during the present year if Bobby could part company long enough with Alistair Simon and his crew to inflict the sort of damage I had come to expect from him. True, the night before Halloween in Yorkville was, as it happened to be in so many communities around the country, a town-wide celebration of paranoia and fear. Without Bobby's antics, it would not be the same. Men like my father, who sat on the porch all night keeping a vigil against all manners of mischief, men who had nothing to show but coats, shirts, and pants stained by tossed eggs and homemade paint bombs, would be deprived of their quota of chaos if Bobby McMahon chose to remove himself from the campaign of confusion and devastation that the youth of Yorkville were morally obligated to uphold on the most holy of nights.

That year on Mischief Night, I sat in my living room, silently counting the minutes of wasted time that slipped by, watching a Halloween special on ABC hosted by Paul Lind. As if that creep factor wasn't enough, my mother and I endured a rather dreadful reading of Edgar Allen Poe's *The Raven* by none other than *Star Trek*'s own William Shatner.

Suddenly, my father's face loomed in the window that looked out onto the front porch, his mug all pale but for a five o'clock shadow.

"What is it?" my mother asked after she opened the window.

"Bobby McMahon's out here," my father said. His expression turned sour when he added, "He's carrying a bag."

In my house, there was a ritual I performed in order to be allowed out on a week night. My father remained forever enmeshed in a number of activities, ranging from the Yorkville Coalition (a united front of like-minded citizens and business owners, who happened to be like-skinned, that was bent on maintaining the community's status quo—read: keeping the neighborhood predominantly white) to rolling with the Kingpins, the bowling team to which he belonged. Rarely home, he had little to say in my comings and goings.

My mother, on the other hand, belonged to no clubs or organizations, racist, bowling, or otherwise. She was a firm believer in the pitfalls of the hive mentality, whether it was military service or some other activity where individuals were stripped of their sense of self for the greater good; even if it was something as seemingly innocent as membership in the local Boy Scouts. Our attic still housed a number of anti-war signs riddled with horrid images and colorful language that my mother carried at demonstrations around Philadelphia when I was just three years old, often taking me along in tow, despite my father's protest. And Mischief Night meant, for her, the biggest chance of infectious hive mentality, the kind that could do irreparable damage if left unchecked. Ironically, she sought to keep me imprisoned in her hive, watching bad television, rather than let me bumble with the other bees, pollinating the neighborhood with mischief.

"What does Bobby want?" my mother asked.

"He seeks the company of our renegade son," my moon-faced father replied.

"Mom, may go out?" I asked.

The ritual begins, I thought.

"What night is it?" she asked.

"Thursday."

"Try again."

"The night before Halloween," I told her. "Two nights before All Saints' Day."

"Let my people go," my father sang through the screen.

My mother slid the window shut and dropped the blinds. What followed was the delicate dance of my pleading with my mother to go out and her parrying my pleas with flat-out refusal since it was a school night. For the past four years, it was always the same: both of us knowing that Halloween at school was a joke—a day for costumes, candy, apple-bobbing, and parades. Well, perhaps it would have turned out that way if I'd gone to a public school, but, despite my being a student at St. Bonnie's where all things Halloween were considered pagan and therefore taboo, that was besides the point. I resorted to desperate measures that night, wailing about democracy or the lack of it under our roof. That's when I heard the front door open. *Yes*, I thought. As it happened for the past four years on Mischief Night, my father assumed the rule of the *deus ex machina* in the tragedy unfolding in our living room.

"Young McMahon awaits your company." My father threw a coat at me.

"Fine," my mother glared at me, "but when the police pick you up again, don't call this house."

Her stress on the word "again" did not go unnoticed by me, or, judging by the look on his face, by my father.

"Uh, I don't get a phone call. I think the police call you," I told her, remembering a few run-ins the brothers Swanson had with the Yorkville PD. "I'm a minor."

"Which is why you shouldn't be going out to cause mischief," she countered.

"Dad!"

"Just let the boy go out," he said.

My mother threw up her arms. "Go," she told me. "Go on. Get out."

I put on my coat, gave my mother a kiss on the cheek, and darted out of the house. Bobby McMahon stood cloaked in shadow beneath the oak tree near the street. He wore a black petticoat, the kind the merchant marines wore when I saw them in Philadelphia near my uncle's neighborhood, and a black knit ski mask pulled up on top of his head, for the time being, that gave the appearance of Bobby having two faces: his ordinary cherub face capped by a sinister black head, eyeless with a permanent scream etched there.

"Joey," he wrapped his arms around me and gave me a hug.

Bobby had made himself scarce since the school year began, choosing to spend all his free time with Alistair Simon. Rumors abounded at St. Bonnie's Catholic School that Simon's flaming crony Geoffrey Morgan had been caught giving a handjob to a guy three times his age. There were several versions of the story, but the only constant in each version was the location—behind the big screen at the Haddonwood Drive-In Theater.

"Honestly, Joe," said Bobby when I quizzed him about the rumor. "Do you think that Geoffrey is some sort of sex deviant?"

I didn't know what to say to that. Two months after Marcella was laid to rest, I saw her ghost nearly everywhere. At night, I had dreams that left my underwear all wet and sticky. My mother and father never bothered to tell me about nocturnal emissions. It wasn't long after my first wet dream about my dead girlfriend that I discovered jerking off. A whole new world opened up for me. Given my penchant for pleasing myself, I was the last person in the world to say what constituted being a sexual deviant.

"Almost all the kids at school are talking about it," I said at last.

"Joe, don't believe everything you hear."

"I didn't say it was true."

"What's the difference?"

"How's your mom?" I changed gears now.

"Fine," he answered. Then, "Hey, speaking of rumors, I heard that you and the brothers Swanson ferried across the River Styx to the forbidden forest."

"Who told you that?"

"It doesn't matter."

There was no sense in denying our recent adventure. I told Bobby the whole story, from stealing Von Braun's little rowboat to Jack breaking the mirror, but I left out the part about Jack turning into a blubbering mess. As I told the tale of our recent expedition to the forest house, I didn't want Bobby going back to Alistair Simon and telling him all about how Jack Swanson nearly had a nervous breakdown.

"I never heard about any house out there," Bobby said when I finished. "I do have to accompany you one Saturday. It all sounds positively scary."

Five minutes later, we hunkered down in an alley on the west side of Yorkville Square. Bobby opened the bag he carried, producing two cartons of a dozen eggs each, two rolls of toilet paper colored powder blue, two bars of Dial soap, and a sleek set of binoculars.

"What's with the field glasses?" I asked.

"When we're finished our mission," he said, "we can climb to the top of Yorkville Public School and watch further mayhem unfold."

I didn't believe him. For as long as I had been friends with Bobby, I never knew him to be a risk taker. Simple mischief was one thing—his once-a-year meltdown when he turned into an egg-tossing, windshield-soaping maniac included—illegal activities like climbing onto the roof of a public school in the dark and other dangerous jaunts were another story. Did his association with Alistair Simon and the Queer Club somehow render his judgment and reason impotent? And if so, what sort of adolescent homoerotic sexual escapade awaited me four stories above the streets of Yorkville? Was Bobby's calling on me that night a mere continuation of the custom we had established on Mischief Night, or was it all some psycho-sexual ruse to lure an innocent like me, fresh from the loss of my love, Marcella, into a rooftop round-robin suck-off initiation into the Queer Club? I feared for the worst. Paranoia seized me there beneath a fire escape ensconced in shadow like—

"Joe, are you listening to me?"

Shit, I thought. *There goes my train of fear.*

Bobby's lips moved, but I heard no sound. Over my friend's shoulder, I glimpsed a reflection on the pane of a barred window.

The reflection smiled. It took a moment for me to recognize the image, that it didn't belong to me, but it was the face of Marcella staring back at me. I knew if I blinked, the apparition would vanish; such was the frail nature of ghosts in a concrete world. In the dark, as Bobby's voice came back to me, the face in the window looked less like a reflection and more like one etched in frost.

Bobby was going a mile a minute about some crazy movie and a group of derelicts who went around terrorizing women and clubbing old men to death with phallic statuettes.

"You're talking *A Clockwork Orange*?" I blurted out.

Over Bobby's shoulder, Marcella's face grimaced in the window before it turned into an oval spot of condensation. Guilt overcame me, as if my sudden outburst about Stanley Kubrick's movie somehow broke the invisible chain between Marcella and me, that the words I spoke caused her eldritch presence to vanish.

"Geoffrey's older brother," Bobby was saying, "goes to St. Sebastian High School. Do you know Stanley?"

"Stanley, of course," I said, knowing I'd never met him. "Geoffrey's older brother."

Bobby made a face, the same expression he mugged whenever he dealt with someone of far more inferior intelligence.

"Stanley Morgan," he stressed the last name for my benefit, "heard that the Clockwork Boys are coming to Yorkville to rumble with some boys from the vo-tech school."

The Clockwork Boys were a gang from Pennington. They got their name not from Kubrick's movie or from the novel by Anthony Burgess, but from a turn-of-the-century gang of the same name that ruled the city of Pennington's southwest side. Through the nineteenth and early twentieth century, the Solaris Clock Company was Pennington's pride and joy, according to the old men at Ben Bazarra's barber shop in the Yorkville Square. My dad told me once that there were three things that I could count on in life: death, taxes, and the gospel according to Mel Benson and Clem Burnett—the two old men who met every day at Bazarra's Barber Shop to match wits in a game of checkers as they spun the oral history of southern New Jersey. It was Mel and Clem who claimed that the advent of electricity was the Solaris Clock Company's undoing. Whatever the case, The Great Depression came along, and the residents of southwest Pennington were subjected to the whims and wild antics of the original Clockwork Boys.

The modern version, like their 1930s predecessors, wore denim overalls and steel-toed boots. On Mischief Night, however, the gang donned bleached white long johns and black bowler hats, along with their trademark steel-toed boots, and they drove around all whacked-out on methamphetamines until they came upon some poor girl they might gang-rape or some unsuspecting man they might kick half to death just for fun.

Two years had passed since the last rumble in Yorkville. The County Vocational and Technical Institute was located in Pennington. The Clockwork Boys recruited from schools like the vo-tech high school, but most of the gang members were dropouts. Every now and then, some teen from Yorkville ran afoul with a Clockwork Boy who attended the trade school, but in school, there were always more Yorkville teens than Clockwork Boys. There were skirmishes on the school grounds, but Pennington Police kept a lid on large-scale fights so the gang fights ultimately migrated to Yorkville where the police presence wasn't as large or as strong as it was in the city of Pennington.

"Who is it this time?" I asked.

"Mike Gruber and that crowd," he told me.

Next, Bobby reached into his bag of goodies. He pulled out a huge folding knife.

"What are you going to do with that?" The sight of the knife made me feel uneasy.

"I thought in the middle of the brawl, I might cut Gruber's heart out," said Bobby. "Maybe some Clockwork Boy will beat him unconscious and let me do the rest of the work."

"That's not you, Bobby. You're—"

"What?" he flipped open the blade. "Queer?"

"I was going to say a poet."

"Oh." He folded the knife and put it in his pants pocket. "Well, thank you."

"Now," I said, "are we going to sit here in this alley all night?"

"To arms!" Bobby cried. "To arms!"

He cracked open an egg carton and hurled one egg after another at the apartment windows overlooking the alley. Before long, I was lobbing eggs too.

Somewhere overhead a window creaked open.

"Hey, you little bastard!" an old man cried.

Bobby launched the last egg in the carton. It sailed through air, almost as if in slow motion, toward the third floor window. The old man didn't stand a chance.

"I'll come down there and stomp your ass," the old man continued. The egg exploded in a parabola of shell and yolk against the man's face. "Ow, damn it!"

"Let's get out of here," Bobby said as he took hold of my arm and led me away.

We took turns shouting war cries as we made our way out of the alley. Bobby stopped in his tracks and loosed a high-pitched scream that made my blood run cold. No sooner did we step foot into the square, we spotted three old-fashioned Studebakers, all painted flat black, cruising down America Road. Each of the occupants wore bowler hats. Bobby grabbed my arm. Three more Studebakers wound their way around the square. In all, I counted twenty-four Clockwork Boys.

Bobby tossed aside his sack. I heard the eggs crack in the second carton.

"What are you doing?" I asked.

"Let's get to the school," he said. "Tonight's party looks like it's going to start early."

There were throngs of kids in the Yorkville Public School yard. Parked at the center of the basketball court on the far end of the schoolyard were six black Studebakers. Along the edge of the court stood two dozen or so teens from Yorkville. Some were vo-tech boys; others I recognized from St. Sebastian's. Among them stood Gale Carbone, his jaw set as he stared straight ahead at the Clockwork Boys. I hadn't seen him since before Marcella was killed.

"Gale," Bobby's falsetto filled the schoolyard.

The outburst brought a round of laughter from the visiting gang. Gale didn't look our way.

An empty bottle whistled neck-over-bottom as it sailed through the air. A Clockwork Boy swung a black cane at the bottle but missed. The bottle exploded against a Studebaker windshield. All at once, everyone held their breath, and before Bobby or I could move, the Clockwork Boys charged headlong at the ad hoc Yorkville gang.

The brawl lasted less than two minutes. Three of the Clockwork Boys threw Gale to the ground. They kicked him with their heavy boots. I thought Gale was a goner. Then, out of nowhere, Mike Gruber jumped into the fray, booting one of the Clockwork Boys in his groin and smashing his fat elbow into the face of another. Gale got up and rushed into a mixed crowd between the Studebakers and the edge of the basketball court. Gruber followed him, but he didn't make it far. The Clockwork Boy with the cane swung his weapon at Gruber's head. The crack sounded like fly ball hit at a baseball game. Gruber fell face-first onto the paved basketball court. Here and there, Yorkville kids were throwing stones, bottles, sticks, and anything else they could get their hands on at four Clockwork Boys, who had kicked a Yorkville boy into a bloody pulp.

As I stood there watching the spectacle, I saw Bobby run full-tilt into the fray toward the four Clockwork Boys. At the basketball court's edge, the steel of Bobby's folding knife glinted beneath the schoolyard lights. His intended target was the Clockwork Boy with the cane who busied himself by taking cheap shots at Yorkville boys who were gaining the upper hand.

The Clockwork Boy with the cane spun just as Bobby was about to attack. He jabbed Bobby in the gut once before whipping Bobby's knife hand. After that, the cane-wielding Clockwork Boy kicked Bobby between the legs. By the time I reached him, Bobby lay on the ground. The Clockwork Boy raised his cane, like a batter looking to knock one out of the park. Suddenly, Gale Carbone, with one eye swollen shut, appeared behind the Clockwork Boy and grabbed the cane with both hands.

A bright flash caught my eye to the right. I turned and saw that one of the Studebakers had been set on fire. Beyond the flames, I spotted the culprit, a flaxen-haired vo-tech girl named Cindy McMasters. A six-pack of Molotov cocktails lay at her feet. Cindy and another girl took turns lighting the homemade bombs and tossing them at the Studebakers.

"I'll take that," Gale said to Bobby.

He grabbed the knife and straddled the now-fallen Clockwork Boy. All around us, Clockwork Boys lay on the ground beaten and bleeding. Some of them were unconscious; others I couldn't tell if they were dead or alive.

"I give. I give," the Clockwork Boy beneath Gale pleaded.

I pulled Bobby away. The heat from the car fires was too much. Looking back, I saw Gale's silhouette over the fallen Clockwork Boy, who screamed over the roar of the flames until his scream became a gurgling flooded mess while his legs kicked wildly beneath Gale's weight until they came to a rest.

"Wait!" Bobby shouted.

Sirens wailed in the distance and drew closer block by block. It would take the police nearly no time at all to get to the schoolyard.

"Come on. Let's go," I pleaded with him.

Bobby took a few steps toward the fallen Clockwork Boy. Gale had already fled into the darkness beyond the car fires. Bobby stood over Gale's victim, doubled over, and puked on the ground after he got a good look.

We left the schoolyard just as the first police car arrived. Halfway down America Road, a fire truck passed us. Bobby stopped and slumped against a chain-link fence. A long howl came up from his throat as he faced the fence and punched it until his knuckles were bloody and raw.

The next day was Halloween. No one went out trick or treating. The smell of burned rubber and oil permeated the air that morning, even though the fires were put out before midnight.

Four days later, I heard that Gale Carbone was picked up for the murder of the cane-wielding Clockwork Boy. News spread like wildfire that Gale pleaded guilty, waived his right to a trial, and was shipped to the same detention center where Tim McClusky was sentenced for the murder of Marcella Carbone. In those days, whether it was an oversight of the judicial system or just plain stupidity, no good was ever to come from such an arrangement, but, in our county, there was only one juvenile detention center, and that's where all the minors ended up who had committed serious crimes.

News came weeks later that Tim McClusky was found beaten to death in a shower stall at the detention center. No one ever said that Gale killed him, but everyone who knew Marcella and her brother understood it to be that way; even Bobby, upon hearing the news, smiled with satisfaction, as if for the first time in our pathetic lives, something resembling justice, no matter how barbaric it appeared on the surface, had finally been dealt to a boy most of us considered sub-human.

McClusky's death happened right after Thanksgiving. There were no significant events until Christmas Eve, when the brothers Swanson showed up on my front porch bearing news. While certainly not as devoid of hope nor nearly as brutal as the autumn proved to be thus far, it turned out to be the strangest all year.

Chapter 20

"Can you come out?" Jack asked.

I studied the agitated expression he wore that told me that he was ready to burst if he didn't share whatever secret he carried from Granny Swanson's to my house. Tim, on the other hand, was a study in non-chalance, happy to occupy his time in my front yard, catching snowflakes with his open mouth. Every couple of seconds, he alternated his curse words by trading up "shit" for "fuck" as more snowflakes missed his mouth and fell into his eyes.

"My uncle's on his way here," I told Jack.

"Uncle Scott?" Tim asked.

"How many uncles do I have?"

"You don't got to be sore about it," said Tim. "For fuck's sake, it's Christmas."

"I have to show you something," Jack announced.

"Joe." My father's voice shook the hallway behind me. "Do you plan on heating the whole neighborhood?"

"Merry Christmas," Tim called out from the front yard.

My father ignored him.

"In or out, son," he told me. "Which will it be?"

I slipped on a pair of boots I kept parked in the vestibule, put on my coat, and pocketed my gloves and hat.

"Out," I told my father.

Gunmetal gray clouds hung low in the sky, breathing snow down all over Yorkville. Christmas had always been a family thing. My uncle Scott came from Philadelphia to Yorkville, one of the few times that he abandoned his bachelor pad and spent more than a few hours with us. One night I heard my uncle say that the city, even though people practically lived on top of one another, was a lonely place during the holidays. Uncle Scott cited as an example the New Year's Day Parade that took place every year in Philadelphia. My uncle said that thousands of people lived near the parade route, and other than exchanging a booze-addled, "Happy New Year," they hardly spoke to one another for the remainder of the year. There were exceptions, of course.

"Like when some cocky bastard grew beer balls the size of grapefruits," my uncle once told me, "and took a fancy to some woman he shouldn't have."

One might argue that Uncle Scott was a lonely man, despite the parade of women that traipsed in and out of his life. Still, he was my mother's brother, and knowing a little bit about my family's history, it seemed that my uncle Scott was less lonely and more inclined to be alone.

City life did not have a corner on the loneliness market. Christmas could be a bad time for anyone, given their circumstance. No one knew that more than the brothers Swanson. Ever since their father was sent to jail, Jack and Tim saw the winter holiday not so much as a time for celebration, but as a time for longing. It was hard for me to sit in my house, knowing that Jack and Tim were at Granny Swanson's only a few blocks away, while I was surrounded by family and gifts. My parents weren't rich, nor, for that matter, were any of the other families in Yorkville. Parents in our little working-class town did what they could. And I would not be telling the truth if I offered here that I found every Christmas of my childhood satisfying, that every holiday wish for a certain toy or game was granted. Every Christmas, I pictured Jack and Tim at Granny Swanson's home with no more than a gift or two each. Jack's grandmother didn't bother to put up a tree. Christmas trees were too expensive, and the artificial ones they sold in town were doubly so. Instead, the boys' grandmother bought practical Christmas gifts for them like new socks, winter coats (but not every year), snow boots, or hats and gloves.

The first year Jack and Tim's dad went away, my mother brought gifts and food to Granny Swanson's house. When Bobby McMahon's father caught wind of my mother's good will, he tried a little good cheer, but whatever bad blood existed between Mrs. McMahon and the Swansons made for a very bad time. Since then, everyone left the Swansons alone at Christmas. It was the one day out of the year that the entire neighborhood acted as if the Swanson family never existed. And while I was friends with Jack and his brother, I was left with no choice but to follow my parents' lead. Still, I never forgot to think about Jack and Tim, to picture them while they opened their gifts that Granny Swanson left on the dining room table. If Jack and Tim were lucky, Granny Swanson purchased them a simple board game, but that money, I found out later on, usually came from Mr. Von Braun. Whatever the case, the boys always ended up losing game pieces, so, even in Von Braun's absence, Jack and Tim managed to exact some sort of vandalism on property purchased by the old German.

The dismal air that plagued every Christmas for the Swanson brothers seemed to dissipate as we drew near to their home now. With each step closer to Granny Swanson's house, Jack and Tim became more elated. They led me around the house to the backyard.

"Radio says the snow's going to get worse," Jack said.

"My dad hopes it's not that bad," I told him.

"What does he care? He doesn't drive."

"Yeah, but it's my uncle Scott," I said. "If it snows real bad, then he might stay over until the buses are running again."

"And that would be bad?"

"Exactly."

"You don't like your uncle?"

"No, he's cool. My dad's another story."

"You don't like your dad?" Jack stopped as we reached the trail that led to the dock.

"Don't be a boob," I said. I was going to tell him that I loved my dad, but with it being Christmas and all, I didn't see the point in insulting my friend by driving the point home.

"Family," said Jack.

The trail that led down to the Swanson dock was barren save for the deep snow already marred by Jack and Tim's footprints. From the trail, I spotted the cold, dark waters of Hobbs Creek. The brothers Swanson led me to the dock without muttering a word. I kept glancing at the creek, wondering if Sean Pullman was still down there. Shivering against the cold, wet snow, I saw, after we reached the dock, what prompted Jack and his brother to come get me.

A small boat drifted in place, moored to the dock by a length of rope fashioned from thin vines. The exterior of the boat was painted dark brown.

"It's Von Braun's," said Jack.

"How can you be sure?" I asked.

"I knew he wouldn't believe it," Tim announced. He moved to the edge of the dock, leaving me alone with Jack.

"Look," Jack whispered, "I know it's crazy. But this boat here in the water is the boat from behind Von Braun's shed. See where it's patched?"

Inside the boat, dark pitch like tar covered the very spot where the little boat took in water on our last trip across the creek.

"I thought it sank," I said.

"It almost did, remember?" Jack held a hand out, palm up, catching snowflakes as they fell. "Well, it would have if we used it to get back. Anyway, we never got to find out. Someone stole it, didn't they?"

"So—"

"That's not all."

"Someone stole a stolen boat out of the woods," I said, "a boat that by your admission wouldn't make the return trip, repaired it, and now they left it here tied to your dock? I don't believe it."

Jack reached into his coat pocket and pulled out a compass, the same one his father had given him, the same one he lost on our first expedition into the forest.

"This was inside the boat," Jack told me. "Someone was out there with us. Someone from that house."

I would have been scared if I didn't feel relieved. A fierce wind blew from the north right over the creek; several snow devils materialized on the dark water's surface, dancing and whirling about before they vanished. I looked across the creek. The landing site we used was barely visible. I felt foolish, expecting to see the feral boy of the woods waving like some fairy in a feel-good movie where mythical creatures come to the aid of poor boys like me and Jack,. But, as much as I hoped inwardly that he might appear, there was no one there. I wondered if the feral boy was orphaned and now lived in the woods. Were his parents killed there? In Yorkville, there were plenty of wild stories about the scrub forest that hugged the far bank of Hobbs Creek. For as long as anyone could remember, that portion of the state forest was always trouble. Older men at our barber shop told stories of gypsies and all manner of transient people who lived in the woods across the creek. It wasn't beyond the scope of possibilities, at least for boys like us, to consider that a child of these mysterious people may have been left behind. At least Jack and Tim had Granny Swanson, even if there weren't as many presents to go around. Suddenly, the Christmas holiday lost its luster, replaced with a mystery more ancient. Forces unseen taunted us.

"The creek will freeze over by late January," Jack said.

"You'll need a place to store it."

"What about your garage?"

"You don't think my dad will notice?"

"I could park the Titanic in there," Jack said, "and your old man would be none the wiser. Besides, it's the last place Von Braun will look for it."

So it happened that the brothers Swanson and I hauled the boat out of the water and spent that Christmas Eve afternoon carrying it through the streets of Yorkville. We took the long way around my block to avoid my father seeing us. The alley behind my house provided adequate cover. From there, we snuck the rowboat into my parents' garage. After that, we parted ways.

In the weeks that followed, I expected my father to confront me about the boat, but he never did, not even when he finally got around to taking down the Christmas decorations and putting them back into the garage. The brothers Swanson and I stashed the boat against the back wall and covered it with an old tarpaulin. If my father discovered the boat, I doubted he knew the vessel belonged to Mr. Von Braun. We were fortunate that the garage was like a vortex where things were stored and often forgotten about, as if a spell of amnesia seized my father every time he opened the garage door.

My mother was another story. Unlike my father, she never succumbed to glamours of any sort. She remembered everything, and she could smell when things were out of place. That winter, I spent all of my spare time running interference whenever she thought about going out to the garage. When she insisted, I always accompanied her, making sure she didn't go near the back wall.

Throughout most of the winter, everything went according to plan. The restored boat lay hidden from the world. Then, as if party to the powers that steered the Swanson brothers and me toward further mystery, fate threw a smoking hot curveball early that spring.

Chapter 21

"Are you shitting me?"

My father was furious when he heard the news. He was the kind of guy who bitched all the time about someone else's good fortune, believing there was a sordid price to pay when the gods smiled favorably upon someone. No good deed went unpunished; that was my father's philosophy.

What made it worse for my father was that the recipient of the gods' favor was my mother. She came home from Stevenson's Supermarket early one evening all charged up about the lottery ticket in her purse.

"How much did you spend?" my father asked.

"A buck," my mother answered.

"Fool's tax."

"I had a dream."

"Only Puerto Ricans play numbers they dream, baby."

"That's not true."

"You're right. It wasn't fair."

"Thank you."

"Old black women, too. Then they go to church and ask God why they lost."

"Dave," she snapped at my father. "Don't talk like that."

"Eileen, come on," he countered. "You don't really believe in all of this...stuff, do you?"

My mother crossed her arms over her chest. She looked pissed. When it came to prejudice, my mother always took the high road. She fancied herself a liberal, a progressive thinker who saw beyond the limits of skin color and cultures. But for all of her peace and harmony talk, she never once went out of her way to help a family in need. On the bus into Philadelphia, she avoided conversation with blacks, Latinos, and other non-whites riding the New Jersey transit system. It was one thing to be prejudiced like my father, and it was something more sinister to preach equality and peace but practice what amounted to racial elitism.

"5-7-7-2," she was saying. "It was the address of this huge glass building. Big metal numbers."

"And?" my father was already losing interest.

"Five and seven equals twelve." My mother touched her forehead with both hands now. "Seven and two is nine. Twelve and nine add up to twenty-one. Two and one equals three. A very powerful number."

My father picked up the newspaper. He opened it as he sat down at the kitchen table. Whenever my mother turned up the heat at home, my father brandished the daily newspaper like a shield, but it was never enough to defend him. And this latest rant from my mother about how she knew her Pick-4 lottery number was destined to win broke down all my father's defenses. He didn't care for number theory, especially a theory my mother believed in, one that was, in my father's mind, tantamount to astrology, palm reading, dowsing, or any other form of divination that hard science could not prove.

Whatever the case, whether my mother's dream was prophetic in the truest sense or not, the next day, to my father's agitated chagrin, 5772 came out as the winning Pick-4 number. Mother played the number straight and in the box. Her winnings totaled over $6,000.

In the 1970s, a $6,000 windfall, especially in a poor neighborhood like mine, went a long way, even after Uncle Sam took his due. For a week, my parents argued over how the money should be spent. My father thought some new furniture might be in order, but my mother disagreed. My father voted for using the money to renovate our house, specifically, closing in the front porch and installing double-pane windows all the way around.

"You know, a sun room," he told her. "And it would keep out the noise."

My mother laughed in his face. That was Friday. On Monday, my father went to work. I went off to school, but when I came home, I found parked in our driveway an avocado green Chevy Nova with big mag wheels.

As colors go, avocado green was all the rage when I was a boy. In the 1970s, there were avocado-green refrigerators, ovens, washers, dryers, and a whole host of countertop appliances like coffee makers, blenders, mixing bowls, and toasters. Likewise, there were telephones, lamps, shades, blinds, sofas, chairs, and bedroom furniture like dressers, headboards, armoires, nightstands, and wardrobes all colored that horrid shade of green. Looking back, I know I inherited my dislike for avocado green from my father. So, it came as no surprise that my mother chose that shade for the first car she ever owned.

"Do you want to go for a ride?" my mother asked.

The car's interior smelled like cherries and leather. My mother drove out of Yorkville and raced down the interstate that led to the Walt Whitman Bridge. The Nova was loud and fast.

"Dad's going to flip," I said.

My mother pulled the car onto the shoulder and slowed to a stop. She gripped the steering wheel, leaned against it, and cried.

"Mom, don't," I told her.

"I'm okay," she sobbed.

"He'll get over it."

"It's not that, Joe."

"What then?"

Not divorce, I thought.

"I'm going to need the garage," she wailed, punching the horn a few times. "He's going to have to do something with all that shit!"

Five minutes later, we made our way back to Yorkville. For the first time, I saw my mother not as the invincible stalwart who made my father's life uneasy, but as someone vulnerable, someone who sacrificed her own needs for her family. Someone who, after all that time, found herself in a position to do something for herself—maybe for the first time since I had been born—and still she was overcome by grief while pondering my father's disapproval. None of it seemed fair.

Two hours later, my father came home. He entered the kitchen through the back door, the way he always did.

"Some jerk-off parked in our driveway." He plopped onto a kitchen chair. "What's for dinner?"

"It's my car," my mother stood defiant, ready for a fight.

A grin slowly stretched across my father's face. I was afraid he was going to flip out. Instead, when he opened his mouth again, he scared me even more.

"Good for you, baby," he said. "That's what you did with your lottery money?"

"We need a car," she told him.

"What about insurance?"

"I can get a job."

"What about Joe?"

"He's too young to work," she quipped. "And he's too young to drive."

"I meant who's going to watch him if you go to work?"

"I can work anywhere. The supermarket. The post office—"

"And what about—"

"—in the middle of the day."

They argued for more than an hour. I got bored and went upstairs to my room. From my window, I looked west toward Hobbs Creek. The house was still out there, as was the feral boy. Was he the one who mended the boat? I decided it had to be him; the alternative, for now, was unthinkable. Otherwise, it meant the house was inhabited by others. If not the house then maybe someone in the forest who was aware of our exploration. Whatever the case, it meant that we were welcome there since they went through the trouble of fixing the boat and giving it back to the Swanson brothers.

I left the window. My parents' voices quieted after several minutes. Lying down on my bed, I pulled out a Dr. Strange comic book, one that I had read countless times already, and gave it another go. Downstairs, the back door opened and closed. I ran to the bathroom to look out the small window next to the sink. My mother and my father stood behind the new car, arm in arm. I went back to my room and picked up Dr. Strange. It wasn't long before I dozed off.

When I opened my eyes again, my room was aglow with orange light from the setting sun. In the spring, with the bedroom window open, and if I lay in my bed just so, I could see dust motes swirling in the twilight that illuminated my room. I used to imagine that angels visited me; that instead of dust motes in the light, they were celestial spirits, heavenly messengers, sent by God himself, who entertained me with their languid dance. Not only me, but all the children of Yorkville who experienced the same, if only they had eyes to see. That evening, instead of angels with bodies of light and dust, another spirit visited me. And like the dust-light angels, she was barely visible, but still, there in that dusky luminosity, something familiar sat on the edge of my bed, within my reach, even though I knew she lived beyond the world now. Her eyes all hallow as she looked at me.

"Marcella." The whisper I muttered broke the spell.

She vanished along with the orange glow as the sun set, behind the forest on the other side of Hobbs Creek, somewhere far west.

Chapter 22

In school, I tried to forget what I saw in my room. For two weeks following the event, I hung around the schoolyard, or, when school let out, I spent the afternoon in the square where I divided my time between Schmidt's Pharmacy and Dave and Di's Luncheonette. There was the new Marvel Team-up Issue with Spider-Man and Vision. I was never a huge Spider-Man fan, but Vision was another story. He was one of my favorites next to Dr. Strange. While I was inside Dave and Di's, I avoided stealing looks at the nudie mags after one day when I thought I saw Marcella's face on one cover. I don't remember the name of the magazine now, but after seeing her ghost in my room, I began to suspect that she was following me, so I avoided my house like the plague when my mom and my dad were both at work.

One afternoon in the early spring, I walked over to Stevenson's Supermarket where my mother worked a checkout register. Whenever I went to see her, she was always chatting up the old ladies and going on about her lottery dreams. The old ladies in town all bought into my mother's psychic ability. We didn't tell my father about my mom's side job, that of the town seer who provided unsuspecting lottery players with potential winning numbers. Every day, men and women stopped in to see her at the supermarket to tell her that a number she provided had hit straight or box, or on rare occasion, both. Some of the winners parted with as much as 20 percent of their winnings; others usually handed my mother a ten dollar bill and told her thanks. Depending on the week, my mother stood to make anywhere from $25 to $50 extra. And in 1977, that was not bad money for dreaming up numbers and sharing them with others.

"Joe, my baby," my mother cried out, "come here and give your mom a hug."

"Don't call me that," I said, embarrassed as I looked around to make sure no one had heard her.

"What do you need?"

"Can I have a dollar?"

"Do you have homework?"

"Do you think those penguins would give me a break?"

"Joe," my mother gave me a stern look. "No need to be disrespectful."

"Sorry."

"Why aren't you home?"

"I don't feel like it."

"Oh, I know the feeling," she said. "Spring was always my favorite season, too. The days are longer. The air is warm. I never wanted to go home when the springtime came. So, what are you doing with the dollar?"

"Buying some new comic books," I told her.

"Here," she handed me two dollars, "but if you're father catches you with all these new comic books, I don't know you."

"Thanks."

The next day, with four new unread comic books tucked safely away in my room, I entered the school cafeteria, still plagued by the vision of Marcella's ghost. If ever there was someone who could help me with all things supernatural, it was Tim Swanson. I chewed over approaching him for the next two weeks.

"Why Tim?" Bobby asked when we sat together to have lunch.

I was lucky enough to pull him away from the fairy brigade long enough to spill my guts about Marcella's ghostly visit that was nearly three weeks old.

"He knows about that kind of stuff," I told him.

"From monster movies and comic books. They are questionable sources at best, Joe."

"Tim says there's a kernel of truth—"

"No." He patted me on the thigh beneath the table. "Tim's got his head in the clouds. What you need is some good old-fashioned research."

So it happened that Bobby led me that Friday afternoon to the Yorkville Public Library. Before leaving the school grounds of St. Bonaventure's, however, he met with Alistair Simon and the rest of his queer club entourage.

"I'm intrigued," was all Alistair said after Bobby informed him of our pending research project. "Are we talking ghosts?"

Geoffrey Morgan and Jonathan Overy both snickered like school girls. That spring, all three of them sported hairdos like David Bowie's alter ego Ziggy Stardust. Kids in Yorkville were always late with fashion, and Alistair, Geoffrey, and Jonathan looked creepy. I read in a rock magazine at Schmidt's Pharmacy that Ziggy Stardust was supposed to be some sort of Martian. There were days when I wondered if the two of them, Alistair and Jonathan, were from a different planet. Their nearly translucent skin, their purplish thin lips, and their delicate mouths, along with their eyes. Each one had eyes that were two different colors: Alistair had one blue and one green eye; Jonathan's were green and brown, combined to give them a rather haunting look.

"It's..." my voice went all weak. At least Bobby didn't tell them I saw Marcella in my room. "My uncle's house in Philadelphia might be haunted."

Alistair and his friends tapped their lips with thin fingers, nodding all around as if they were well-versed in all matters paranormal.

"You mean the fireman?" Geoffrey suddenly spoke up. "Him I have to meet one day."

"A real hero," Jonathan added.

"Okay, you little hens," said Bobby, "run along now. Joe and I have work to do."

The fastest route to the public library was straight into the square, but Bobby insisted that we avoid that section of town. As the months went by, it had less to do with the memory of the abuse he suffered when Tim McClusky got a hold of him as it did with Alistair Simon insisting that the square was no longer "fashionable." Ever since news of McClusky's demise reached Yorkville, it seemed a collective sigh of relief escaped the mouths of young queers, bookworms, and introverts all over town. No one had seen any of McClusky's goons, not since the gang fight with the Clockwork Boys. It was just as well for Bobby and his new friends.

A few blocks away from the library, I heard the soft shuffle of someone running behind Bobby and me. Geoffrey Morgan, all red in the cheeks, double-timed it as he led his two mates toward us.

"Robert," Geoffrey panted. "Joseph, wait for us."

"Honestly," Alistair was saying, "do I need this aggravation? You know how my suit pants chafe my legs."

In the decades that followed, Alistair Simon would shed his suits for blue jeans and work boots and go to work for PSE&G as a line man. He would call himself Al, and, when he was able, he would seduce younger, confused coworkers. Alistair would find working outside quite suitable, keeping him tan and fit. For now, however, he was still a scrawny, pale kid who loathed physical exertion.

"Good Lord," Jonathan Overy mumbled, "my back feels like it's bleeding."

"You're not bleeding," Geoffrey told him. "You're sweating."

"I'm perspiring," he concluded. "And it's not even gym class."

"I forgot to tell you, Joseph," said Geoffrey, ignoring his friend's panic attack. "I'm having a birthday party next Saturday. Do stop by. And bring Jack if you want."

"I'll mention it to him," I said. "Thanks."

Bobby's elation at the prospect of me being inducted into their close-knit society was too much for me. He droned on all the way to the library about how lucky he was to make friends with Alistair and his two cohorts. He was still talking when we entered the library, so much so that his rant took old Mrs. Perjowski by surprise. The librarian was an old, skeletal crone whose sallow, withered face looked as if it might crack if she smiled.

"Mister McMahon," Mrs. Perjowski accentuated each syllable, "please keep your voice down."

The beauty of having a smart, adolescent, gay friend was never turning to anyone for help with detail-oriented research. Bobby, like others of his ilk, seemed hardwired for the fastidious attention to detail I needed. From the moment he sat me down at a rickety old table on the library's second floor, Bobby's whole demeanor changed. Gone was the flippant arrogance he flaunted when he was in the presence of Alistair Simon's band of fairies. Replacing that arrogance was the purpose-driven state of mind I knew before he started keeping company with the three dandies, consumed now, not so much with the desire to learn as much he was with the desire to teach. Seeing the old glint in Bobby's eye led me to believe that his fascination with Alistair and the other fairyfolk would be a passing thing. The reality, I knew, even at my age, was that Bobby's leanings toward homosexuality was a permanent part of him, that his desire for members of the same sex would wane no less than the freckles on his alabaster cheeks.

"We'll start with these." He gently placed a short stack of hardback books down on the table.

The first book, thick as a bread loaf, was authored by a man named S.E. McClintock. The tome was published by New Moon Press in 1939. For the most part, McClintock's book dealt with hauntings in and around old sites in England and Scotland. Brief outlines were included beneath each chapter heading in the table of contents. I was about to lose interest when beneath the heading for Chapter 37 I saw the following:

Bird spirits: Eso-Ornothological Practices Through History

I turned to page 485 and discovered a daguerreotype that looked so familiar, I nearly dropped the book. Housed in Mason jars on shelves were a variety of dead birds. Reading on, I found out that many cultures, going all the way back in antiquity, saw birds as either the souls of man or as the carriers that conveyed a man's soul to the next world. In ancient Turkey and Persia, for example, it was widely believed that vultures preying on the dead did so in order to take the soul to the next place. Burying the dead, especially in arid climates, according to McClintock, was unheard of, for in order to reach the proverbial final resting place, the recently deceased were left in the open air climate, away from villages or other dwellings, as carrion so that the body could be picked clean, thus eliminating the flesh and blood cage. Afterward, the revered vultures would transport the soul to the world beyond. The author also made brief mention, almost an afterthought, of the practice involving shamans in antiquity who captured birds believed to be the souls of their dead enemies and stowing them away in sealed urns; a practice, McClintock maintained, that crossed over into dark or black magic.

"Bobby, look at this!"

"Wait."

His nose was buried in a book about New Jersey haunted houses. I stood up and hovered over him, keeping my place in the McClintock book, and glimpsed the pictures he perused. Most of the images were of old farm houses. Haunted house books were always like that. Some stand-alone house in a remote area infested with spirits and all manner of otherworldly ghoulies and demons; never once did I come across a book about haunted row homes in a poor neighborhood like mine. Maybe it had something to do with ghosts that acted like mice and bugs, an eldritch infestation, moving from one house to the next. From what I gathered, ghosts and other disembodied spirits weren't as industrious as insects and vermin. Even ghosts, it seemed, didn't want to be caught dead in a place like Yorkville.

"Bobby," I said, thrusting the McClintock book into his face, "check this out. When me and—"

"This is interesting," he swatted the book away and showed me his. "In a town called Raritan, there was an old mill haunted by an entity that two local children saw again and again. One of the children, a boy, never wavered in his story. The other witness, a girl, claimed she could no longer see the ghost after she turned thirteen."

"So, what? I wait a year or two, and it will all go away?"

"Let me finish," he said. "The girl fell victim to a vicious assault. Though it doesn't say so in this book, one can only imagine that she was raped. There were many documented cases of the paranormal variety in which a witness suffers a calamity and no longer sees or hears or otherwise experiences the ineluctable touch of the unknown."

I closed the McClintock book. "So, ghosts come to warn us?"

"You are not listening," said Bobby. "The girl is inconsequential here. I was going to say that the boy, the other witness, got in touch with a local priest after the entity allegedly told him that he had never been baptized."

"But priests don't even believe in ghosts."

"Precisely. The boy took it upon himself to steal holy water from the local church and sanctify the old mill on his own. After he did, the ghost was banished for good."

Banished, I thought. That didn't sound good. I wasn't sure I wanted to sever ties with Marcella that way. There were no guarantees that I'd ever see my love again if I went around my parents' house sprinkling holy water in every room. Plus, it would have been my luck that I get pinched stealing holy water, and who knew what kind of punishment a crime against the church might carry. Every week, the good sisters at St. Bonnie's told us that bad behavior in the classroom would be rewarded in Hell. How much of a chance did I stand if I stole from my local church? No, I decided then—given the chance I may never see Marcella again, not on Earth and perhaps not in Heaven or whatever else lay beyond the pale—that I would rather be haunted by my love's shade—regardless of how insubstantial her ghost may be, regardless of how much I longed to smell her, to touch her, to gaze upon her fragile beauty, perhaps in the autumn morning light at the schoolyard—rather than be left only with the memories of Marcella that may fade as they succumb to time's passing.

Bobby was still going on about New Jersey farmhouse hauntings when I realized that we were no longer alone. Over my friend's left shoulder, deep in the stacks, Marcella's face bore the luminescent quality of the moon. Only her upper body was visible. She wore the dark dress my parents described from when they went to Marcella's viewing. The apparition lasted a few scant seconds before it vanished.

"I need to get home," I said.

Bobby closed the book. I held the hefty McClintock tome in my arms.

"You're checking that out?" Bobby asked.

"I can read, you know."

"I think holy water's the cure," he said, adding, "but only for isolated incidents in one location. We can't go around the countryside sprinkling stolen holy water, now can we?"

"No one is stealing holy water."

"I'm just trying to help."

"Well, don't."

"Are you seeing this ghost of yours anywhere else?"

"No," I told him.

Until that day, I never kept anything from Bobby. The lie, I must admit, felt good.

"Because if that were the case," he went on, "then it wouldn't be a haunting so much as you being delusional."

Chapter 23

Crazy or not, I found out I had more pressing issues than Marcella's ghost when I got home. First, I found a note from my mother telling me she had to work that afternoon. She landed another job at Schmidt's Pharmacy. The pay, I knew, wasn't great, but it was enough to pay insurance on the car and leave her a little left over for spending money. What started as a part-time gig at eight hours a week was quickly turning into a full-time job. My mother's insistence on picking up extra hours sent my father into a tailspin.

"So your family suffers," he told her, "because you are too damned dependable?"

"If Mr. Schmidt needs my help—"

"Eileen, that's all I've heard for the past month," my father said. "Mr. Schmidt this, Mr. Schmidt that."

"You're jealous of an old man?"

"Don't be ridiculous."

My father could say whatever he wanted, but it was evident that the situation worked his last nerve. The jealousy lie not in Schmidt's taking up so much of my mother's time, nor even some deranged sexual tryst between my mother and the old man (Schmidt was old enough to be her father); no, the source of contention for my father lie in Schmidt's ability to strike out on his own, to start a business and be successful, something that a career Bolshevik proletariat like my father was diametrically opposed to all his life.

I scrapped my mother's note. No sooner than I did, the phone rang.

"Joe?" my father asked when I answered.

My father challenged the authenticity of everyone's identity he spoke to on the phone, as if the phone company manipulated the telephone lines just to frustrate him. His greetings always came in the form of a question. Never once did he call my name out declaratively, never once. With both feet planted firmly on the ground as he spoke on the telephone, he did he acknowledge me as his own. Perhaps it had to do with some secret delusion the old man harbored, envisioning, no doubt, that whenever he dialed our number, he didn't reach our house but a different one in some alternate universe where I wasn't really me and no one had ever heard of him.

"—out of the garage," he was saying. "If it's not too late."

"Wait," I told him. "Say that again."

An audible sigh crackled like static electricity. My father had never been a big fan of the telephone. In the years that followed, he would become one of those technophobes who looked upon the home computer as a passing fad like sea monkeys, pet rocks, mopeds, or lava lamps.

"Joe, pay attention," he snapped. "You know I don't like to repeat myself."

"Sorry."

"And don't apologize."

"Okay," I said. "I'm not sorry."

"Now you're just being uncouth."

"Yes, sir."

"And don't patronize me."

"You got it, buddy."

"Watch it," he warned. Then, "If you have anything stashed in the garage that doesn't belong there, try to remove it this afternoon before dark."

Did he know about the boat? Or did he think I was some adolescent go-between for drug dealers in our neighborhood? Whatever the case, I called Jack Swanson after I talked to my father. Telephoning the Swanson residence was always an ordeal because, inevitably, it was Granny Swanson who answered the phone. And when she spoke, her tone made her sound like a switchboard operator for the hearing impaired. Granny Swanson never quite grasped technology.

She spoke on the phone as if it were a rickety, old field radio, and she was calling in a fire mission at Normandy Beach.

"Did you say Joe?" Granny Swanson screamed in my ear. "There's no Joe here."

"No, Jack."

"Why, of course. Jack's here!" Suddenly, there was a muffled struggle replete with scratching noises over the phone that ended with Granny Swanson screaming, "Stop it! You are hurting me!"

When Jack got on the phone, I explained the desperation in my father's voice when he requested we remove the boat.

"Did he say 'boat'?" Jack asked.

"Yes," I lied. If I hadn't, I feared that generalities and innuendo would have only slowed us down.

Fifteen minutes later, someone pounded on the front door. I peeked out the living room window that overlooked the front porch.

"Okay, Clancy," came the worst Irish accent I'd ever heard, "take the boys and surround the house."

Jack stood on the front porch. He raised his fist to pound on the door a second time. Tim stood on the sidewalk with a large red wheel barrow that looked as if it was held together with dirt, rust, and spit.

"Okay, boy-oh," Jack pounded on the door. "The jig is up. Come on out with your hands in the air!"

Tim looked up and down the street. Then, confident that no one was watching him, he picked his nose. Where most kids my age used their index finger or pinky finger to do the deed, Tim was by far the most dexterous nose-picker, a consummate boogie miner of the highest order who used all ten fingers in quick succession. And for the likes of Tim Swanson, nose-picker extraordinaire, there was no brushing snot from his fingers on his pants, his shirt or some nearby object. Wiping, as Tim saw it, was strictly for amateurs. A regular ecosystem unto himself where nothing went to waste, Tim licked his fingers clean every time the way a normal kid might after eating fried chicken.

"When do we get to ride in your mom's new car?" Tim asked when I met him and his brother in the yard.

"I don't know," I told him, picturing my mother freaking out over Tim's nose-picking virtuosity.

"It looks fast."

My mother's car sat in the driveway. She didn't take it anywhere if she could walk. As spring lurched toward summer, my mother kept after my father about using the garage. At first, my father resisted, citing a lack of storage for all the crap he collected over the years. My mother's constant harassment, however, soon broke down his defenses.

"What's wrong with the basement?" she asked one night while my father grilled hamburgers in the backyard. "Or the tunnel?"

My father spun around on his heels like some checkpoint Charlie, brandishing the spatula as if it were a lethal weapon.

"What tunnel?" I asked.

At last, I thought, *some closure to the mystery surrounding the submarine door behind our furnace.*

"There's no tunnel," said my father. "I'll use the basement."

Once the old man started cleaning out the garage, transporting his second-hand treasures to the basement, I knew it was only a matter of time before he discovered the boat. As far as I knew, he never found it. My father was very methodical in his laziness. He relocated only those items that prohibited my mother from parking her car inside the garage. Along the back wall, there was enough clutter left over to successfully camouflage the boat, but, given my father's frantic phone call, I did not doubt that my mother would push him until she received total victory, winning the garage for herself. My father and I both knew that she would never quit, not until every last piece of junk belonging to him was moved out.

"How should we do this?" I asked Jack.

He looked at me like I was retarded. When he spoke next, he did so slowly and deliberately, as if English was my second or third language.

"We go into the garage and pull out the boat," he said.

"How do we carry it?"

"Joe, did you get hit on the head today?"

"That's what the wheelbarrow is for," Tim piped up now. He examined his fingers for any last vestiges of mucus-laden tiny treasures.

"I don't think—" I started to say.

"You stand the boat up nose-first in the wheelbarrow," Jack explained. "Tim will push. You and me we hold either side of the boat. Easy-peasy."

The transport wasn't so easy-peasy after all. Halfway down the block, we discovered that the laws of physics weren't on our side. Tim couldn't steer the wheelbarrow worth a damn, and Jack and I struggled against the awkward weight of the boat. Between Tim's jerky attempts at steering and the overall deteriorating condition of the street, the whole thing turned into a royal mess. We dropped the boat, twice. Jack and Tim nearly got into a fist fight over it the second time it happened. In the end, we abandoned the wheelbarrow (a disposable "loaner" the Swanson brothers had "appropriated" on their way to my house) and carried the boat like a rowing crew team carrying their racing shell. We stopped and switched positions twelve times, one of us on the nose, the other two on the left and right rear sides, holding the boat upside down over our heads.

As if the journey wasn't bad enough, the moment we reached Granny Swanson's house, we ran into Mr. Von Braun, who busied himself with yard work. I could see the expression on Tim's face. Somewhere between flight and fight, he looked like he was ready to shit a brick. We put the boat down on Granny Swanson's lawn.

"Hey," Mr. Von Braun said, "nice boat."

Jack pretended not to hear him. He indicated that we keep moving, but Tim already had shoved his hands in his pockets.

"Good afternoon, Mr. Von Braun," I called out. "Planting some rosebushes?"

"Azalea," he responded. Then, "You boys going out on the creek?"

"No," Jack told him. "Just getting ready for the summer when it's warmer."

"What about life jackets?"

"Is it going to be a wet summer?" Tim asked, distracting the old man.

"No, son," Von Braun replied. "A dry one at that."

"You don't say."

"I do," he said. Then he looked at me. "Joe, how's your mother's new car?"

"Just fine," I told him.

Von Braun turned his back on us. "I had a boat just like that," he said when he walked away.

"We have to tell him," I said to Jack when the old man was gone.

"Go ahead, Joe," he said. "You march up right into Nazi headquarters and tell Hitler's right hand man that we stole a boat from his backyard. Go on, go rat on your friends."

The matter was closed for discussion. The last leg of our journey to the dock behind Granny Swanson's house was made in silence. Once we made it to the dock, Jack sent Tim back to the house to retrieve a padlock and chain.

"We wouldn't want anyone stealing your stolen boat," I said.

"Is that what happens when you start hanging around the queer brigade?" Jack asked. "You get all righteous on me?"

"What are you talking about?"

"Never mind."

I looked past Jack to the other side of the creek. Standing on the far bank, flanked on either side by tall fir trees, the feral boy raised a large stick in the air. He pointed at me before gesturing to the wide expanse of woodland behind him.

"Jack," I whispered, "look across the creek."

The feral boy pointed his stick in our direction once more and motioned to the forest again.

"Did you see that?" Jack asked.

"What?" Tim stood behind us now, giving me a scare. "The forest boy?"

"You've seen him before?" I asked.

"I see him all the time."

"Why didn't you say anything?"

"Because," said Tim, "you guys wouldn't believe me if I did."

"We shouldn't tell anyone else about this," I said.

"You're right," said Jack. "I think we should go over there this weekend. Tell your parents—"

"Yeah, I know the drill," I said. "Listen, I should get back home. If I'm not doing my homework when my mother comes home, there will be hell to pay."

I left the brothers Swanson on the dock. When I reached Tanner Street, Mr. Von Braun was nowhere in sight. I made it home before my mother did. It wasn't always a bad thing being home by myself after school. Five minutes after I entered my house, I felt a chill air all around me. It turned out that I wasn't alone.

Chapter 24

It wasn't the emptiness that I felt, nor was it the cold that descended upon me like fog from a mountain. These attributes I experienced whenever Marcella came calling. What got me was the hopelessness that overcame me when I considered her soap-scented flesh, her sweaty palm in mine, and how I could never again know those attributes.

Sunlight slipped through the blinds in the living room window. The coldness washed over me, and she appeared in the shimmering sunlight. Only her torso and part of her face were visible that afternoon. During the weeks since she first appeared to me, it was always that way. Sometimes I could only see her face; other days it was obscured, and just part of her body showed itself; a leg here, an arm there; never once a full-body apparition. Even in death, Marcella knew the gain of leaving a little to the imagination. I knew nothing about the rules of the afterlife. Often, she looked like she was ready to speak, but she never did. At times, it was difficult to tell if she saw me. Marcella acted as if she was somewhere else; whatever reality she was in now had camouflaged the one where I still existed. That afternoon, however, things were different. Whatever questions I had, whatever doubts I harbored concerning these visitations, there were all answered.

"Joey," her voice sounded like static on a ham radio. "I miss you."

Her words brought tears to my eyes. My first instinct was to grab her and hold her close. But when I took a step forward, she shimmered and nearly vanished.

"Do you..." a big lump welled in my throat. My voice quit on me. "It's not the way you think."

"I was going to ask if you remember dying?"

"Sorry, I thought you were going to ask if I miss living," said Marcella's ghost.

"Do you?"

"Yes...and no."

"You don't remember anything?"

"No," her voice echoed now. "We are not permitted."

"By who? God?"

"Joey, don't be silly. All of us, even where I am, are so far from God right now. It's like He's..."

"What?" I pleaded after a moment of silence. "Not there?"

"Not like that."

"Is he dead like that crazy philosopher said? The guy Bobby is always going about?"

"No, no. But I'm not permitted to talk about it."

"What's it like where you are? Are you in Heaven?"

"That comes later."

"Your brother," I started to say but decided it would be better if she didn't know.

"What about Gale?"

"Nothing. He misses you."

"That's not what you were going to say."

"Gale killed Sean McClusky," I blurted out.

I didn't mean to, but I was afraid that if I kept that information from her, she might vanish and never visit me again.

Marcella shifted in the light of dusk now. *Did she know where she was buried*, I wondered.

"My brother—," she started to say.

"Where do you think Sean is? With you? Oh God, I'm sorry," I told her. "I hope not."

"Not everyone ends up in the same place."

"Maybe he's in Hell."

"Oh, Joey," she whispered, "you don't know anything."

I heard the front door open, but I was still enthralled by my visitor's presence. The noise sounded like it came from far away, as if someone down the street entered their house. My fear was the sound that would scare her away.

"There is no Hell?" I asked.

"On this side, there's much more to learn," Marcella told me. "If Hell exists, I haven't seen it."

"What about angels?"

"A few."

"With wings and flowing robes? Or do they look like flying babies?"

"Oh, brother."

"What?"

"I call them angels," she said. "They may be devils for all I know. You have to be on this side to understand."

"I want to go with you," I pleaded. "I...I can kill myself and—"

"No, Joey. It doesn't work like that. You will be somewhere even further from me now."

Marcella's visage blinked off when the sunlight faded from between the blinds.

"Joe," my father stepped into the living room. "Are you talking to someone?"

"Uh, no," I answered. "Why?"

"I thought...no, never mind."

"What, Dad?"

"Nothing," he waved his hand. "I thought I heard a girl's voice, that's all."

Sure, Dad, I thought. *She's a ghost.*

It occurred to me that perhaps he did, indeed, hear Marcella's voice. Explaining the situation would have been difficult. Worse, how could I convince him that the disembodied voice he thought he heard belonged to my dead friend? Somehow, telling him "it's okay. I heard it too" just didn't cut it.

"No girls, Dad," I told him.

He turned to exit the room. "That's strange," he said. "I swear I heard a girl's voice."

"Hey, Dad," I switched gears on him now, "can I camp out at Jack's this weekend?"

"That depends."

"On what?"

"On how much homework your teacher assigns."

I had two options: cram all the homework in on Saturday morning or just flat out lie to him. That would have been easy, but my father had met Sister Mary on numerous occasions, and he knew enough about her to figure out that she would never let a weekend go by where she didn't hand out assignments to her students. Of course, I could have further embellished the lie and told my father that Sister Mary was out sick. That part of the story, I'd have to wait until Friday afternoon to tell. Still, my only obstacle was my mother. My father was the easy part, but my mother possessed an almost preternatural ability to tell when I was lying. Maybe it had something to do with some psycho-spiritual link between mothers and their children; a metaphysical bond formed between us when I was still swimming around in her womb. Or maybe my father was that much of a jerk that he didn't care if I lied to him.

"When does Mom get home?" I asked.

"Don't change the subject," my father said.

"I'll do my homework on Saturday morning before I go out."

"What about church?"

"What about it?"

"Joe, you know you have to go to mass."

"But you don't."

"Listen, son, when you get to be as old as me, you can do whatever the hell you want. But until then, you do as I say."

"Fine," I gave up. "Saturday afternoon."

"With whom?" My father folded his arms across his chest and did his best to give me a scary look. He knew as well as I did that there was only one person in our house who intimidated me.

"Bobby McMahon."

"Okay," he dropped his arms. "But you have to finish your homework before you go anywhere on Saturday."

After that, my father and I jawed about me getting rid of the boat. I did my best not to act surprised when he mentioned it. He told me he couldn't recall giving me permission to allow the Swanson brothers access to his coveted garage. I came up with an intricate and elaborate story about how I asked him around Thanksgiving. I counted on him getting tired of me weaving my tapestry of lies before I had to come up with an ending that tied it all together in a nice neat knot.

Chapter 25

That evening, after my mother returned home from work, there was a knock at the front door. My father opened the door, and Uncle Scott entered the foyer with a strange woman in tow. A commotion followed as my uncle attempted to convince my father that his friend needed a place to stay for a few days. My mother entered the fray after that. Suddenly, my father was outnumbered two to one.

The woman on Uncle Scott's arm looked no older than my mother. Her eyes, which she never took off me as the other three adults argued, were large, slightly slanted, and colored emerald. At first, I wasn't sure if the woman was entirely human. My uncle introduced her as Svelanka.

"Just until things cool off," my uncle announced. "No more, no less."

"Is Svelanka more or less married, Scott?" my father asked.

"It's not like that."

"Says you."

"Do I need this?" my uncle looked at my mother.

A smile crossed Svelanka's face.

The original row intensified as Scott lashed out at my father, calling him every name under the sun. Svelanka tried to pull my uncle out of the house, but he stood his ground. For a second or two, it looked as if my father and Uncle Scott might come to blows. My mother boxed me out of the foyer, like a basketball player trying for a rebound, and ushered me upstairs.

"Time for bed," she told me.

"What about dinner?" I asked.

I was already halfway up the stairs when my mother relented. In the foyer, Uncle Scott spoke of the one thing that my father safeguarded even more than his collection of junk.

"All I'm asking," Uncle Scott said, "is for you give me a hand. Just help her get through the gate."

Gate? I thought. *What gate?*

"The door behind the furnace?" I called out.

"Joe," my mother said, "don't ask about things you don't know about."

"Where does it go?"

"Bed," my mother said after my father shot me a look. "Now."

I did as I was told. Something in the old man's eyes me told he wasn't playing around. I'd never seen him look so grim.

In my room, I pulled out an old copy of Roger Zelazny's *Nine Princes of Amber*. Tim Swanson gave me the book some months ago. I liked science fiction that leaned more toward hard science rather than the kind that borrowed from the fantastical. In Zelazny's *Chronicles of Amber*, the central characters came from a world called Amber, and they were able to shift between realities. I read five or ten pages, trying to ignore the discussion going on downstairs, but my mind kept coming around to the steel hatch in the basement. If my uncle knew about the hatch, then it was no real secret. Or maybe it was, and I was being kept out of the loop for a reason. My eyelids grew heavy just thinking about it.

An hour passed, and the conversation downstairs quieted to the point where I thought Uncle Scott and Svelanka had already left. Slowly, I opened my bedroom door. It occurred to me that my mother may have taken up position in the hallway, waiting to pounce the moment I stepped out of my room. It wouldn't have been the first time she thwarted my attempt to escape. That night, I made it all the way down the stairs into the first-floor hallway before someone else stopped me in my tracks.

To my right, the dining room was cast in near darkness. In the far corner of the room stood Marcella's shade. My parents' voices mixed with Uncle Scott's and his friend Svelanka's as they spoke quietly in the living room. I heard the clink of ice in glasses and knew that they were drinking. For now, all was forgiven between my father and Uncle Scott. I made a mental note to find my way into the basement later, perhaps hide among all the curios my father moved down there from the garage in recent days, and see if Uncle Scott had talked my father into allowing him to open the hatch behind the furnace. Marcella moved to the window that looked out over the front yard. I padded softly into the dining room.

"I always liked your yard, Joe," Marcella kept her back to me.

"Do my parents know—"

"No one knows I'm here but you."

"My dad thought he heard a girl's voice earlier," I whispered.

"He can't hear me."

"When will you go to Heaven?"

I looked to my left. My mother and father were seated on the sofa. Svelanka paraded back and forth, telling them a complicated tale about her life as a young girl. She sounded foreign, but I couldn't place the accent.

"Oh, Joe," said Marcella. "Not everyone aspires to Heaven."

I walked deeper into the dining room and sat down on the floor between the window and the table. Marcella faded in and out of view, but I knew from the cold that she was there.

"Who wouldn't want to go?" I asked.

"There are other places."

"So you say."

"You don't believe me."

"Why wouldn't I? I have no other evidence to refute—"

Marcella laughed. "You sound like Bobby," she said.

"Sorry," I offered.

"Don't be. Just don't question me about things you know nothing about."

I didn't remember Marcella ever being mean to me. The afterlife, such as it was, was taking its toll on her. Her last statement called to mind what my mother said to me earlier that evening.

"Do you know what's behind the door in my basement?" I threw out.

"It's locked," she replied.

"Yes, but you're a..."

"Ghost?"

"Well, yeah. Aren't you?"

"If you want me to be."

"I was reading a book about ghosts in the library," I said, "and it said that the reason some ghosts stick around..."

"After a person dies?"

"Yes."

"It's okay, Joe. I know I'm dead."

"Didn't want to offend."

"Don't be an idiot."

"Anyway," I said, ignoring her last comment, "some ghosts stick around because they feel they have some unfinished business."

"What business would that be?"

"You're the ghost. You tell me."

"I would have liked...oh, never mind."

"Come on. Tell me."

"It's stupid."

"I'm sitting here begging a ghost," I told her. "Nothing can be more stupid than that."

"I would have liked to kiss you, Joe," Marcella said. "Just once."

That changed everything. I wondered what might happen if I did it right there. Would I die from kissing a ghost? I took a step toward Marcella. She didn't move. Slowly, I moved as close as I could, but it was no use. The hairs on my arms stood up, and the whole room smelled like my mother's hair dryer when it was left on for too long—not a burning smell, something else entirely different. I stood face to face with Marcella now, but, in such close proximity, a force pressed on me like a strong wind. My stomach went all sour, and I thought I was going to vomit. Still, I pressed in closer. My vision blurred. I sensed Marcella lean forward. Our lips met. I didn't know shit about kissing girls other than watching some of the teen boys make out with their girlfriends behind The Roost. It was different than what I saw on television. I feared that Marcella's lips might feel ice cold, but they were not. I expected my first kiss to taste all sweet like candy canes at Christmas or cotton candy in the summertime, but it turned out to be far worse. When I kissed Marcella's ghost, all I tasted was dirt. Right at the moment, the whole room went ass over tea kettle. I blacked out.

When my mother woke me up, I had no idea of how much time had passed. She found me beneath the dining room table.

Before my mother roused me, I dreamed I was in the company of angels, living effigies of the ceramic seraphim my mother kept on a shelf in her bedroom. Only, unlike the statuettes my mother owned, the angels beneath the table were as tall as me, with large, dark wings and menacing faces. I had no idea how we all fit underneath the table since there were six of them, but dreams had a way of making a thousand angels on the head of a pin look like amateur hour. The physics of us all occupying the limited space didn't bother me as much as what the angels told me.

Those savage seraphim in my dream shared secrets with me— deep, dark secrets they made me swear never to repeat. When I woke, I couldn't remember any of those secrets save for one. They told me that Marcella was on her way to Heaven, never to return from the twilight of lost souls. No explanation was given, no reason why. During my dream, I figured that interrogating angels was not a safe bet, especially for a boy who knew better than to question God's messengers. They were, after all, the very ones who kicked the Devil out of Heaven. I stood no chance.

It saddened me to think that I would never see Marcella again. Still, I couldn't bring myself to cry about it. Even after my mother woke me up, I knew I couldn't tell her about the dream. Not the angels beneath the table, not the last kiss, and not Marcella's departure. It was for me and me alone.

"Where's Uncle Scott?" I asked when I crawled out from beneath the table.

"Never mind him," my mother said.

"What about the Russian girl?"

"Svelanka?"

"Yeah, her."

"Never mind that one either. And she's not Russian." My mother fought to hold back her laughter. "What were you doing sleeping beneath the dining room table?"

"I don't remember."

"You know, this isn't the first time."

"What do you mean?"

"The first time I found you underneath the table, you were four years old," she told me. "You don't remember that?"

I shook my head.

"You were so cute, Joe," my mother went on. "I found you one morning. It was early before your father went off to work. You told me the angels made you do it. I thought that was so precious, I told everyone."

"Were you drinking tonight?" I asked.

My mother grabbed my hand. "Let's go, young man," she pulled me toward the hallway. "Time for bed."

Chapter 26

After all those long months, the little boat still smelled of fresh paint. Tim sat lotus-position at the bow, with Jack rowing in the middle. Bobby huddled close to me at the stern. The fact that Bobby agreed to join the excursion astounded us. I knew he feared drowning more than anything else, but he volunteered to come along as soon as he caught wind.

"Can't you row any faster?" Bobby asked.

Jack quit rowing. "You want to take over?"

"No."

"Well, then shut the hell up about it."

"Bobby can't swim," Tim said. He leaned left and let his hand slip into the murky water.

"No shit, Sherlock," his brother said. "Tell me something I don't know."

"We're drifting with the current now," Bobby announced. "It's going to take longer if you don't start rowing again."

"Joe?"

"Yeah, Jack?"

"Tell his highness to button his cock hole."

"You wish, Jack Swanson," Bobby replied.

"Your mother, maybe," Jack told him. "But not you."

"As if she'd have you."

"Guys," I said, "enough already."

"Finally," Tim said, "the voice of reason."

Jack began rowing again. I sat back, looking up at the clouds all white and pristine as they drifted across the blue sky. On the other side of the creek, the trees were thick with green leaves that swayed in the light wind.

Our packs, the pop tent the Swanson brothers owned, and a fishing tackle box that belonged to Bobby were stored in whatever empty space there was on the small boat. It was a tight fit. The row boat, given the weight, sat low in the water, and everyone was agitated.

When he showed up at Granny Swanson's house that Saturday afternoon, Jack couldn't believe it.

"You selling Avon?" he said to Bobby, who stood on Granny Swanson's porch.

"Very funny," Bobby said, coldly.

"No fishing on this trip," said Jack. "Besides, we don't have rods."

Only after Bobby explained the contents inside the tackle box did Jack understand.

Tim was tasked with gathering food supplies. Rather than raid Granny Swanson's pantry, he took it upon himself to use the old newspaper bill collection routine, hoisting envelopes with a couple of bucks each in them from inside mailboxes, which were left for the paperboy. I expected Tim to come back from Stevenson's Supermarket laden with potato chips and Tastykakes. Instead, when Tim returned and laid out his bounty on the dock, there were cans of pork and beans, hotdogs, buns, sodas, marshmallows, and a tin mess kit.

"Is it going to rain tonight?" Bobby asked.

Presently, we were only fifty yards from the far bank. The afternoon was already waning. The woods beyond the creek bank were thick with shadows. Our original plan had been to set out under cover of darkness, but luck came our way when Granny Swanson told her grandsons that she was taking a bus into Philadelphia to do some shopping. So rather than wait, we seized the opportunity to set off early and strike camp in the forest before nightfall.

There was something fishy about Granny Swanson's claim that she was traveling to Philadelphia. The brothers Swanson sensed it immediately since their grandmother hoarded money like a miser. We noticed, too, that Mr. Von Braun wasn't out tending his garden.

"There's no great mystery there," Bobby said.

"How do you figure?" Tim asked.

"Your grandmother and the old German are going out on a date."

"Granny and Von Braun?" Jack asked. "No way."

"Sure," Bobby kept at it. "Probably come home tonight and do it."

"Watch your mouth. That's my grandmother you're talking about."

"What? Old people do it."

"The hell you say."

"Not as often," Bobby explained. "Perhaps not with the sweaty fervor usually reserved for the young."

"Stop it, Bobby."

"Do you think Granny Swanson prefers top or bottom?"

"Top or bottom of what?" Tim asked.

"Stay out of it," his brother told him.

As the boat drifted into shallow water, I kept thinking about that conversation. For a twelve-year-old boy, it was hard to imagine romance between two elderly people. But it made sense in a strange way. The only time Granny Swanson ever showed a modicum of happiness was when she happened to be in the presence of Mr. Von Braun. Maybe there was some merit to what Bobby had said, but then innuendo was always more interesting than the hard truth. So, it was anyone's guess what transpired in the hearts of two old neighbors.

Suddenly, the boat skidded to a halt. The four of us jerked forward.

"Land ho!" Jack shouted.

"There's no dock?" Bobby cried, crushed by the possibility that he might have to get his feet wet.

Tim removed his sneakers and knotted the laces together. Jack followed suit. The brothers slung their sneakers over the shoulders. Next, they rolled their jeans up to their knees. Tim jumped into the creek first, standing in shin-deep water. Jack was out of the boat next. Bobby and I removed our shoes and rolled up our jeans. Jack, Bobby, and I emptied the boat of its contents, conveying our packs and other supplies to the shore while Tim held the boat in place. Once all of our gear was on dry land, we went back into the water to help Tim pull the boat ashore.

Jack lost his footing and fell face-first into the water that parted in two and lapsed back over him. He remained beneath the water a few seconds. When he came up again, his face was covered with mud.

"Son of bitch," he spat.

"Jack, are you alright?" Bobby stepped toward him.

"Leave me alone," he told him. "We have to go back."

"What for?" Tim asked.

"I'm soaking fucking wet. That's what for."

"Maybe you shouldn't have taken a dive."

"Idiot," said Jack. "There's a sink hole. I tripped."

"It's getting late," Tim reminded him.

"Push the boat back out," his brother ordered. "I'll be back as soon as I can."

"Jack, wait," Bobby spoke up. "We can build a fire and dry your clothes. I have plenty of flammable stuff in the tackle box. Matches, charcoal briquettes, lighter fluid, the works."

"What? Barbeque my clothes? Get the fuck out of my way," Jack was already pushing the boat back into deeper water.

The three of us stood on the bank, watching Jack row like a madmen out into the middle of the creek. Soon, we moved into the cool shade of the treeline. Bobby sat on his backpack and put on his socks and sneakers. I did the same, as Tim picked up a stick and drew smiley faces in the dirt.

"You know," said Tim, "it would be cool if we found a world where all the kids were our age. Imagine if we ended up shipwrecked—"

"*Lord of the Flies*," Bobby mumbled.

"What?"

"It's a novel by William Golding," he said. "Kids from a private school end up being marooned on an island. They separate into two factions as they degenerate into savagery."

"So even in a world without teenagers and adults, we'd still fight one another," said Tim.

"Bingo."

"That sucks."

"All it takes is for, say, a kid like Jack to pick on a weaker kid like me," Bobby explained.

"Jack wouldn't do that to you," Tim assured him. "I wouldn't let him."

"In your world?"

"Yeah," a smile stretched across Tim's face as he thumbed his chest. "In my world."

"No monsters?" I asked.

"Joe, don't be a moron," said Bobby.

"I guess there will always be monsters," Tim concluded. "Even in my world. You can't help it."

The conversation shifted away from possible worlds to town rumors. We made ourselves comfortable beneath three trees that stood near one another, propping our heads on our packs. The sunlight dappled through the green canopy overhead. One by one, in no certain order, we fell asleep.

I don't remember what time it was when I woke up to the sound of Jack grunting as he pulled the boat onto the bank. The sun had already receded far behind the trees. Random shafts of late afternoon sunrays shone like fallen pillars of light where dust motes whirled.

"A little help," Jack called out.

The three of us stood up slowly, as Tim wiped sleep from his eyes. Bobby stretched his arms wide, yawning as he let out a roar. We helped Jack carry the boat into the treeline. After we set it down, Jack reached into the boat and pulled out a spare pair of sneakers. He threw the sneakers at his brother.

"Don't mention it," said Jack.

"I was going to say thanks," Tim told him.

"Sure you were."

"So," Bobby spoke up as he checked his fingernails for crud, "how far off is this fabled house?"

"We camp first," Jack said. "Right, Joe?"

"That's the plan." I gathered fallen branches to cover the boat.

"Then we go at night."

"Wait until you see the stones."

"Do I get to go this time?" Tim asked.

"Of course," Jack said. "We might need a sacrifice to the Old Ones."

"Don't mock them."

"Oh, I'm so scared."

"There's a certain truth to every fiction," said Tim. "Just remember that."

"Your brother's right," Bobby added. "What are we talking about?"

"H.P. Lovecraft," Jack said. "My dad had a book of his stories. Tim keeps it hidden because Granny Swanson thinks that Lovecraft induces nightmares."

"Did you ever read Robert E. Howard?" Bobby draped his arm over Tim's shoulders and led him toward the woods.

"Don't they make a cute couple," Jack said to me. Then, "Hey, Tim, don't forget your gear."

Jack and I turned the boat upside down between two trees. Next, we set about camouflaging it with the fallen branches I had gathered. It was harder this time around because they were dead branches without any leaves on them. So, Jack suggested we tear down fresh branches from saplings and other smaller trees near the creek. As we did so, Bobby and Tim stood off in the shadows, deep in conversation, as they shouldered their packs. Once Jack and I finished, we stood back and admired our work. Satisfied that the boat was well-hidden from plain view, we grabbed our packs and joined them.

One hundred yards or so into the forest, we found an old fire pit. There were empty beer cans strewn about, and Tim unearthed an old skin rag from beneath a half-burnt log. There were pictures in the magazine of women with enormous boobs and big hips. The quality wasn't the same as I had seen in *Playboy* when I snuck peeks at the magazine stand inside Dave and Di's Luncheonette. All the women in Tim's magazine had crooked teeth and stretch marks. None of them seemed capable of staring straight into the camera. In many of the photographs, some women pressed men's cocks between their fat boobs; other women had penises in their mouths while they held their boobs in their hands. Tim started to tuck the magazine into his knapsack, but his brother took the magazine from him and flung it away.

"Come on," Tim whined.

"See that over there?" Jack pointed to something behind the fire pit.

The four of us circled the pit. There, in the rotting leaves, was a pair of boy's briefs. Jack found a stick and used it to lift the underwear into the air. The briefs looked small enough to fit any one of us, and they were covered with dirt and grit, but it was the backside stained all rusty brown from dried blood that had caught Jack's attention.

"Gross," Tim said. "That's shit."

"No, it's not," Jack dropped the underwear into the fire pit. "That was blood. Some pervert drifter probably raped a boy just like you."

"Hey, Jack," Bobby said. "What do you say you just lead the way to the camp site?"

"I'm trying to make a point."

"We know you are."

"This is a bad place."

"We know," Bobby and I said at the same time.

Jack broke out his compass. When he did, I thought about that first trip into the woods. In daylight, what was left of it, even I knew it would be easier to find our way. And so we followed Jack as he led us deeper into Franklin Forest, into the dusty twilight that hid the great old house from the rest of the world.

Chapter 27

Shadows swayed on the periphery of the firelight like ghosts dancing around our secluded campsite. The four of us sat on one side of the fire; our packs along with the tent and poles remained where we left them earlier that evening. Jack had chosen a dry rise with only four large oaks on it. The trees stood like silent sentries; ever watchful, they were, of what may lurk in the darkness unseen by human eyes.

For dinner, we ate hot dogs, along with pork and beans straight from the can. Afterward, we spent a good hour farting up a storm. Reluctant at first, Bobby joined in, rendering the loudest ones.

"What time is it?" I asked.

"Half-past nine," Bobby answered.

He was the only one who owned a watch. It was a pocket watch his grandfather once owned. According to Bobby, his grandfather bought it when he returned to the states after serving in the army. His unit was responsible for training resistance fighters in France during the German occupation. Bobby never talked about his grandfather. To get any information out of him was like pulling teeth without using a local anesthetic—struggle and pain the whole way. The only reason I knew anything at all about the pocket watch's origin was because Mr. McMahon had told me the whole story about his father who bought the watch, one of the last the Solaris Company ever made, after he returned home from the war.

"Where's Bobby's grandfather now?" I had asked Mr. McMahon when he finished telling me the story.

Bobby and I had been sitting with him in the McMahons' living room. Mr. McMahon had been reading *The Wall Street Journal*. He had lowered the newspaper when I had posed the question. I still remember the hate in his eyes when he had answered.

"He took off when I was about your age," Mr. McMahon had said. "Presumably, back to Europe. But no one, not even my mother, knew for sure."

"Did you ever hear from him again?" I had asked.

"He sent a postcard from Morocco," he had told me. "Something about being on his way to Mount Ararat. Do you know Ararat?"

"Where Noah's Ark ended up after the flood, right?"

"Very good, Joe."

"What was there?"

I had felt the tension in the room rise when I had asked that question. Bobby, sitting next to me, had started bouncing his leg beside mine.

"I'll be damned if I know," Mr. McMahon had concluded. He had raised his newspaper again, concealing his face. "Maybe the mouth of madness."

Bobby hadn't talked to me for a week after that. When he did, he acted as if the conversation never took place. A week later, his father bestowed upon him the Solaris pocket watch, and with it, the bitter memories Mr. McMahon carried with him ever since his father took off and vanished into the world.

"I think it's time," Jack was saying as I stared into the flames.

"I have to shit," Tim announced.

"Hey, Davey Crockett," his brother said, "use the excavation tool and bury it."

"Why? Deer shit on the ground."

"Are you a deer?"

"Okay," Tim stood up and retrieved a roll of toilet paper and the little shovel from his brother's pack.

Once Tim retreated to the privacy of the dark behind an oak tree, Bobby and I helped Jack douse the fire with dirt.

"Scatter it," Jack said when we finished, "and stamp it for good measure."

"We're not setting up the tent?" Bobby asked.

"Nope," he replied. "We'll bring it with us. Maybe camp close to the house."

We had no map, not even a crudely drawn one rendered during our last visit. So, we had to rely on Jack's compass, the stars, and our collective memory of the landscape. Once Tim finished his business, we shouldered our packs and moved out, heading northwest according to Jack's compass.

A full moon cast a pale light across the forest, turning trees, shrubs, vines, and the pine needle-covered ground into a shade of whitish gray. We walked single-file for an hour or more until we came upon a steep grade that led toward a dry stream bed. Atop the ground that led up from the bed, I spotted the feral boy. He looked the same as he did the first night I saw him: skin like white birch bark and hair, even from far away, a mess of tangled locks, twigs and leaves in the moonlight.

"Is it him?" Tim hissed.

"Who?" Bobby asked. "Where?"

The boy was gone.

"Jack," I said, "we have to cross here."

"But this—" he started to say.

"Trust me on this," I led him across the ravine and up the hill on the other side.

No sooner had we reached the top, the forest thickened. Huge trees bowed toward one another in the moonlight. Thickets, vines, brambles, and bushes blocked our way. The four of us argued about the best course to take. In each direction we searched we were met by a natural perimeter. In some places, the barrier was several yards thick.

It was Bobby who found the passage. He wandered off, heading north along the ridge that bordered the stream bed. While Jack, Tim, and I attempted to crawl our way through the thick brush, we lost sight of him.

"Where's Curious George?" Jack brushed dried leaves from his shirt and pants.

"Bobby!" Tim shouted.

No answer. *Great,* I thought.

"Hey, Bobby McMahon!" Tim called out into the dark.

"Quit yelling," his brother told him.

"Should we split up?" I asked. I wasn't happy about the prospect, but returning without Bobby was a predicament I didn't want to face. "What if he fell? What if he knocked himself out cold?"

My panic turned out to be premature. Bobby came toward us, twirling a stick like a baton as he whistled some marching song.

"I think I found a way around," he said confidently.

"Check out Jungle Jim," said Jack. "Okay, show us."

Sure enough, Bobby did find a way. The opening was situated a couple of hundred yards north of where we stood. When we got there, a well-worn path stretched through the brush and off into the darkness. The passage turned out to be narrow, so we moved single-file with Jack in the lead.

On the other side of the barrier, we found an even mix of pine, oak, and ash trees. Compared to the forest that bordered Hobbs Creek, the trees just beyond the barrier looked ancient. A soft bedding of pine needles beneath our feet cushioned every step. Even with Jack, Bobby, and Tim with me, I couldn't help feeling scared. There was an absence of sound in that place that I never experienced until that night.

"Maybe we should camp here," Bobby suggested.

"No good," was all Jack said.

He whipped out his compass. In the moonlight, his expression went all sour as he slapped the compass a few times.

"It's gone all haywire again," he said, quietly.

"What do you mean 'again'?" Bobby asked.

Jack handed him the compass. "See for yourself."

Bobby opened the compass, turning it left and right. Convinced that we weren't pulling his leg, he gave the compass back to Jack.

"What would do that?" he asked.

Jack closed his eyes and sniffed the night air. Bobby looked nervous now. Tim and I stood there, a little dumbfounded, as Jack spread his arms out wide.

"What are you doing?" I asked.

"Trying to remember," Jack answered.

"It's okay if we're lost," his brother told him. "We can find our way—"

"We're not lost."

"I'm just saying."

"Will you shut the hell up?"

"Maybe we should just follow this path," I suggested. "The last time—"

"There are paths like this throughout the forest," said Jack. "What makes you think this is the right one?"

Tim and Bobby just started down the trail. Jack and I followed. I could tell he was pissed off. The only thing I had to go on was seeing the wild boy. It occurred to me that the feral boy might lead us into some sort of trap, maybe a crazed witch (or witches) who might cook us alive in a big cauldron or a band of bloodthirsty vampires. But why would such evil creatures need a go-between? Couldn't witches ride brooms and enchant us? And vampires changed into bats and wolves and Christ knew what else all the time, according to Tim. It was best to concentrate on the matter at hand. Still, I had faith that the feral boy wouldn't let me down. He did, after all, lead me to the bridge that one night.

With the moon now hidden by the thick canopy, visibility was piss poor. I couldn't see two feet in front of me. The trail wound its way around giant oak trees, and often the path split in two, going a long way like that before converging once more. We walked single-file for most of it. At some point, the trail led upward to another rise. Jack broke out his compass again, muttered something under his breath, and put the instrument back into his pocket.

At the top of the rise, the moon cast a pale light on everything. Jack slapped me on the shoulder. Less than fifteen yards from where we stood, there was the arch fashioned from two bent trees. Beyond it, the footbridge extended over the shadowy ravine into darkness.

"This is our campsite," Jack announced.

"Oh, thank God," Bobby exclaimed. "I'm completely famished. My blood sugar is all out of whack."

"What the fuck is he talking about?" asked Jack as he dropped his pack on the ground.

The rest of us followed suit. Tim moved forward and inspected the arch. In the moonlight, he looked like an explorer who had just discovered El Dorado or some other forgotten ancient city.

Jack and I busied ourselves putting up the tent. Tim joined us. He looked agitated as he broke out our rations.

"Timmy," said Bobby, "are you okay?"

"Me? Sure. Why?"

"What's up, little brother?" Jack asked.

"I thought I saw some kid on the bridge," his brother confessed.

"What did he look like?" I asked.

"He looked like Sidhe."

"Who the hell is Sheedie?" Jack asked.

"A mythical race said to live in Ireland before the Celts came," Bobby spoke up.

"Well, aren't you the walking history book."

"More like mythology book," Bobby corrected Jack. "If you want to be technical about it. Of course, when faced with an inferior mind—"

"Whatever," Jack said, then added, "Are you sure, Tim?"

"I saw it, alright," Tim said. "What if it was a ghost?"

Jack took his brother in a neck lock and gave him a playful squeeze. "You and your books," he said. "Don't worry, brother. I'll protect you."

Chapter 28

By Bobby's watch, it was already after midnight when we set out over the footbridge. Vines crisscrossed the bridge like giant spider webs. We made it no more than ten feet across the bridge, winding our way over and under the vines, when Jack abruptly quit and headed back toward camp.

"Be right back," he told us. "I'll catch up."

I thought Jack had to relieve himself, but he returned in no time, carrying his coveted excavation tool. He swung the collapsible shovel like a madman, hacking through the vines and knocking them aside. As he did, the bridge moaned like a dying giant.

"Stop," Tim grabbed his brother's arm.

Jack turned to face him. When he did, Bobby shined a flashlight in his face. Jack's eyes looked crazed and sweat covered his brow.

"Let go," said Jack.

"No," I told him, "listen."

Bobby turned off the flashlight. The bridge creaked and groaned. I started once more to weave my way through the vines. Tim let go of Jack's arm and followed me.

"For all we know," I heard Bobby tell Jack, "these vines may be holding up the bridge."

Along the way, Tim shined the flashlight on several intricate images carved into the bridge's railings and support poles. Bobby commented on several of them, but in the dark, the carved images appeared more sinister, and I sensed just how uneasy Bobby felt.

Several minutes later, all four of us reached the other end of the bridge. My hands were raw from pushing aside the rough vines. Bobby was the last one to step off the bridge. He tucked his hands in his armpits; the darkness did little to conceal the pained expression he wore. Earlier that afternoon, I had suspected that Bobby would be reduced to a sniveling sissy by the time night fell. The longer we spent in the forest, however, the more he proved me wrong.

"I can see the stones," Bobby exclaimed and darted past Jack and me into the darkness.

"Bobby, wait," Tim called out.

The marked trail looked pristine, as if groundskeepers worked every day to keep it clear of leaves and the ever-creeping vines that choked most of the surrounding forest. Bobby waited for us twenty yards down the trail. Once we caught up to him, Jack and Tim walked ahead of Bobby and me. We moved slowly, covering another fifty yards, when Bobby grabbed my arms with both hands.

"Look," he whispered, "to the right by the split tree."

An oak adjacent to the trail rose up into the darkness, and it was split into a perfect Y-shape. At first, I could not see what had excited Bobby so much, but, as my eyes adjusted, I saw what had stopped him in his tracks. The pale glow of a moonstone along the trail's edge revealed a short man, no taller than Tim, who wore a leather apron and earthy tones of dark green and brown. The little man's mouth was oddly shaped, as were his large, pointed ears and feline eyes. His face with its snout for a nose and thick facial hair resembled less a human and more like a wolf or fox. The little man leaned against the oak as if he were some hobo waiting to hop a freight train. He executed an about face, spinning silently on his heels, and vanished into the shadows.

"Jack," Bobby hissed, "did you see that?"

"See what?" Jack asked. "The bogeyman?"

"Never mind."

Jack quit walking. He turned around to face us, holding his little shovel at his side.

"What did you see?" he asked.

"A man," I answered. "He had—"

"A fox's face," Tim spoke up.

"You saw him, too?" Bobby grabbed Tim's hand.

Tim shook his hand free and nodded.

"Well," said Jack, "I didn't see shit."

Bobby wanted to wait and see if the fox-faced man would come back. At one point, he started to move down the trail into the treeline where the little man stood only moments ago, but, unable to accept that we had seen anything at all, Jack stopped him.

"Look," he told us, "if the little guy joins us on the trail, that's fine. But I don't want anyone wandering off into the dark."

"But Jack," Bobby started to say.

"I don't know what the deal is here in these woods," Jack cut him off. "You and Tim are all hip to how magic works and all that shit."

"Right."

"Wrong. What are you going to do, Bobby? Throw a net over the man with the fox head and drag him back to town?"

Bobby opened his mouth and quickly snapped it shut. "I understand," he said.

"No, I don't think you do," Jack announced. "All three of you. By rights, I'm the oldest. And that means we do what I say. And I say I don't want anyone wandering off on their own."

"Maybe there's a whole other world out there," Tim blurted out.

"This isn't a story book, little brother," he said. "Now can we all agree that the trail is marked for a reason?"

The three of us nodded in unison.

"Good," Jack went on. "It's getting near dawn. So, can we go now? Bobby and Tim, you guys still want to see the house?"

"Yes," Tim mumbled.

"Come on, Jack," I said.

"No, Joe," Jack snapped. "I'm sick of this shit." He poked Tim in the chest first then Bobby. "If you guys are too scared just say so."

Tim said nothing as he pushed past and started down the trail. Bobby and I were next. Jack followed us some ten yards behind, but at that point, I didn't care if he came along at all. I knew that it was Jack's nature to protect his younger brother. In his life, there were no options. It was just him and Tim, and they looked out for one another as best they could. Sure, they fought like all brothers do, but deep in their hearts, they knew that it was just the two of them against the world. Still, I didn't think it was right that Jack acted as if the whole expedition was his idea. If it hadn't been for me, he would have never seen the footbridge, and if it wasn't for the bridge, we would have never found the house.

Bobby stopped several minutes later to examine the moonstones that lined the trail on either side. He squatted over one and ran his fingers gently over its surface.

"It appears to be some kind of naturally phospherescent rock," he said.

"Thanks, Mr. Spock," said Jack as he moved on up the trail.

"Jerk," Bobby whispered as he stood up.

"Come on," I put my arm around his shoulders. "Wait until you see this place."

The wide lawn in front of the house appeared, the way it did the first time we discovered it, as if it had been mowed and manicured that very day. I imagined some ghoulish groundskeepers, undead landscapers, working through the night at breakneck speed as they edged the boundaries of the lawn, trimmed bushes, and raked dead leaves. Suddenly, the shadows between the trees that bordered the expansive lawn looked more menacing. The idea of ghouls doing their yard work by the light of the moon seemed implausible, but after seeing the feral boy and the fox-faced man, there was no telling what the house and the property held in store for us.

Bobby was the only one who acted as if we were being watched. I fought hard to keep such thoughts out of my mind; otherwise, I would have fled in no time flat. Bobby walked across the lawn as if he were crossing a minefield, slowly lifting one foot and setting it down before moving the other, as if each step may have been his last.

"The place is abandoned," Jack told Tim.

Together, the Swanson brothers marched across the lawn to the front steps. Bobby stopped at the man-made pond, watching the murky waters for a sign. I left Bobby there and joined the brothers Swanson. The porch looked as dilapidated as I remembered it. Turning, I watched Bobby as he made his way around the pond's edge; all the while, he kept his eyes trained on the water. Behind me, Jack and Tim ascended the stairs up to the porch.

"The door's closed," Jack said.

From where I stood, I saw something move in the pond's silt water that sent a subtle ripple from the center out to the sides where the water lapped against the jagged rocks bordering the pond. That was enough to make Bobby give up his investigation. He darted around the pond and ran past me straight up the stairs and onto the porch.

Jack and Tim argued over who was going to find a way into the house. Frustrated, Jack tried the doorknob and found that he could turn it, but, even with Tim's help, the door did not budge.

"Didn't you say it was open the last time you were here?" Bobby asked.

"Yeah, that's right," Jack grunted as he tried the door once more.

"Maybe someone shut it."

"And maybe it was the wind."

"Or the fox-faced man," Tim added.

What followed was a four-way argument over whether or not someone occupied the house. I was under the impression that some old recluse lived there. A human shut-in, not the garden variety fairyfolk that Tim argued. Leave it to the younger Swanson brother to offer up that there may have been a myriad of creatures dwelling inside the three-story mansion. Bobby sided with Tim on the issue, which only frustrated Jack even more. No matter what stance the other three took, Jack was convinced that there was a natural explanation, one that didn't involve creepy, old recluses (that was mine), nocturnal undead (Bobby's), or clever fairyfolk (Tim's). Jack maintained a perfectly good explanation not only for why the door was shut but the reason why no one was able to open it.

"It's an old house," he concluded. "Maybe the ceiling fell in behind it."

"Hard to tell from out here," Bobby said.

"Only one way to find out," he countered.

As if the brothers were clairvoyant, Tim removed his shirt, balled it around his fist, and punched out the stained glass in a window overlooking the front porch.

"That'll do it," said Tim.

"What the hell do you think you're doing?" his brother asked.

Tim didn't answer. Instead, he reached through the broken window and released the lock. He slid the window open, and put his shirt back on.

"Who's first?" he asked.

Bobby's gaze remained fixed on the man-made pond. He moved away from the open window, distancing himself from the possibility of entering alien territory alone. After he sat down on the porch steps, Bobby's focus remained locked on the pond.

Jack slapped me in the arm. "Get a load of this guy," he whispered.

"I'll go," I said.

"No way."

"You want to go instead?"

"What?" Jack asked. "Are you scared now?"

"Don't say Joe's afraid," Bobby told him. "Especially if you are not volunteering."

"Shut up, fairy queen."

Bobby stood up. Slowly, his gaze shifted from the pond to Jack.

"Don't call me that," he said.

"Queen?" Jack asked. "Or fairy?"

Bobby bowed at the waist and charged into Jack, striking him with his head right in the stomach. Tim and I separated them before Jack could do any real damage. Once we did, Bobby returned to his perch on the steps.

Jack rubbed his stomach as he worked to catch his breath. "Little bastard," he wheezed. "I didn't know he had it in him."

Rather than argue any further, I pushed aside the moldy curtain in the open window and wormed my way into the house. As long as I kept the curtain open, I was able to hear Jack and Tim discuss their next course of action. Once I let the curtain drop, however, all of the sounds from outside the house ceased.

I regretted not having the flashlight, but asking Tim for his would have been an admission of fear. So, I let my eyes adjust to the darkness for several seconds before I took another step. When I did, I discovered that I was standing in the library where Jack had found the jarred birds. I was happy to have the darkness around me; thankful that I didn't have to see those jars in all their gory detail.

Across the room, a heavy curtain blocked the wood door that led out into a hall. When I reached for the curtain, I felt cobwebs. Worse, something crawled across my hand before I flicked it into the dark. I stifled a yelp. The last thing I wanted was for the mansion's occupant, or occupants, to know that I was inside. I wanted to believe that I was alone in the house, but it was best to be safe. Besides, crying out loud over a bug on my arm would have given Jack enough ammunition to last until the following Christmas.

The door out of the library didn't budge. The cast iron handle felt cold to the touch. Whether I pushed or pulled, the door moved only a fraction of an inch. It was then I remembered my last visit to the house, and how the doors leading out of the library slid open.

Outside the library, the foyer was dark and cavernous. It took every ounce of self-control not to yell out. What I wanted more than anything in that moment was for some entity, living or dead, to make its presence known to me. Turning, I saw the vague outline of the grand stairwell. Closing my eyes, I took in the silence until I remembered Jack's screams the day he saw a dead boy's reflection in a mirror on the second floor. The same dank smell, one of wet earth and rotting leaves, filled my nostrils.

I found a trunk pushed up against the front door. I tried my best to move the trunk, but it was too heavy. If Bobby and the Swanson brothers were going to join me in the house, they would have to crawl through the window like I did. That a heavy trunk had been pushed in front of the door meant nothing in regard to whether the house was occupied. There were all manner of transients and bums, according to my parents, who hid out from the law in Franklin Forest, going all the way back to the colonial days. I convinced myself that one of these vagrants had used the house and moved on.

After I climbed back out of the window, I found Jack and Tim seated on the porch steps. Bobby was gone.

"What gives?" Jack asked. "I thought you were—"

A sound like rumbling thunder drowned him out. The porch beneath us vibrated.

"We should get out of here," I told him.

Jack and Tim looked at each other.

"No way," they said.

"Where's Bobby?"

"He went to take a leak," said Jack.

"You let him go alone?"

"He wanted privacy," he answered. "Besides, what am I going to do? Hold it for him?"

Tim found this funny, and he suppressed a laugh, causing him to snort like a pig.

"What about the fox-faced man?" I asked.

Before either of them could answer me, Bobby appeared in front of a treeline behind the rock-bordered pond. He waved. The brothers Swanson and I left the porch and joined him.

Suddenly, the front door of the mansion opened with a crack like a tree splitting in two. The noise echoed against the woods.

"Run!" Tim pushed Jack and me toward Bobby.

"What's going on?" Bobby asked as he ran backward.

"I don't know," I told him.

"Why are we running?"

No one answered him. We didn't stop running until we reached the footbridge. Only after we started across the bridge again did I tell the three of them about the trunk blocking the door.

"That noise," said Tim.

"Someone must have moved the trunk," Jack concluded.

"Maybe we should head back to the creek," Bobby offered. "The front door was opened by someone inside the house which means that same someone, maybe more than one, lives there."

"Calm down."

"So we're not going back to the creek?"

"No," Jack said. "We go back to camp. In a few hours, the sun will be up. Then we go back to the house and see what's what."

Bobby pursed his lips and shook his head. I tried to tell him that we'd be foolish to come this far and turn back, but, judging by the look on his face, I knew that he wanted nothing more than to retreat to the comfortable confines of his attic bedroom surrounded by his books. Early on, Bobby proved that the forest wasn't going to get the best of him, but, in this new, eldritch surrounding, his fortitude slipped away. He had a look in his eyes I had not seen since that night with Sean McClusky. He was scared. It wasn't until we reached the campsite that I found out why.

Chapter 29

Once we put the bridge between us and the house, I felt confident that we didn't need to retreat all the way to the creek. Jack and Tim set about gathering new tinder and wood for a fire. The forest took on a more primal look than I remembered it had only a few hours ago. The full moon was gone now, and the darkness appeared deeper within the woods. Once Jack and Tim gathered the wood, they had a hard time getting a fire started.

"Let's see that tackle box," I told Bobby.

Bobby opened the box and produced a large can of lighter fluid. He handed me matches and the lighter fluid, which I poured over the kindling in the fire pit Jack had made with his excavation tool. I lit the match and tossed it onto the kindling. Flames erupted with a poof and a blast of heat. Afterward, each of us took turns feeding first twigs and then small branches into the flames before Jack placed logs on the fire.

I was relieved that the campfire fought back some of the darkness, and I suspected that my friends felt the same way. The firelight reached all the way to the bowed trees that formed the arch at the bridge entrance. I tried not to look at the vines and the shadows beneath the arch. When my gaze lingered too long there, the darkness shifted as if something alive was staring back at me. Bobby and Tim sat facing the campfire huddled close together. Jack unrolled his sleeping bag and stretched out lengthwise, keeping his back to the bridge.

"Tell them," Tim said, at last.

Bobby lowered his head. He remained silent, gathering his thoughts. When he finally spoke, his voice sounded distant, filled with fear.

"I'm not sure how to say this," Bobby began. "You guys saw him too, so you know I'm not making this up."

"Who did we see?" Jack asked, already half-asleep.

"Mr. Foxman," he answered. "He's what we call a wood sprite. He says there all kinds, ranging from nymphs to naiads, ogres to orcs. There are also kelpies, selkies, and brownies."

"The fox man told you this?"

"When I was taking a leak earlier tonight," he said. "He asked me my name, and he told me to call him Foxman."

Jack turned to face Bobby and Tim. "You're telling me you're out there in the woods, taking a piss," he said, "and you were talking to this...thing?"

"Sprite."

"Whatever," the older Swanson said. "Bullshit. That's the kind of thing someone would say who wants to back out of this trip."

"No, it's not," said Tim. "Just hear him out."

"Foxman told me that we shouldn't ever go inside the house," said Bobby.

"What the hell, Bobby," I sat up straight. "I was inside that place, alone!"

"I know," he replied. "But by the time I got back, I really had no way of telling you, because you guys were all running helter-skelter."

Jack turned onto his back and looked toward the bridge.

"Look," he hissed, nodding at the arch. "Don't move. Just look!"

They stood on either side of the bridge entrance. Some of their faces were concealed by shadow; others were not. They had almond eyes that flickered against the firelight. Some stood six or seven feet tall and were reed-thin; others were short and stout. There were broad-shouldered brutes with coarse hair covering their bodies, and there were lithe winged creatures, some of which were only a foot tall, whose bare skin looked translucent, and they each bore an internal, eldritch light that glowed pale yellow-green or vibrant blue. All of the creatures who stood on two legs, regardless of their size, wore cloaks and chainmail, leather breeches and aprons, or simple hooded capes.

It was Tim who stood up first. He was halfway to the fantastical crowd before the rest of us could move. Three winged creatures came toward him, fluttering around as the light inside them turned from greenish yellow to a ghostly pale blue. As soon as Jack reached his brother, the winged creatures changed. They grew larger, more fierce looking. A shrill whistle from within the fairy crowd called them off just as Jack picked up a large stick to defend himself.

"Let's get the hell—" Jack started to say when the Foxman stepped out of the otherworldly crowd.

"Hear me," the little man held his hands in the air, as if supplicating to some primitive deity. "The boundary is no more. Go your way. Forget what you have learned about us and this place."

I stood next to Jack now. He and I watched as the Foxman and the others retreated into the shadows and vanished. Several seconds passed before any of us moved. The only noise in our camp came from the fire where burnt wood crackled.

Then Bobby wigged out, packing his things hastily in a desperate attempt to escape. He shouldered his pack and took hold of his tackle box. Jack tried to talk him into staying, to show him how irrational he was behaving, but Bobby insisted on leaving.

"I want to go," Bobby repeated this mantra over and over.

Together, he and Jack performed an awkward dance as Bobby tried to flee the camp site, and Jack blocked his every move.

"Where would you go at this hour?" Jack pleaded with him. "Your parents will flip if you went home right now. And then what will you tell them?"

"I just want to get out of here," Bobby told him as tears streamed down his face.

"It will be morning soon."

"But I want to go now."

"Why?"

"What if they come back and kill us?" asked Bobby. "Did you ever think of that? What if they enchant us a-and pull us into the fairy realm? Christ, Jack. You don't know about these things. Throughout history there have been hundreds, no, maybe thousands of cases where—"

"Bobby, come on," Jack said. "If the Foxman and his crew wanted us dead, that would have happened already. And as far as the so-called fairy realm goes, I don't know much about that kind of stuff, but I'd bet we're already in it."

"What boundary was the Foxman talking about?" Tim asked, taking the opportunity to step between Bobby and Jack.

"Does it matter?" Bobby's voice cracked. "We're doomed."

"Come on, man," Jack said. "This is the United States. One nation under God. You think those fairies are any match for Jesus?"

Bobby dropped his tackle box and slid his knapsack from his shoulder. When the pack landed at his feet, he kicked it aside.

"That's the stupidest thing I've ever heard," he said.

"But it's true, isn't it?" Jack kept at him.

"Do you see Jesus anywhere out here?" Bobby screamed at him. His voice echoed through the woods. "Don't you understand how this goes? Tim, tell him. Do you know what these things are? Some say they are fallen angels, Jack. Do you think a few kids like us from Yorkville are any match for them?"

"I think you're over-reacting," the older Swanson brother said.

By now, Bobby's eyes were filled with tears. He broke down into a blubbering mess. There was nothing any of us could do. For several minutes, Bobby simply lay on the ground where he collapsed into hysterics. Jack shrugged and went about the business of stoking up the fire. Once the fire was roaring again, lighting up the entire camp site, I felt better. It took me about that long to offer Bobby any comfort. He was my best friend, but there were times when you had to let emotions run their course. That's what my mother used to tell me. And it seemed to me that this was one of those times. Bobby lay on the ground, curling his body into a fetal position once he rolled over to face the fire. I squatted down next to him and patted him on the shoulder. No sooner than I did, he jumped to his feet.

"Bobby, listen," I started to say.

He ran off into the shadows beyond the fire's ring of light. I heard him offer up a muffled curse in the dark when a twig snapped. Then, somewhere in the shadowy woods, several branches shook as Bobby cried out.

"Quit running!" Jack shouted, then muttered, "Come on, Tim. Let's go find him."

"Wait," I told him. "I want to go."

"Just stay here, Joe," he said. "We'll find him faster. Plus, I think it's safer near the fire."

"You're serious?"

"The Foxman and the others didn't come near it," said Jack. "Maybe they are afraid of fire. We'll be back, soon." He and Tim were already trotting off into the dark. "Don't worry."

So, I waited alone. After thirty minutes with no one in sight, human, fairy, or otherwise, I lost interest in keeping the fire lit. I took every natural sound in the forest to be the Foxman or one of his fairy henchmen. I imagined several gruesome scenarios where those monsters would take us out one by one. Before long, I crawled into the tent where I felt even less safe since I couldn't tell if anyone was sneaking up behind me.

Perhaps an hour passed in this fashion before I heard Tim calling out my name. I crawled out of the tent to meet him near the fire pit. His face looked ashen, and his breath smelled like vomit when he spoke.

"Bring the flashlight," was all he said.

Chapter 30

Making my way across the pristine lawn, I saw the body as it floated face-down in the man-made pond. There was no need to shine the light over the body to know that it was Bobby. Jack stood shin-deep in the water like some sentry guarding the dead. He made no attempt to hide the fact that he was crying. When he saw me approach, Jack pulled Bobby up from the water and over the jagged rocks at the pond's edge. Gently, he lowered our friend's body down on the ground.

The halo of light from the flashlight revealed that Bobby didn't just slip and fall into the pond. There was a gaping wound in his chest the size of a fist. The wound appeared to have already stopped bleeding, as if someone or something had cauterized the hole.

Tim broke down into tears; only, instead of slipping into hysteria's grip, he sat down quietly next to Bobby. Holding Bobby's head in his hands, he wiped the dirt and grime from our dead friend's face.

"Turn off the flashlight," Tim whispered.

I obliged him. The front lawn was dark now. A cool breeze blew, rustling the trees in the distance.

"We shouldn't stay here," I said.

"I'm going up to the house," Jack announced.

Before Tim or I could stop him, Jack ran full-tilt toward the house. By the time I caught up to him, he was kicking and punching the front door.

"Open up!" he screamed over and over again. "Open this goddamn door, you murderers!"

I ran up the stairs onto the porch and tried to stop him, grabbing his arm in an attempt to pull him away. For my efforts, I received a swift punch in the gut before he shoved me aside. I stumbled and fell onto my hands and knees.

It was then I heard Tim scream. He had followed me to the bottom of the porch stairs and was now pointing toward the pond.

Over his shoulder, I saw a long tentacle, gray and slick and thick as a fence post, slither beneath Bobby and wrap him up in its grip before it pulled him into the pond. The dark surface rippled a moment. After that, the water turned placid again.

Jack helped me to my feet and offered a lame apology, which I ignored, wincing from the pain I felt. Together, we joined Tim and proceeded cautiously back toward the pond. Halfway there, we stopped in our tracks when a pale blue glow appeared beneath the water.

"This is bullshit," Jack muttered as he turned and headed back to the porch.

"Jack, wait," said Tim.

The pale blue glow intensified, turning the pond's surface into a crude mockery of the daytime sky. The phenomenon lasted a few scant seconds before the light faded.

Tim took another step forward. Then he took one more before the pond's surface broke, and a pale, thin arm shot into the air and a scrawny hand gripped the rocks bordering the pond. Tim and I stood shoulder to shoulder as we watched our dead friend slowly emerge from the dark waters.

"Bobby!" Jack shouted as he bolted toward the pond.

Once he pulled himself over the jagged rocks, Bobby McMahon crawled forward on his hands and knees, a look of both wonder and fear etched on his face. Jack pulled our friend to his feet as Tim removed his shirt and offered it to Bobby, but he refused it. I knew at first glance that something was hideously wrong with my best friend. His eyes were the giveaway. Bobby once told me that the eyes were the windows to the soul. He quoted little snippets all the time from one of the numerous books he had read. And whenever he did, there was a certain light in his eyes. Even after his ordeal with Sean McClusky, that light was still there. Now, peering into those Irish eyes, I saw that the light was gone. Bobby looked back at me with the eyes of a dead man. I almost pissed myself.

"Joe," Bobby croaked as he slumped in Jack's arms.

The gaping hole in Bobby's chest was still there, exposed to us all through his shirt, now torn to ribbons. The Swanson brothers laid him down on the ground. Bobby attempted to cover the wound in his chest, tugging at the tattered remains of his shirt.

"You're freezing," said Jack. "Let's get you out of here."

"Okay," Bobby replied, weakly. He stretched out his hands for us to take hold.

I took Bobby's right hand. Tim grabbed his left. It felt like I was holding a chunk of ice.

"Doesn't it hurt?" Tim asked.

"What?" Bobby fingered the hole in his chest. "This? Maybe, I don't know. I can't feel anything."

Tim and I escorted him, standing on either side, while Jack followed. Bobby shuffled like an old man, but after a few steps, he was able to hold his own. His breath, however, was shallow and labored. I wondered if air escaped through his chest every time he drew a breath. As we neared the edge of the lawn and saw the moonstones come into view, Bobby's condition worsened. Bobby gripped his chest like he was having a heart attack.

"I can't," he gasped.

"Bobby, come on," said Jack. "You have to try. I swear I'll take you right across the water. We'll find your...we'll find you help. I swear."

"No," Bobby pivoted on his heels and headed back away from the lawn's edge. "I don't think I can leave here."

"You didn't want to come here in the first place," Jack reminded him. "I'm telling you, we're going to take you home."

"Bobby," I said, "don't you want to see your mom and dad?"

"I can't picture them anymore," Bobby said. "Is that weird? Oh my God. I don't remember anything. I mean I know you guys, but I can't picture mom or dad. I can't see my house. I can't remember."

Tim took Bobby by the arm. "It's a fairy wound," he said. "It's like what happened in *The Fellowship of the Ring*."

"The what?" Jack asked.

"Tolkien, you dumbass," his brother snapped. "Remember when Frodo got stabbed by one of them wraiths?"

"You're telling me a wraith did this?"

"I don't what did it, Jack."

"Then don't make shit up."

"I'm not making this up," Tim stood his ground.

Bobby shook loose from his grip and headed back toward the mansion. We followed him as he skirted the pond and trudged toward the house.

To our shock, a young girl was now sitting on the porch stairs. Her long dark hair was pulled back in a bun, and her eyes were slightly slanted; up close, as we stood at the foot of the stairs, it was evident that she was born with Down's syndrome. The girl's dress was a simple long-skirted one, with a high collar and long sleeves; it was reminiscent of nineteeth century farm girls whose pictures I saw in a history book at school. She offered a slight smile as Bobby walked up the steps and sat down beside her, as if he were visiting some long-lost country cousin. Behind her, the front door to the mansion was wide open.

"Who are you?" Jack asked.

"Adele." Her voice sounded like a four-year-old. "I live here."

"Where are your parents?" Tim inquired.

Adele cocked her head. Whatever had caused Bobby to forget his parents had also done the same thing to her.

I noticed her bare feet. They looked dirty and calloused. Suddenly, without any of us prodding her, she stood up and motioned for us to follow her into the house.

Bobby took her hand when Adele offered it. Tim and I followed them. Jack took up the rear again, stopping once to look back at the pond.

"Wait here," Adele told us and went into the house.

A yellow globe of light illuminated the vestibule just inside the doorway. Adele looked ghostly as she held a lit lantern in her hand. She stepped onto the porch and bade us to enter the house.

"We have a flashlight," Tim told her.

"Oh, we don't care much for electric light." She took hold of Tim's hand.

"We?" Jack asked.

"You're the one who broke open the jar." The girl pointed a finger at him. "You hurt us."

"I didn't—" Jack started to say, but Adele cut him off.

"Is nothing sacred to you?" she asked.

"What's so sacred about a bunch of crummy jars?"

"There were very fragile things inside," Adele answered. "Some of them were old. Older than you, older than this house, this land."

"They were just pickled dead birds."

"You are wrong," she said, then added, "Don't touch things that do not belong to you. It's bad for you."

Inside the house, Adele brought us into the library where the jars filled with various dead birds lined the shelves from top to bottom. I noticed there was only one empty space among them.

"Jack," I whispered as I stood next to him, "didn't you break two of them?"

"Maybe," he said. "I forget."

"The brothers wait here," Adele said. Then she pointed at Bobby and me. "You two come with me. I want to show you something."

Adele held her lantern up and led us toward the door. Tim snatched the flashlight I kept tucked in my belt as we exited the library.

Across the hall, Adele led us into a den with sliding doors. She placed the lantern on a table and slid the doors shut. Next, she stood before us, allowing the lantern light to make her more visible, and reached behind her head with both hands. When she pulled the snaps apart on the back of her dress, it sounded like small caliber gunfire. Her eyes never blinked as she pulled her sleeves off and let the top portion of her dress fall to her narrow waist.

Chapter 31

Between Adele's little bud breasts, there was a gaping wound. Only, her wound appeared to be much older than the one in the middle of Bobby's chest.

"He will live here now," Adele told us. "Don't worry. We have fun here."

"I can't go home?" Bobby asked.

"This is home," she told him.

"What happens if I leave?"

"The borders are protected," said Adele."It's the way of things."

"What does that mean?" I asked.

"You tried, right?" she said to Bobby now. "The ache in your chest?"

"Yes." Bobby held a hand there, protecting himself.

"No one leaves the grounds once they get the mark. It's the way of things."

"You keep saying that," I told her, "but that doesn't explain—"

"The pain?"

"Well, yes. That too."

"In here," she went on, "in this house and out on the grounds, inside the border, we remain. Beyond the border lies obliteration. Never go past the markers, Bobby. You will be lost forever."

There was a look of confusion on Bobby's face. The sheer panic of the situation did not faze him. I, of course, was scared shitless, but to Bobby, it didn't seem to matter. It was as if he was no longer capable of suffering genuine emotion. Whether it had something to do with his heart being taken from him, if indeed that was what happened, or the trauma of undergoing some secret magic beneath the water that turned him into a living cadaver, he was in no shape to fathom the fate that awaited him. It pained me to watch him remain aloof over the notion of never seeing his parents again.

"Why does this place smell so old?" I blurted out, a feeble attempt to concentrate on something else.

"I don't smell anything," Bobby said.

Adele pulled the top of her dress up and fastened the hooks in the back. In the lantern light, Adele's eyes looked dead like Bobby's. It was hard to tell where the pupils ended and the irises began. I couldn't look into Adele's eyes for too long; they mirrored the mystery and the madness that ensnared the mansion and its occupants. I feared she might turn me into something less than human.

"How long have you been here?" Bobby asked.

"It's hard to remember," Adele answered. "I came to this place on my father's carriage."

"When was that?" I asked.

Adele's expression changed. She looked as if she was desperately trying to remove gum from the roof of her mouth with her tongue. Her eyes rolled in the back of her head. I had to look away.

"Joe," Bobby stood close to me and whispered, "I should be scared. But I don't feel it."

His breath smelled like wet ash. It was all I could do to keep from throwing up on my shoes.

"I'm sorry," Adele said, regaining a semblance of her former self. "I have no memory of that time except for the carriage. I loved that carriage. I was a like a princess."

"The...uh...sun is coming up," I said as I saw the light outside the window.

"We shouldn't keep your friends waiting," she told me. "The others won't like them being here alone."

"Others?"

"The shy ones," she told me. Then she took hold of Bobby's arm and pulled him close. "We should all go to the garden in the back."

"I'm tired," said Bobby. "And I want to get home."

"But you can't go home," she reminded him. "Not now. Not ever. It's—"

"I know," he said. "It's the way of things." There was no emotion in his voice. "But I don't want to stay here."

"This is your home now."

"No, it isn't," he argued. "Joe will know where I can go. Won't you, Joe?"

"Leave us," Adele instructed me.

There was a menace in her voice. Bobby's face looked contorted. I knew he was doing his best to silently plead with me, but it all felt like the time in the alley behind Schmidt's Pharmacy when I cowered and left him alone. Without saying another word, I exited the room.

Panic set in when I reached the hallway. The Swanson brothers were not there. I pictured Jack and Tim crawling from the mucky pond with holes in their chests. The main door down the hall was wide open, and early morning light illuminated the front porch. I felt relieved when I heard the brothers talking outside.

"Where's Bobby?" Tim asked when I joined him and his brother on the porch.

"Inside," I said, "with Adele."

"Did they do anything to you?" Jack asked.

"No," I told him. "Are you guys okay?"

Jack started for the front door, striding across the porch like John Wayne, but he didn't get far. Adele met him at the threshold. In the early morning light, she looked like a normal girl.

"What happened to Bobby?" Tim asked.

"He's been through so much," Adele told us. "The others will care for him and see that he sleeps."

"I want to see him before he goes," I said, stepping close to Jack so I could peer over Adele's shoulder.

Down the hall, a gaggle of pale children, all of them dressed in ragged, rotted clothing, escorted Bobby up the grand staircase. Adele cocked her head and offered a faint smile as she stepped forward. I saw Bobby turn and look back at us as if he were sleepwalking. The front door slammed shut behind Adele. And that was the last time I saw my best friend, Bobby.

Adele snaked her way past us, indicating for us to follow her, and started down the porch steps. The three of us fell into step behind her. She turned right at the bottom of the steps. Her slender hips shook from side to side as she made her way around the mansion.

The garden behind the house was bordered by an outer hedgerow that stood taller than Jack. Past the hedgerow there were stunted, gnarled trees devoid of leaves growing in dusty, ashen earth. Dried, brittle vines stretched between the deformed trees. Adele stood beneath one of those trees, waiting for us. Behind her, dense green vegetation and wild flowers stretched for as far as the eye could see. What stopped me in my tracks was not the ring of dead trees and withered vines, nor the flowers or the rich greenery that lay beyond the dead space. Directly behind Adele, there were three men, tall and thin, with skin like tree bark that attended the begonias, lilacs, and other flowers. Around the wood men flew miniature winged women, similar to the winged fairies we saw in the woods the previous evening, no larger than dolls with hair like autumn leaves. The winged women's skin was colored like the underside of an oak leaf. When the morning sun caught the wings just right, a myriad of colors sparkled like a prism.

"Don't be afraid," Adele said. "There's so much more to see."

Chapter 32

A dead girl's invitation to a magical garden can only lead to ruin. That knowledge nearly cost me my life.

Tim walked toward the tree men without hesitation. He was more at ease than Jack and I were; it was as if his young life so far, with all of the comic books and sci-fi fantasy novels, with all of the horror movies and Saturday morning cartoons, was prelude to meeting the eldritch inhabitants of Adele's secret garden.

In almost no time, Tim vanished deep into the garden, surrounded by winged fairies, the tree men, and other peculiar ones. I looked around for the Foxman and the feral boy, but they were not among the many fantastical creatures who worked or roamed the garden. Beside me, Jack grew more agitated with every second that passed.

"I need my brother," Jack told Adele.

"Nonsense," she said, taking Jack by the arm. "There is so much to see here, but it only lasts the first hour of dawn."

"Where is Tim?"

It was rare that I saw Jack melt down into a panic. He looked like he was on the brink, but it was short-lived. Suddenly, Tim came running toward us as two fairy women flew on either side of him.

"Jack!" he cried. "There's a fountain back there. You have to see it."

"Okay," said Jack.

"They want to take me to the cave where they live."

"I don't know about that, Tim."

"Come on, Jack. Time is almost up."

"Fifteen minutes," his older brother said. "And don't make me come look for you."

"You are such a good brother," Adele said once Tim retreated into the recesses of the garden.

Jack grimaced. As if sensing his ill feelings toward this strange new world, Adele held his arm more tightly. When she lay her head on his shoulder, I wondered if he smelled death on her the way I did, or if some slow-working enchantment had finally begun to take effect on him.

I turned from them and looked back at the mansion. A light mist obscured most of the house except for the two towers that rose up like ghostly minarets. More than anything, I wanted to be back in my own house, curled up in my bed with a comic book, only, something different than the standard fair of Dr. Strange or The Incredible Hulk. Looking up at the towers, I thought about Bobby and how he was cursed to live within the property borders. I thought about the malevolent magic that had robbed him of his heart, and perhaps even his soul. It wasn't hard to surmise how, upon learning that he was gone for good, Sister Mary Ianella would have Bobby's desk removed from the classroom the same way she did Marcella's.

Our predicament weighed heavily on me that morning. The only thing worse than having a friend die was having a friend turned into a soulless zombie. Still, Adele appeared to have come to terms with her situation. In time, I hoped that Bobby would learn to do the same. Whether it was a condition of the magic or not, being imprisoned maybe for centuries, no matter how you cut it, was a fate worse than death. Immediately, I thought about Marcella and how, even though she stuck around between Yorkville and the afterlife for awhile, she eventually moved on in death to where she belonged. The angels I dreamt about were very clear on that point. As I stood there in the garden, I prayed that I would have the same dream about Bobby, that the angels would speed their way to him and break the bond that held him between life and death. When they whisked him away from the clutches of Adele and the so-called shy ones, only then would I rejoice.

But dreams never got anyone out of a tight jam. Worse, Bobby's walking corpse was worthless without a soul. My mind kept coming back around to those sealed jars in the library with the dead birds inside. Somewhere deep inside the mansion, hidden behind Adele and the shy ones, was the culprit responsible for turning Bobby into what he had become. The blinded birds in their jars kept gnawing at me that morning. I wanted to press Adele for information, but I was afraid that if I stepped out of line I might end up like Bobby.

A rich scent like hyacinths drew my attention away from the towers in the mist. Three little winged women with skin the color of blueberries flitted above my head. I felt tired, all of a sudden, and I found it difficult to keep my eyes open much less remain on my feet. The miniature women led me to an ancient-looking oak tree where, with their aid, I lay down beneath the monstrous limbs and fell asleep.

In a dream, Marcella came to me bearing a bloody heart that beat in her hands as she held it. Adele was in my dream, too, and she tried to wrestle the heart away from my ghostly love. At one point during the struggle, the heart slipped from Marcella's hands and fell to the ground. The organ was coated with dirt and dried leaves. As it lay there on the ground, the heart began to spasm until a bird beak broke through the serous membrane. A sparrow, all smeared with dark blood, freed itself from the confines of the dirty heart and took flight. The sparrow flew high into the mist over the mansion and vanished.

When I woke up, the sun was directly over the garden. I had no idea what time it was. The garden was empty. The fantastical creatures that had inhabited that place were gone. Somewhere behind me came the sound of trickling water. I got up, feeling a little unsteady, and followed the hypnotic sound until I discovered the stone fountain bordered on all sides by lilacs and hydrangea.

Jack lay face-down in front of the fountain. Adele was nowhere in sight, though I suspected that she watched my every move now. I kicked Jack's foot.

"Come on. Wake up," I told him. "Tim, where are you?"

No answer.

"Jack, I'm not kidding." I tried once more to rouse him. "Let's get out of here."

There was no response. I knelt down at Jack's side and turned him over. His face was covered with dirt, and his eye sockets were crammed with broken sticks. His mouth was agape and stuffed with dried leaves and acorn shells. His head rolled to one side. When I let it go, Jack's head hit the ground with sickening, hollow thud like a wood bucket dropped on concrete.

Slowly, I back away from Jack and retreated deeper into the garden. When I did, the garden grew larger, denser than it first appeared. I turned around every few steps and saw the towers of the mansion looming in the distance. Even though Adele and the others may have been watching, I felt relieved to know that there was a landmark I could use to find my way out.

A worn path led to a grotto hidden by vines and scrub brush deep within a cluster of mahogany trees. As I skirted the grotto and delved deeper into the garden, I glimpsed Tim's T-shirt and jeans beneath the undergrowth. I tore away the vines thinking he was trapped beneath, but it didn't take long to realize that the thing entangled in the vines was not Tim. Instead, I discovered a scarecrow effigy of Tim made from bound sticks stuffed into his clothes.

"Tim!" I shouted. "Tim, where are you?"

I called out several times, but there was no reply. A few yards behind the grotto, I discovered a stone marker like the one I spotted on the lawn during the first expedition several months ago. I turned back and, keeping the towers in sight, made my way out of the garden.

Vines crept from the garden across the backyard and up the steps of the mansion's back porch. Several times I got my feet trapped in those vines, as if they were deliberately trying to pull me back toward the garden.

The woodwork on the small porch and the trim bordering the roof over it were carved with faces of creatures that resembled the ones on the bridge. The door on the back porch was locked and all the windows on that side of the mansion were shuttered and rusted iron rings several inches in diameter and intertwined with vines and ivy were nailed in place around each of the first-floor windows and the back door.

I made my way around to the front of the mansion. On the lawn, I spotted a familiar face. Adele's expression never changed as I began pushing her away from the mansion. I kept shouting at her, cursing her, shoving her across the lawn. She looked at me with her beatific eyes, as if it were impossible for her to admit the evil I had witnessed in the garden. At last, we reached one of the obelisks at the lawn's edge.

"No, wait," were her last words.

I pushed her past the stone obelisk. A look of sheer terror seized her as her body went rigid. She collapsed, toppling over backward. Slowly, her skin turned chalky like gypsum and started to split open. Seconds later, her body turned into a ruined husk and caved in on itself. Adele was barely recognizable save for her old peasant dress. I kicked her remains into a thousand pieces and stomped on her dress until it lay flat against the ground.

Afterward, I ran screaming into the woods.

It wasn't until after I cleared the web of vines at the footbridge that I realized there was only one thing left to do.

A ring of stones marked the place where Jack and I had lit our campfire the previous evening. The ashen charred logs and sticks reminded me of Adele's body after I pushed her beyond the boundary marker. I kicked the cold ashy remains of the fire pit until all evidence was gone.

I found Bobby's tackle box next to the tent. Inside it there was a can of lighter fluid, still half-filled with flammable liquid, and a box of matches. I pocketed the matches and carried the lighter fluid close to my chest, as if it were some venerated relic entrusted to me from a higher power. There was no doubt in my mind, no matter how confused and scared I was, that twelve ounces of lighter fluid would not be enough for what I intended to do. So, I left the camp site and headed deeper into the woods.

By the time I reached the old hobo camp site near the creek, the place where Tim found the skin magazine and Jack found the soiled underwear, it was already late in the afternoon. I found two ten-gallon cans of gasoline sticking out of the dirt. The gas cans were heavy, and it took me nearly all afternoon to transport them both back through the woods. When I reached the footbridge, I left one of the cans there after I camouflaged it with fallen branches. After that, I made my way across the bridge, winding my way through the vines that crisscrossed the passage, and headed up the marked trail.

The front lawn looked as pristine as ever as I trekked toward the mansion. With each step I took, I expected a gang of ghoulish children to empty out of the house and surround me. Nearing the porch now, I made sure to give the pond a wide berth, unsure if the thing under the water sought its victims regardless whether it was day or night.

The front door was wide open. I marched up the steps, carrying the gas can. Every impulse told me to drop everything, to forget everything, and just run for my life, but, as I stepped over the threshold, it became evident that there was no one about. Adele talked about the fairies in the garden and how the visitation lasted only during that first hour of dawn. Tim once told me that there were two types of magic, that whatever magic still existed saw a sort of gradation throughout the day. The dead children like Adele and Bobby were probably kept not as slaves or anything as sinister as that, but as play things for whatever was behind the magic. I remembered how Bobby once told me that fairies cared little about the affairs of men. Tim was of the same opinion, having read more about that sort of thing than I ever did.

Inside the mansion, I climbed the grand stairs, careful to tread lightly so as not to give myself away, and doused the second floor landing with gasoline. From there, I made my way down and splashed more fuel on each step until I reached the ground floor. Next, I created a short trail from the stairs halfway down the foyer between the library and the other rooms. The gas can went dry, so I used the lighter fluid to continue the trail all the way to the front door, making sure to wet the door and its frame.

The first match I lit and tossed went out before it hit the floor. I had better luck the second time around. The next lit match landed in a puddle of lighter fluid and ignited. As the flame spread down the foyer to the grand stairs I sidestepped the fire and slid open the library door. A draft fanned the flames even higher, causing them to spread across the floor and engulf the heavy curtain draped behind the library door. I wanted to grab whatever old books I could, tear them to pieces, and feed the flames, but the fire spread faster than I anticipated. The acrid smoke filled the ground floor and burned my eyes. I coughed as I fought back the urge to vomit. Half-blind, unable to breathe, I abandoned the library. The fire crept up the grand stairs and fanned out to the wood railings on either side. I bolted out the front door, leaping through the flames that licked the threshold.

Once I made it past the pond, I turned to see the fire I created. It was a glorious one. The windows in the library burst into a thousand shards of glass. Flames licked the top of the windows and the main doorway, working their way higher up the façade, scorching the gray stone edifice. Before long, the doorway was one large mass of fire that spilled out onto the porch. When the porch roof went up in flames, I started back toward the trail.

From the property's edge, I ran for all I was worth through the woods all the way back to the footbridge. It felt like forever, as I weaved my way through the vines that covered the bridge's span. *Had they grown thicker,* I wondered. My hands, my arms, my face, and my neck suffered scratches and cuts as I plowed my way through the last of the vines before I reached the other side.

The other gas can remained hidden where I left it. I used the gasoline in the second can cautiously as I wetted down the far side of the bridge nearest the path marked by the moonstones; then for the third time that day, I made my way through the mess of vines, stopping now and again to spill gasoline over the floor beams, the verticals and whatever vines that were in the way. The last quarter of the can I saved until I moved back to other side. Once the can was empty, I tossed it aside and dumped the remainder of the lighter fluid.

I lit a match and tossed it. A short whoosh was followed by a slender flame that shot up from the first bridge beam just as a breeze blew, nearly extinguishing the small fire. I took another step closer, confident that I would have to use more than one match. That's when the breeze quit, and the flames shot up over my head. Thick, black smoke billowed toward the carved arch that marked the bridge entrance. The fire then laced its way through the vines, jumping along the floor beams to the other side until the flames grew high enough to ignite the verticals and the railings. Backing away from the bridge, I realized the fire was not going to be confined there. Flames licked their way from the vines to the trees on either side of the bridge. Soon, the fire spread to the surrounding brush.

It was hard to breathe, but I stuck around and made sure that the fire completely destroyed the bridge; otherwise, my work would be all in vain. I walked backward, peering over my shoulder every so often for fear of running into the Foxman or the feral boy or some other eldritch creature, until I found a spot some twenty yards away from the bridge. The smoke wafted from the blaze and choked me. I used my shirt to cover my nose. It wasn't long before I heard wood snap and a great groan as the heat and the flames weakened the bridge. After that, a great ball of fire engulfed the bridge before the structure crashed down into the ravine below.

Fire crept up from either side of the ravine, moving back toward the mansion grounds and toward me. I turned tail at that point and started back through the woods, running in a blind, choking fury. For a hundred yards or more, I felt the heat of the forest fire on my back. Once I put enough distance between me and the fire, the heat dissipated. I kept running, however, until I saw the creek through the woods.

I didn't know what time it was when I uncovered the small rowboat and dragged it to the creek bank. An eastward wind blew through the forest. In its wake, thick smoke drifted like fog all the way to the water; the familiar landscape of the state forest and the banks of Hobbs Creek turned, through my doing alone, into a surreal realm where I was a lost soul wandering alone in a dark wood.

Rowing across the creek was not easy. The forest behind me was now reduced to a veritable mountain range made out of smoke whose peaks vanished into the evening sky.

Epilogue

Drawing near to the dock behind Granny Swanson's house, I heard voices along the bank, familiar voices that belonged to Von Braun and others who lived on Tanner Street. Once I made it to the dock, several arms reached down and hoisted me up.

"Good lord," I heard Granny Swanson say.

"I'll take him to his parents," Von Braun said. "You call the police."

"Where are my grandsons?" Granny asked.

"Gone," I managed before I broke down into tears.

Von Braun didn't say a word to me, but he kept his long, clammy hand on my neck as we walked back to my house. Fortunately, my parents were home. Von Braun excused himself when my mother flipped out over the gasoline odor that she smelled on me. My father thanked Von Braun and ushered me into the house.

"We'll be calling the police," Von Braun called from the yard.

"You do what you have to do," my father told him. "We're not going anywhere."

Inside the house, my father beat the old man to the punch and called the police himself. I heard more voices outside the house. My mother sighed as she looked out the dining room window, her hands clenched in fists as they rested on her hips. Curiosity seekers, no doubt, were already gathering as news of my work spread. Off in the distance, fire trucks blared their horns as they raced toward the forest to extinguish what I had created. My mothered stripped me out of my smoky, gas-soaked clothes and marched me up the stairs to take a bath.

Once I finished cleaning up, my mother left me alone in my room to get dressed. I turned out the light and collapsed naked on my bed, slipping dreamless into unconsciousness.

Whatever sleep I managed to acquire was cut short by the sound of voices downstairs. It was still dark out, so I got up, put on some pajamas, and left my room. At the top of the stairs, I felt dizzy, thinking about the grand stairs in the mansion and how the fire spread so quickly.

The walk down the stairs was difficult on account of how weak my legs felt. In the living room, I found my parents, their eyes swollen and red, along with Granny Swanson, Bobby McMahon's parents, and two police officers. They all stared at me for a long time without saying a word. They didn't have to. It was evident by their expressions that they all believed I was guilty for setting what would go down in Yorkville history as one of the biggest fires in Franklin Forest.

"We need to ask you some questions, son," one of the police officers said.

It was Malone. The cop who came between me and McClusky in the alley the night I found out Marcella was dead. Malone looked older than the other officer. He was short and portly now, not at all like I remembered him. I decided I liked him compared to the other one who was younger, skinnier, and dead in the eyes.

"Can I have something to eat?" I asked.

"Monster," Mrs. McMahon mumbled.

All hell broke loose as my mother sprung from her seat. The young, skinny cop slid between the women as my father took hold of my mother and Mr. McMahon pulled his wife back.

"Just bring him in," Malone said once the women were separated.

His partner took me by the arm. I looked at my dad, but he was too busy trying to restrain my mother. Malone and the skinny cop led me out of the house as the adults hailed curses and accusations at one another.

That night, I rode out of Yorkville in the back of a police car that smelled of cigarettes and cheap cologne. On the way to the station, we drove through the town square. Passing Schmidt's Pharmacy, I stared out the window, waiting to see the Swanson brothers high-tailing it out of the alley next to the pharmacy, only steps ahead of fat Sean McClusky, or a glimpse of Marcella, very much alive, outside The Roost with Annie Gallagher and Kim Whalen, any familiar face to remind me that my world hadn't turned completely upside down. Instead, the alley was empty, and the windows of The Roost were dark. That was the last time I ever saw Yorkville Square.

There was no incarceration to speak of, not for a twelve-year-old like me. In the days that followed, my thoughts always returned to the forest house and the ghastly garden behind it. I barely remained aware of what was going around me, even when the police testified at a hearing that I seemed cold and unresponsive. I became a ward of the system, and no one believed my story. Instead, they turned me into a fall guy for the deaths of my friends and for starting the forest fire.

At my hearing, there was much talk about how I was little more than a psychopath, a mad monster whose mind was fractured beyond repair, a butcher who harbored no respect for human life. The more I pleaded for my story, the real story, to be heard, the more they ignored me. They painted me as a crazy boy who showed no remorse for his actions by embellishing in some made-up world, a psychotic ensnared in an intricate web of lies.

When the hearing was over, I went to the county juvenile detention center. I met with psychiatrists and social workers, and they were all convinced that I killed my friend Bobby and hid his body so that he would never be found. Likewise, they assumed I killed Tim Swanson also, even though his body was never recovered. They said I killed Jack and mutilated his body beyond recognition. And in order to hide the crime, I lit the fire that had subsequently consumed nearly one-quarter of Franklin Forest. I pleaded with the authorities and my parents to find the burned out forest house, but either they didn't believe me, or they were too scared to go and see for themselves.

I begged them repeatedly to back to the forest. I even volunteered to guide them to the mansion in order to prove my innocence. Somewhere out there in the forest, trapped perhaps in some borderland between the world we know and another world ruled by chaotic, primal forces, were two of my friends.

In the end, my desperate attempts served to further enmesh me in the imposed prison of insanity. But is it madness to know the truth of things? Even when the truth tests the sanity of others?

Most nights, I didn't sleep. Most nights, even with the medication they gave me, I saw Adele in the dark. Behind her, lurking in shadow, are the silhouettes of the feral boy and the Foxman. I saw Bobby in the dark, too; his eyes devoid of life as they darted left and right, searching for his way back to a home he no longer remembered. I pictured the ghosts of the brothers Swanson as they roamed freely until angels carried them out of this world. It wasn't hard to imagine Jack and Tim in spirit form haunting Von Braun's home for their own selfish enjoyment. During those hours after midnight, when I lie awake in the dark, I hoped that my friends' ghosts stepped lightly over the ashes I created, lest they stir up the ruinous past.

About the Author

Richard J. O'Brien was born in Camden, N.J. He served in the army, attended Rutgers University, and worked a variety of jobs before attending graduate school. In 2012, he received his MFA in Creative Writing from Fairleigh Dickinson University. Currently, the author lives in Pennsylvania and teaches English composition at Mercer County Community College, Rowan College at Gloucester County, and others. Visit him at www.obrienwriter.com.